INTERTWINED

The Chronicles of Laili Island

Samantha Edwhan

Edwhan NZ

First published by Edwhan NZ Limited 2025

Copyright © 2025 by Samantha Edwhan
Cover and Illustrations by Samantha Edwhan

First edition

Paperback ISBN 978-0-473-75718-2
eBook ISBN 978-0-473-75719-9

www.edwhanbooks.com

Acknowledgements

Special thanks to Sally for helping to edit my book, and to Ciara for her mutual interest in this world.

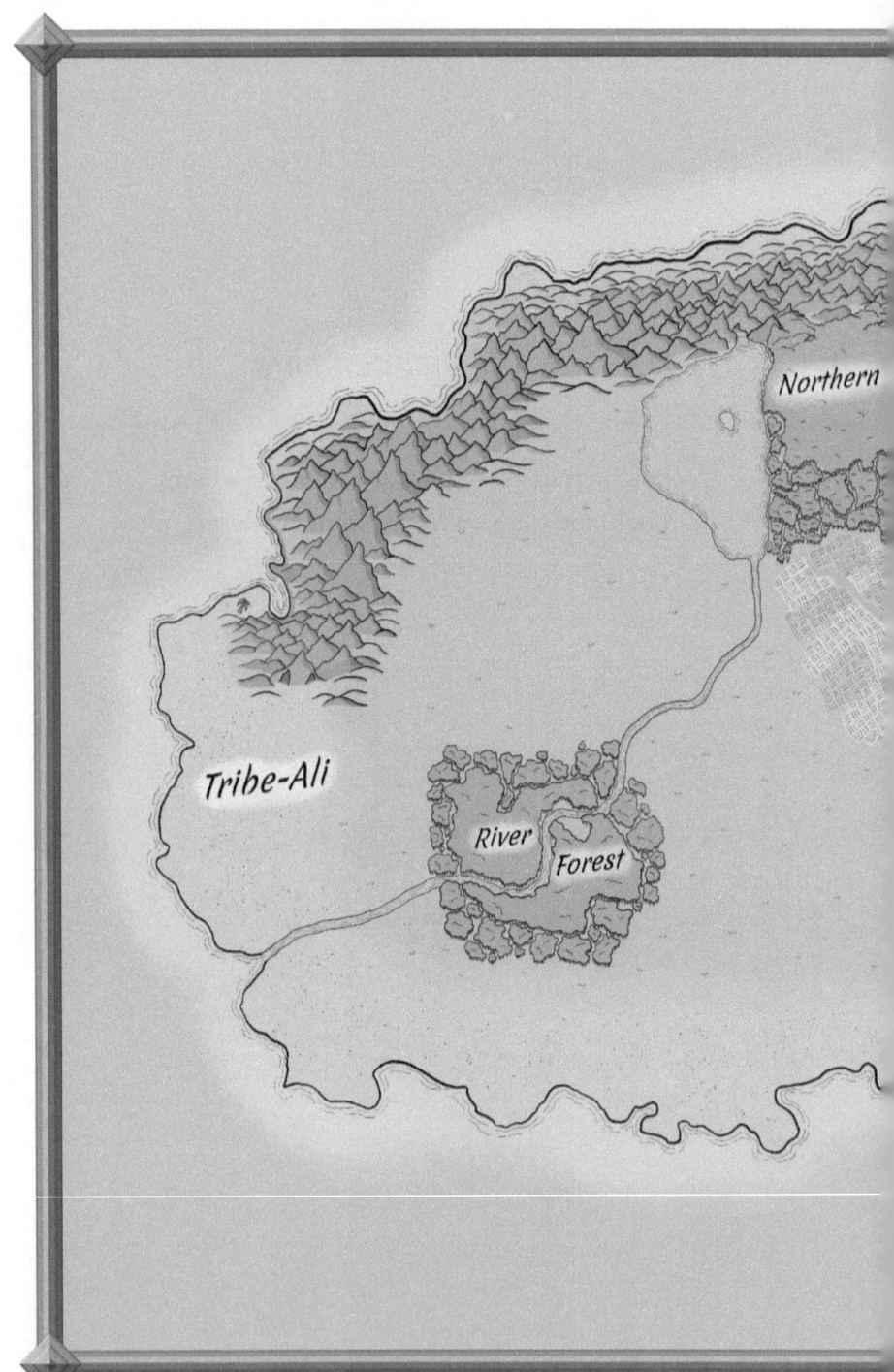

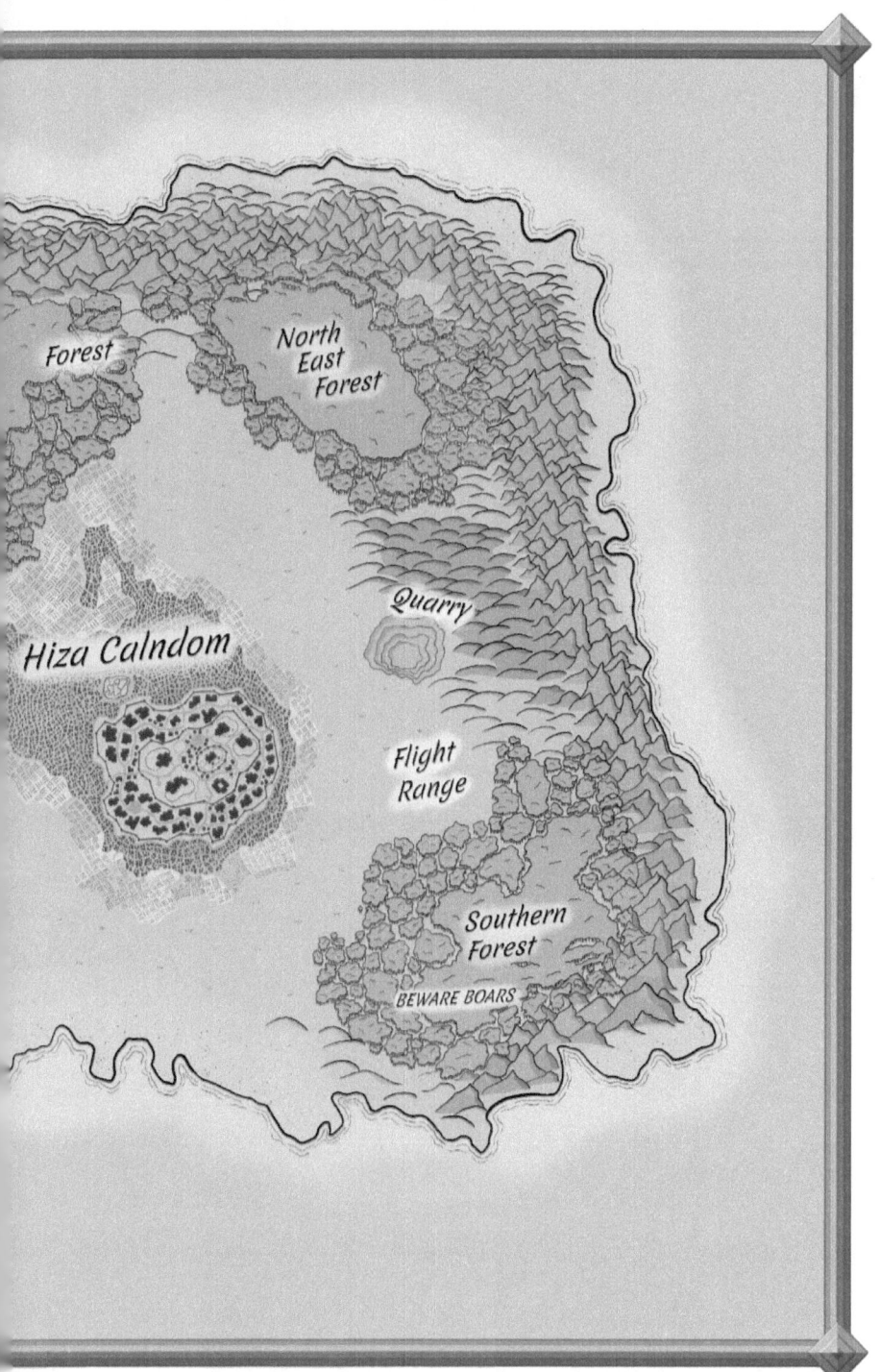

Types
of
Dragons

Water Dragon

Depicted by Lucas

Colours: Varies from blue to green. Can be light or dark in colour.

Unique Traits: No horns. Fins for ears. Webbed feet. Can breathe underwater and on land.

Trivia: Prefer swimming to flying. Can control water movement but not water temperature. Most commonly live near water.

Ice Dragon

Depicted by Zina

Colours: Typically pale shades of blue. Can also be white or grey.

Unique Traits: Resistant to cold environments. Can freeze their whole body without dying.

Trivia: Prefer colder settings. Can freeze water into ice and shape it at will. Can use ice breath in battle.

Rock Dragon

Depicted by Heather

Colours: Varies from brown to grey. Typically darker shades.

Unique Traits: Can move any form of stone with their mind. Thicker skin for protection against accidental rockfalls.

Trivia: Can navigate tunnels easier than other dragons. Rarely suffer from claustrophobia.

Fire Dragon

Depicted by Tanner

Colours: Can be red, orange, or yellow. In very rare cases, they can also be blue.

Unique Traits: Can heat bodies to keep warm. Can ignite themselves for short periods of time without dying. More resistant to smoke inhalation than other dragons.

Trivia: Prefer warmer settings. Can use fire breath in battle.

Nature Dragon

Depicted by Victoria

Colours: Typically green. Sometimes brown.

Unique Traits: More peaceful than other dragons. Can understand the needs of plants and animals or force their movement.

Trivia: Make great farmers. Prefer to be surrounded by nature.

Lightning Dragons

Depicted by Priscila

Colours: Typically yellow with highlights of other colours. In rare cases, can have yellow as secondary colour with a different primary colour.

Unique Traits: Can summon lightning from the clouds. Can charge their body to hold lightning for an attack. More resistant to zaps than other dragons.

Trivia: Prefer living under the open sky. Often skilled flyers. More likely to be claustrophobic than other dragons.

Dragons with No Element

Depicted by August

Colours: Can be any colour. Colours tend to be based on genetics.

Unique Traits: More innovative and perceptive than other dragons. Extremely adaptable.

Trivia: Can fill any role that does not require elemental abilities. More commonplace than each of the other elements.

Prologue

It was a sunny day on Laili Island. On the beaches of Tribe-Ali, dragons went about their day. The adults cared for hatchlings and hunted for food, the young dragons played among the dunes, and down where the sand met the water, two fledglings were walking side by side.

"The water looks wonderful today," Evelyn said, gazing out over the ocean.

"I don't think it's warm enough to swim yet," Alita told her.

"Says you." Evelyn grinned at her. "I could take a dip in the middle of winter if I wanted to."

Alita shivered at the thought of the ice cold water. "I'd rather stay on the beach."

Evelyn turned back to the water for a moment longer. "When the sun sets tonight, it'll look quite nice. Maybe we can sit by the river outlet later to watch."

She turned to Alita with a smile. Alita smiled back at her. "That'll be nice. But there's plenty of things we can do before then."

Evelyn raised an eyebrow at her. "Such as?"

Alita responded by scooping up some wet sand and splatting it on Evelyn's head spike.

"Hey!" Evelyn yelped.

Alita laughed as Evelyn shook her head vigorously. A few grains of sand stubbornly clung to her head. Evelyn shot Alita a glare before pouncing on her and knocking her to the ground. Alita yelped and broke into a fit of giggles.

"You're heavy, Evelyn!" she exclaimed.

Evelyn grinned. "Do something about it then."

Alita frowned playfully at her and focused her attention on the sand. She could feel each and every grain, right down to the rock and sediment beneath the surface. Alita willed the sand to move, forcing it up so that Evelyn tumbled over. She rolled down the newfound slope and into the water. Alita sat up, already laughing. Evelyn flailed around until she was upright and glared at Alita.

"That was mean!" she complained as she clambered out of the water.

Alita giggled. "You told me to do something."

Evelyn froze the water on her fur and shook herself. Alita covered herself with her wings as freezing drops of ice hailed over her.

"That's cold!" Alita whined.

"Wuss," Evelyn said, smiling.

"Ice lover," Alita retorted playfully.

Evelyn rolled her eyes and shook her head. Alita noticed a distant look appear in Evelyn's eyes, staring right past her shoulder. Alita turned and spotted two older Ice Dragons approaching. The first was Chieftain Clyde. She could recognise his blue skin and straight horns anywhere. His ears were pointed and he had that light patch of blue on his throat like Evelyn did.

As they neared, Alita got a better view of the dragon beside him. He was larger and wore a silver crown, inlaid with opals, and a thick blue-grey cloak that covered his shoulders, wings, back and tail. The wooden button holding the cloak together was etched and painted with a silver-grey dragon wing. Alita had only heard of High Caln Griffin Silver, the ruler of Hiza Calndom, but she knew this must be him.

"Evelyn," Chieftain Clyde said, a smile on his face, "High Caln

Griffin has come with good news."

"What news?" Evelyn asked.

"I have chosen you to be my heir," Griffin said. His voice was surprisingly deep.

Alita and Evelyn exchanged a wide eyed look. They had both heard that the High Caln was looking for a Prinze. Who would have thought he'd choose Evelyn?

"What do I have to do?" Evelyn asked. There was a tiny wobble in her voice.

"You will come to Hiza Calndom and live in the castle with me and my family," Griffin explained. "You will become Prinze and I will train you to become High Caln."

"Can Alita come too?" Evelyn asked.

"I'm afraid not," Griffin said. "Alita will be staying in Tribe-Ali. This is her home."

Alita caught the creeping fear in Evelyn's eyes as she glanced over.

"But she's my friend." Evelyn frowned. "And this is my home too. Why can't I stay here?"

"Prinzes and High Calns must live in the castle. Hiza Calndom will be your home from now on. The castle is the safest place on Laili Island," Griffin explained. "You will enjoy leading your subjects. Come."

Griffin spread out a wing. Evelyn looked at Alita, then Clyde. Alita felt her chest tighten as Evelyn's indignant expression gave way to defeat.

"W-wait!" Alita stammered. "You can't just take her away."

"This is the way it has to be," Griffin told her.

"Then take me too." Alita did her best to frown up at him.

"Alita." Clyde placed a wing on her back. "Evelyn will make a good High Caln one day. I'm sure she'll be back to visit sometime."

"But she's my best friend," Alita protested.

"I know." Clyde's tone was hushed and gentle. "But now she has a duty to Hiza Calndom. Don't be sad. Be proud for her. This is a once in a lifetime opportunity."

Alita felt tears prick in her eyes and squeezed them shut. She was losing her best friend. Alita pulled away from Clyde and wrapped her wings around Evelyn in a hug.

"Promise you'll visit me," she whispered.

"I will," Evelyn said. "You won't be able to stop me."

Alita sniffed and stepped back. Evelyn forced a smile at her. Alita managed to smile back. Griffin wrapped his wing around Evelyn without another word and turned away. As they took to the sky and flew away, Alita felt her tears roll down her face. She didn't know if she would ever see Evelyn again. Alita could only hope that she visited often.

Chapter 1

Seven years later

Alita stared at the rabbit across the field. It was a bit far away but she was sure she could catch it. She just had to get close enough for a good head start.

A shadow passed over the rabbit. Alita looked up in time to see a grey-brown dragon dive down and pin the rabbit beneath his feet, taking it out easily.

"Liam!" Alita yelled at her brother. "I was going to catch that."

"I had a much better advantage than you," Liam protested. "There's no way you could have caught it on foot from so far away."

"I'm sure I could have," Alita muttered.

Liam rolled his eyes with a smile. "Sure you could. There's no point fighting over it now though. We should take it back to the beach."

Alita nodded and turned for the beach. A gust of wind swept past her as Liam immediately took flight again. Alita shook her head and followed suit, leaping into the sky.

"Clyde won't be happy that we only caught a single rabbit," Alita said. When Liam shrugged, she added, "We'll have to hunt for an elk or deer later."

The flight home only took a few minutes. Alita smiled as she looked down at the view beneath her. Flat stretches of grassland gave way to sand. Beyond that, the ocean stretched into the horizon. The sun reflected off the waves, making the water sparkle.

Alita landed on the sand and pre-emptively used her ability to manipulate rocks and dirt to steady herself. Dry sand wasn't the most stable thing to land on, but Rock Dragons like her and her brother could make any ground stable.

Liam landed beside her and started for the caves up the beach. Dragons of all colours and elements were scattered around them, but the youngest ones were kept in the caves for protection. Alita followed her brother. Ahead of them, she recognised Chieftain Clyde approaching.

Clyde had been Chieftain of the Tribe for as long as Alita could remember. He treated everyone with respect and was strong enough to keep other male dragons from taking the title. After so many years of being Chieftain, Clyde had mastered how to hold himself. With his head held high, tail straight behind him, and his wings tightly folded at his sides, Clyde radiated authority. The only other dragon Alita had seen with the same sense of power was the High Caln of Hiza Calndom.

"Greetings Liam, Alita," Clyde said once he'd reached them.

Liam nodded, unable to speak with the rabbit in his mouth. Alita dipped her head respectfully.

"How was your hunt?" Clyde asked.

"It went okay," Alita said. "I know we only caught a rabbit, but I'll go out again later and catch something bigger."

"I see." Chieftain Clyde paused for a moment then said, "Alita, I would like to talk to you. Alone."

Liam threw a wary look toward his sister, then ducked his head and quickly trotted away.

"Have I done something wrong?" Alita asked. "I-I know I didn't catch the rabbit. But I'll make sure to catch something bigger before the end of the day."

"This isn't about hunting, Alita," Clyde said. "You are twenty years old now. It's time you contributed eggs."

"Oh…" Alita dropped her gaze to the ground. "Chieftain, I

understand that you need more young, but... I'm not ready to have eggs yet."

"Alita, I am not as young as I used to be. Every year, I am faced with more and more dragons who are younger and stronger than me. It takes a lot of skill and effort to stay on top," Clyde explained.

"I understand, Chieftain." Alita glanced up at him. "But surely there are other dragons who can give you eggs this year."

"There are," Clyde said. "However, you still need to make up for your disloyalty last year."

Alita looked at the ground again. She spotted the scar on her foreleg from the incident in question. "I know, and I'm doing everything I can to make up for that. But I'm still not ready for eggs. Perhaps I can spend more time contributing through hunting?"

Clyde sighed quietly. "Very well. As long as you are ensuring the mothers and young are fed, that will be sufficient. Perhaps you could spend some time teaching or caring for the nestlings as well."

"Of course, Chieftain," Alita said, dipping her head.

Clyde turned and walked down the beach. Alita watched him go, reflecting on the conversation. It was hard to follow the laws of the Tribe at times like this. Clyde had been Chieftain since before Alita had even hatched. He was a father figure for her. The thought of giving him eggs twisted her stomach. But she wasn't allowed to choose any other male dragon as a mate. She had definitely learned her lesson there.

Alita sighed and turned for the caves. She almost jumped when she saw Liam standing next to her.

"Are you alright?" he asked.

Alita quickly relaxed from the brief scare. "I'm fine. How long have you been standing there?"

"I just came back from the caves. I thought I'd check on you. Did Clyde give you a hard time?" The worried tone in Liam's voice made Alita want to roll her eyes. Ever the protective big brother.

"No. Just a conversation. It's fine," she said.

"He's been asking a lot of dragons for eggs lately," Liam said quietly, "I wasn't sure if he'd ask you."

"What makes you say that?" Alita asked.

"Well, you've never been a big fan of the Tribe's culture," Liam reminded her. "I figured Clyde knew that so he might not try to force it on you."

"It's fine, Liam," Alita said.

She didn't want to dwell too much on her opinions of the Tribe. She might not like some parts of her life, but she could leave whenever she wanted. At least, that's what she wanted to believe. The thought of leaving on her own for life in Hiza Calndom scared her, though. There was no guarantee that her life would be any better there. For now, she would stay in the Tribe. But Alita hoped that a new Chieftain might arise soon.

Chapter 2

Alita went out hunting again shortly after her conversation with Clyde. She returned to the beach a few hours later, triumphantly hauling a deer by the neck. It was too heavy to fly with, but she was able to drag it on foot across the sand.

She hauled her catch into the caves. The main area only had a few dragons in it, mostly older dragons, though a pair of nestlings were tumbling around near one of the cave walls. The slender Ice Dragon watching them stood up and approached Alita with a smile.

"Looks like your hunt went well, Alita," she said.

"Thanks, Kelda." Alita stretched out her neck and back. "I wish I could say catching it was the hard part, but dragging it back here was definitely more difficult."

"Well, you still managed it," Kelda reassured her. "I'm sure this will be more than enough for the nestlings."

Alita glanced at the pair of nestlings rolling around the cave. "Looks like those two are having fun."

Kelda glanced back at them, then smiled. "Yes. They don't seem too bothered by their mother leaving them with me while she sees Clyde."

At the mention of Clyde, Alita remembered the conversation she'd had with him earlier. Her stomach twisted in knots again.

"Uh, well, I guess I should get going," Alita said, awkwardly backing towards the exit. "Got lots to do if we're going to feed everyone, right?"

Kelda's expression softened. "Oh, Alita. He finally asked you, didn't he? Don't worry, dear. Clyde won't force you if you're not up to it. Just keep working hard like you always do."

"Thanks, Kelda," Alita said. "But I think I'll go now."

Alita hurried out of the cave. She needed to escape the reminders of eggs. Despite Kelda's reassuring words, Alita knew Clyde would push for it again, sooner or later.

"Alita!" Liam's voice pulled Alita from her thoughts. She spotted him sitting near the water, waving a wing at her. Alita made her way over to him, noticing the pair of fish at his feet.

"Did you go swimming?" she asked him.

"No, silly. One of the Water Dragons dropped it off for us," Liam told her. "I saw that deer you took into the caves. Nice catch!"

Alita couldn't help but smile. "Thanks."

Liam pushed one of the fish towards her. "Here. We should eat if we want to keep our strength up."

Alita nodded and settled down beside him to begin eating. But as she did so, she felt Liam's gaze on her. Curious, she glanced at him.

"Is something wrong?" she asked.

"I was just wondering how you're doing," Liam said. "You were pretty shaken up this morning."

"That hasn't really changed much," Alita admitted. "I don't know how I'm going to deal with eventually having eggs for Clyde. It just feels... wrong."

"I know what you mean," Liam said.

"How can you? It's not like you're ever going to have that problem," Alita pointed out.

"Perhaps not. But I'll never be able to have eggs at all. Not if I stay here." Liam stared at his fish. A hollow expression appeared in his eyes.

"Why don't you move to the Calndom then?" Alita asked.

Liam smiled at her. "Well, why don't you?"

Alita opened her mouth, then closed it again. She didn't have an answer for that. She looked around the beach, recognising the dragons she'd grown up with all her life. She had friends and family here. But she didn't want the life that would be ahead of her if she stayed. So why didn't she just leave?

As Alita surveyed the beach, she spotted a dragon swoop down from the sky and land beside Clyde near the dunes. The dragon's horns were long and straight and sharp behind her golden crown. Her pale blue cloak hid most of her body from view. But Alita could never forget the face of her old friend.

"Is that Evelyn?" Liam asked, noticing her after a few moments. "What's she doing here?"

"Must be official leadership stuff," Alita muttered.

She looked down at her half eaten fish. She still remembered the day Evelyn had left, years ago. She had promised to visit. Yet, she never did. Alita squeezed her eyes shut as memories flooded her mind. There was no way Evelyn had flown all the way to the Tribe just to visit old friends. She couldn't possibly be the same dragon.

"Alita, are you alright?" Liam asked.

"Alita?"

Looking up, Alita saw Evelyn smiling down at her. Had she crossed the beach that quickly? Or had Alita been within her own mind longer than she'd realised?

"It's so good to see you," Evelyn said, still smiling.

"Uh... yeah," Alita agreed hesitantly. "G-good to see you too."

"I wasn't sure if you'd still be here," Evelyn said.

"Where else would I be?" Alita asked.

"Well, several dragons go to Hiza Calndom each year," Evelyn explained. "I had a feeling that you'd be one of them once you were old enough to leave."

"R-right." Alita averted her gaze. She didn't need to tell Evelyn that she was starting to seriously consider leaving. It's not like she would do anything about it.

"Since you're still here, though, I wanted to ask you something," Evelyn began. "There's been a lot going on in the castle lately. Tensions are rising, everyone's worried about my safety. Griffin wants me to have a bodyguard. I told him I'd want to choose one personally. So, I came out here to see if you wanted to come back to Hiza Calndom with me to be my bodyguard."

Alita stared at Evelyn. After all this time, was Evelyn just trying to pick up where they'd left off? She blinked several times, thinking she must be imagining all of this. It was too coincidental. But Evelyn was still there, and the question was still in the air. Alita sat upright and pushed her fish away from her.

"Why didn't you visit?" she asked.

Evelyn blinked. Her eyes widened just a little. "Visit?"

"When you left, you promised you would visit," Alita reminded her.

"Oh." Evelyn dropped her gaze for just a second. "I tried to, Alita. Really, I did. But Griffin wouldn't let me leave Hiza Calndom. I have a strict schedule I have to follow. The only reason I was able to come now was because Griffin allowed me the day to find the bodyguard I wanted."

"So, what would happen if I said yes?" Alita asked.

"Well, we would go back to Hiza Calndom together," Evelyn explained. "You'll get a little training from our head of guard and you'll start work tomorrow."

"That's very sudden. Are you sure you've thought this through?" Alita asked. "I'm not exactly intimidating."

Evelyn laughed lightly. "I trust you more than any other dragon, Alita. I know you'll keep an eye out for dangers. Bodyguards tend to be Rock Dragons anyway. You'll fit right in."

"But I'm not anything special." Alita stared down at her feet in the sand. "I'm dirty, I don't have proper posture, and I'm clumsy on a good day. Why would you want me?"

"You're *not* clumsy, Alita. I used to tell you that all the time. And posture and dirt are easy things to change. I want you to be my bodyguard. Just say yes," Evelyn then added. "Plus, it'll get you away from Tribe-Ali and the impending future of having eggs for the Chieftain."

"How do you know I don't like it here?" Alita asked. "What if I actually love it here and want to stay?"

Evelyn made a sound that seemed like she was trying not to snort out her laughter. "Alita, I know you. Just because it's been seven years doesn't mean I forgot what you're like. Plus, Clyde mentioned it when I arrived."

Alita glanced across the beach to where Clyde was talking down a pair of male dragons. Why would he say something like that? If his intention was to have as many eggs as possible, why would he tell Evelyn that Alita didn't want eggs?

Evelyn stretched out a wing, getting Alita's attention again. She looked at Alita expectantly.

"What do you say?" she asked. "Do you want to come with me?"

Alita thought for a moment. Would it be better in Hiza Calndom? At least she'd have Evelyn with her, so she wouldn't be completely alone. But then she'd be living in the castle. How different would that be from here? Would it be worth it to leave? What if she was forced to come back? Would Clyde take her back? Would he still be in charge then? Would *any* Chieftain take her back?

Liam nudged Alita with his wing. "I think you should do it. It's a good opportunity, and I think you'd be much happier there."

Alita glanced at him. "Are you sure?"

Liam nodded. Alita turned back to Evelyn. If Liam thought she would be happier in the Calndom, perhaps she should agree to it. It was likely to be better than staying in the Tribe forever.

"Alright, I'll go with you," Alita said, hoping this wouldn't be a massive mistake.

Evelyn smiled. It wasn't an open mouthed grin, but she did look delighted. Perhaps she had been taught to refrain from showing too much emotion. Alita didn't focus on that thought for too long though, as Evelyn quickly got her up and hurried over to Clyde to inform him that they were leaving. Alita only had time for a quick goodbye to her brother before she and Evelyn were in the sky, flying for the Calndom further inland.

Chapter 3

Evelyn was quiet the whole flight to Hiza Calndom. Alita followed her in silence, unsure if she should ask any questions. Where would she even begin? She knew the Calndom was different from the Tribe, but just how different would it be?

The sun was starting to set when they finally arrived. Evelyn swooped down to land on the street as they approached a large, silvery fence. Alita landed beside her and stared up at it. It was the height of three dragons stacked on top of each other. At regular intervals, the silver metal connected to thick stone pillars. Atop each pillar sat an armoured dragon. The dragons were so still that Alita thought they were statues for a moment. Then she spotted one look down at her and shivered. She realised they were watching for anyone who might try to fly over the fences.

Evelyn led Alita up to an extravagantly designed gate. The thin metal curled and spiralled into various patterns and connected at the centre for perfect symmetry on either side. Alita noticed two dragons standing in front of the gate. They were covered in metal plates and chain link armour. Alita could barely make out their eyes in the shadows of their helmets.

Evelyn strode up to the guards and said, "Evelyn Caldwell, Prinze to High Caln Griffin. I have returned from my visit to Tribe-Ali. This is Alita, my new bodyguard."

The guards dipped their heads respectfully. "Welcome back, Prinze

Evelyn. May the rest of your journey be safe."

They then turned and pushed open the gate. Evelyn indicated for Alita to follow and trotted through the gate. There were two more armoured dragons on the other side who pushed the gate closed again. Alita sped up a little to trot beside Evelyn.

"So, um, when do I start being your bodyguard? And how?" she asked quietly.

"Not until tomorrow," Evelyn replied. "It's getting late and there's a few things we need to sort out before you can start."

"What things?" Alita asked.

"I need to inform Griffin of my choice so that he knows who you are. Then we can sort out getting you cleaned up and fitted with a suitable outfit," Evelyn explained.

"I need an outfit to be a bodyguard?" Alita asked. "Wouldn't that be restrictive and limit my movement?"

"Perhaps a little, but once you get used to it, you'll find it's much safer to wear a vest in case of attack," Evelyn said.

"How likely is it that there'll be any sort of attack?" Alita asked. "Those gates look well-guarded."

"There's an increasing risk of attack the closer we get to my wedding day," Evelyn explained.

"You're getting married?" Alita asked. She'd heard weddings were commonplace among richer Calndom dragons.

"Yes. I'm betrothed to Laird Luana Everhart," Evelyn said.

"Who's that?" Alita asked.

"She's the daughter of the last High Caln. Her mother and Griffin arranged for us to marry," Evelyn explained. "There's fears regarding the Duchies trying to take the crown by force. That's why Luana and I are betrothed. Once she moves into the castle, she'll be able to hear anything they do, which will stop them from trying to kill Griffin or myself."

Alita stared at Evelyn with wide eyes. "You say that like it's normal."

"I've spent seven years living with Griffin's family, Alita," Evelyn told her. "It's not news to me that they're jealous or vengeful. They only have a right to the crown if there's no Prinze and the High Caln dies." When Alita gave her a blank look, Evelyn added, "Don't worry, I'll explain everything to you. I think Chieftain Clyde is the only one from Tribe-Ali who knows how the royal family works."

They returned to silence as Evelyn continued to lead Alita through the streets. A few dragons were still out, but most paid no mind to them. Alita noticed most of the dragons wore cloaks similar to Evelyn's. Each one was a different colour and Alita finally noticed the wooden buttons holding the cloaks in place. Each cloak had one large button, which was carved and painted with a symbol. Alita glanced down at Evelyn's button and spotted a blue diamond shape. It was coloured to look like ice.

"It's the crest I chose when I took on a surname," Evelyn said. noticing Alita looking at the button, "Every noble family has a crest and surname. Every noble wears a cloak made out of any fabric or colour they choose. Most choose to keep family colours similar. Griffin's family all have grey-blue cloaks made out of fleece. I don't know why Griffin chose fleece though. I tried one of their cloaks once, it's heavy and warm. Not something I thought an Ice Dragon would choose."

"What about your cloak?" Alita asked.

"Mine is made out of silk," Evelyn said, "It's much lighter so I don't feel hot all the time."

Alita nodded. "So, your surname is Caldwell then?"

"Yes, Caldwell," Evelyn stated. She lifted her head a little, though she didn't look prideful.

"Evelyn Caldwell," Alita muttered to herself, testing the name. She didn't think it fit very well, but she decided not to say that to Evelyn.

They soon came to another fence. It looked the same as the first one, though Alita noticed the guards here looked a bit more intimidating. Evelyn told them she was returning from Tribe-Ali with Alita and they let them through the gate with no hesitation. Alita found herself walking closer to Evelyn as they continued down the street.

"Where are we anyway?" Alita asked.

"The Noble Districts. The fences keep the noble families and royal family separate from everyone else in Hiza Calndom," Evelyn explained. "Working within the Noble Districts is considered an honour."

"Are we getting close to the castle?" Alita asked. The sun had almost set entirely by now, making it hard to see much more than shadows.

"We are," Evelyn said. "There's still one more gate, but once we've reached it, you'll be able to see the castle."

"Why are there so many gates?" Alita asked.

Evelyn sighed quietly before replying, "It's all about ranking, Alita. The first gate protects everyone; all fifty noble families plus the royal family. The second gate protects the five highest ranking noble families and the royal family. The last gate protects only the royal family and those who live in the castle. The more important you and your family are, the more protection you get."

"And who decides who's important?" Alita asked.

"The laws and traditions that have been in place since we first founded Hiza Calndom thousands of years ago," Evelyn said, "It all ties into the royal family and how the crown is passed. The High Caln chooses an heir and teaches them how to rule the Calndom. When they die, their chosen Prinze becomes High Caln. The Prinze must be married before they can become High Caln, though, to prevent corruption. Their spouse acts as an advisor and, in most cases, gives the High Caln eggs. Those are the Duchies and they pass on the lineage of their family and reap the rewards of their parents' positions.

"Of course, the Duchies are also useful to the High Caln in the event that they die without a Prinze," Evelyn continued. "In that case, one of the Duchies is chosen as High Caln. But once a Prinze becomes High Caln, the previous royal family moves into one of the five manors in the Higher Noble District. That's where they live until their rank is pushed down through the natural course of High Calns dying and their families' becoming nobles. Once a family becomes sixth in rank, they move to the Lower Noble District, where they stay until they become fiftieth in rank. That's when they drop their surname and become regular citizens. Of course, by that point, it's been about so long that the original dragons of that family are long gone."

"That sounds very complicated," Alita said. She wasn't even sure she had understood everything.

"It's actually quite simple. Everyone gets a turn living a good life." Evelyn looked at Alita, her indigo eyes narrow. "Would you prefer we had a system where dragons had to please the higher powers to remain in their rank?"

"No..." Alita said uncertainly. "But it sounds like rankings change a lot. How do you remember which dragons are in which rank?"

"The rankings only change when a High Caln dies and their Prinze takes the crown," Evelyn explained. "That normally only happens every three to five decades or so."

They emerged into a wide, circular area of cobblestone. The moon was almost full and the sky was clear, filling the area with silver light. Evelyn turned and led Alita up to the final gate. Alita realised she could see the shadow of the castle looming behind it. There wasn't much distance between the gate and the entrance to the castle.

Evelyn explained the same thing to the guards here as she had twice before. The guards welcomed her and opened the gate. Alita couldn't help but notice how tired they seemed. As she and Evelyn went through the gate, Alita spotted a group of guards come out of the castle. They nodded to Evelyn respectfully as they passed and continued to the gate, where they swapped places with the other guards. The worn out guards followed Evelyn and Alita into the castle.

Chapter 4

The castle was far more extravagant on the inside. Though it was dark, the walls were lit by torches. The outside of the castle was definitely built out of stone. Alita could feel that much. But the walls inside were made out of wood, and the floor was a glossy marble, which reflected the firelight of the torches onto the floor.

Evelyn headed straight for a grand staircase, directly ahead of them. Alita followed her, though she noticed the guards behind them go into one of the rooms they passed. Evelyn led Alita up the stairs and down a corridor on the right. At the very end there was a spiral staircase. It was much narrower than the grand staircase behind them. Evelyn didn't hesitate to start climbing the stairs. Alita followed behind slowly. This was the first time she had been inside an actual building. Being surrounded by walls gave her an uncomfortable tingling feeling deep in her gut.

The stairs led to a small room, which had a single door opposite them. Evelyn pushed it open and glanced behind her. Alita realised she was waiting for her and sped up a little. The hallways behind the door were much wider than the ones on the lower floor. Evelyn and Alita followed the hallway around a corner. Evelyn turned to a set of doors beside her and pushed them open.

Alita was starting to wonder how much longer they would have to navigate the castle when she realised this room was a library. There were shelves loaded with books from floor to ceiling. A low table sat across the room and there was a desk in the far corner. The desk had a few lit candles and an open book. The dragon at the desk was large and blue. His horns were long and straight, like Evelyn's, but had an extra spike halfway along the top. His blue-grey cloak sat heavy on his shoulders.

Evelyn cleared her throat and said, "Griffin, I have returned with my bodyguard."

High Caln Griffin turned to look at them. His cyan eyes were faded with exhaustion. He stood, head high, silver crown glinting in the dim light.

"That is good to hear," he said. He looked Alita up and down. "A Rock Dragon is a good choice. What is her name?"

"Alita," Evelyn replied.

"Alita," Griffin said the name slowly. Alita suppressed a shiver at how uncomfortable it made her feel. "That name is familiar..."

"She was my friend before I became Prinze," Evelyn explained.

"Ah, yes." Griffin looked down at Evelyn. "I hope you know what you are doing. Do not let emotions interfere with your decisions."

Evelyn rolled her eyes. "I know. I would trust Alita with my life. She'll only need a little instruction to take on the role."

Griffin sniffed. "And a bath."

"That too," Evelyn muttered.

"Very well. Take Alita down to the guardroom and tell Heather of her arrival," Griffin instructed. "Then, go to bed. It is getting late."

"You should go to bed too, Griffin," Evelyn said, turning to leave.

Griffin merely grunted and turned back to the desk. Alita watched him for a moment before quickly following Evelyn out of the room. Once back in the hallway, Alita shook her wings and shivered.

"Are you cold?" Evelyn asked.

"Uh, yeah," Alita lied. She didn't want to admit that High Caln Griffin freaked her out.

Evelyn eyed Alita for a moment, then smiled. "Griffin's quite large for a dragon. It's okay to be intimidated by him."

Before Alita could respond, Evelyn turned and trotted back to the spiral staircase. Alita followed her briskly all the way back to the ground floor. There, Evelyn led her to one of the rooms they had passed earlier.

Inside, Alita recognised the forms of dozens of sleeping dragons. They all had one blanket each on the floor and a second blanket pulled across their backs. The few dragons that were awake, sat near the entrance. Alita recognised one of the guards from earlier kicking off the last of his armour before crawling into one of the pairs of blankets.

A dragon the same height as Alita stepped in front of her. The dragon had short ears and horns that curled down and around like a ram's. Her skin was dark brown, though her neck and belly were a lighter grey-brown.

"Heather," Evelyn said. "This is Alita. She is my new bodyguard."

Heather raised an eyebrow at Alita, then turned to Evelyn. "Are you sure this is a dragon you want to follow you around? She doesn't look anythin' like a guard."

"She's from Tribe-Ali," Evelyn said. "I trust that you'll teach her what she needs to know."

"Very well, Prinze Evelyn." Heather bowed her head so that it was lower than Evelyn's. "I will have her ready to serve you by mornin'."

"Thank you, Heather," Evelyn said with a nod. "Alita, I'll see you bright and early."

"Er, right. Night, Evelyn," Alita said.

"*Prinze* Evelyn," Heather corrected sternly.

Alita shot Evelyn a questioning look. Evelyn nodded before leaving the room. Alita turned back to Heather.

"Alright, Alita," Heather began, "first thin's first, you need a bath."

Chapter 5

Heather dragged Alita across the ground floor of the castle to a new room. Upon entering, Alita saw a large, rectangular pool of water. Warm, damp air clung to her body in the form of little droplets. She had never seen a bathhouse before, and she had certainly never expected them to be so big, but Alita was able to recognise it regardless.

A freckled blue dragon was alone by the water's edge. He scrambled to his feet when he saw them.

"Greetings Heather," he said. "Bit late for a bath, isn't it?"

"It's not for me, Jai, it's for this one." Heather waved a wing at Alita. "She's Prinze Evelyn's new bodyguard."

"Ah, yes. I heard she was getting a dragon from Tribe-Ali today," Jai said. "Hop in and we'll get to work."

Alita looked at the water, then at Jai and Heather. "I can bathe myself."

"I'm sure you can," Heather said. "However, new workers in the castle must gain our trust. Especially when that dragon is in charge of keepin' our future High Caln safe."

"Don't worry, I've been washing dragons for years," Jai said. "Once I'm done, you won't have even a grain of sand on your skin."

Alita blinked at him, then looked at Heather. "Is he serious?"

"It's his job." Heather shrugged. "He's only supposed to wash the royal family, but we're all in this together."

Alita realised she wouldn't be able to talk them into leaving her be. With a sigh, she approached the water and carefully slid in. The water was oddly warm, but not hot. Alita wasn't sure how she felt about the temperature. She was used to the chilly waters of the ocean. But as Jai started scrubbing her head and neck, she found herself relaxing into it.

After the bath, Alita dried off and followed Heather back into the castle. The drier castle air hit her in a cold blast. The cool marble floors beneath her feet didn't help. Each step felt like ice crawling up her legs. Heather stopped at the door next to the guardroom.

"This is the servant's quarters. Wait here," she told Alita before going inside.

She came back out a few minutes later with another dragon. He was skinny and tall. His legs looked almost too thin. He had pale yellow skin and horns that pointed down, behind his head.

"This is Henry," Heather said. "He's in charge of fittin' the guards with their armour and vests."

"I just need to take some measurements." Henry lifted a forefoot to show the flexible measuring tape he was holding. "I'll be able to find a premade vest for you by morning."

"Okay." Alita stood straight, making sure her wings were folded correctly.

Henry wrapped the measuring tape around the base of her neck and pulled it until it was just starting to get tight. He muttered something then wrapped it under her chest, pulling it up between her shoulders and her wings. He muttered again and pulled the tape away. Lifting one of Alita's wings with his own, Henry stretched the tape across her side, muttered a third time, then stepped back.

"You're actually about the same size as Heather," Henry said. He looked at Heather. "I think she'd fit into one of your old vests."

"I guess I'll have to pull them out," Heather muttered. "Thank you, Henry."

"Anytime." Henry smiled before heading back into the servant's quarters.

Heather turned back to Alita. "I'll go over the correct posture in the mornin'. You need your sleep."

Alita nodded, silently agreeing with her. It was late at night, perhaps around midnight. Alita was starting to feel drained from the long day. Heather took her back into the guardroom and pointed out a bed for her to sleep in. Alita curled up on the blankets, not bothering to pull one over herself, and fell asleep within seconds.

Chapter 6

Evelyn entered her room with a weary breath. It had been a long day, flying all the way to Tribe-Ali and back, but it was all worth it to see Alita again. Evelyn hadn't had the chance to visit her since becoming Prinze.

Her room in the castle was fitting for a Prinze, even if it was a bit extravagant for her. The two walls that met the outside of the castle were built of old stone, carefully stacked together and regularly maintained. The other two walls were made of wood and painted blue to match Evelyn's element and skin colour.

Sitting down, she leaned back a little to fiddle with the button on her cloak. It was a pain to get off without help. But her personal servant, Lily, had the day off so Evelyn could make the trip to Tribe-Ali in peace. She had needed that solitude to mentally prepare for the conversation ahead. As much as she had hoped to be met with enthusiastic agreement, she knew there was a chance Alita wouldn't leave the Tribe. She could be a completely different dragon after seven years or may have even left Tribe-Ali in that time.

Evelyn was relieved that hadn't been the case. Alita was still her old friend from seven years ago, and they could begin rebuilding that friendship now that they were together again.

Finally pulling her cloak's button out of its clasp, she let the fabric slide off her back. She was too tired to be bothered moving it. Lily would be washing it tomorrow anyway, there was already a clean cloak sitting on a hanger in the corner of the room.

Evelyn walked over to a small table that held only an empty stand. It was sculpted perfectly to hold her crown when she wasn't wearing it. Although she was rarely without her crown, she certainly wouldn't sleep with it on. She slid it off her head and horns and placed it carefully on the stand, relieved to be rid of the weight for the day. She never understood how Griffin managed the weight of his silver crown. It could be that the lighter material wasn't such a weight to bear. She had been expected to wear gold due to resource limitations, but maybe the physical weight wasn't what wore heaviest on her at all. Evelyn wondered if she would ever be rid of the crown, or if she could get it changed once she was High Caln. Griffin wouldn't be able to control her choices then.

Utterly exhausted, she crawled onto her bed, which was thankfully right next to the table. It was soft, and sinking into the pillows and blankets reminded her of being wrapped in her mother's wings on the sandy beach of Tribe-Ali.

Things were so much simpler when she was younger. Evelyn was raised by her mother and aunt, alongside her cousin. Whenever she wasn't with them, she would be hanging out with Alita and her family. They had other friends too, but Evelyn could barely remember their names anymore. Alita had been the only dragon from her youth to stay on the forefront of her mind all these years.

She rolled around on the bed a bit, trying to get comfy. None of the usual tricks were working. She had tried pulling one of her sky blue blankets over herself and even pulled her favourite pillow under her chin for support, which always helped her to fall asleep when she felt restless. After trying every possible position at least three times over, she found herself staring at the portrait of herself across the bed. She'd never been fond of seeing herself in paintings, let alone in her own room, but Griffin had insisted that it was tradition. After seven years, Evelyn wasn't sure how true that was. The nobles didn't seem to follow it, but perhaps it was just a royal family thing.

Evelyn considered rolling around some more, so that she wouldn't have to look at the painting. However, her aching muscles finally won the battle for rest and she allowed herself to settle into sleep.

Interlude I

Modesty looked over the edge of the castle's parapet. The moon was almost full in the clear sky above her, taunting her with its light. A cold breeze brushed her wings. She relished its icy touch. She didn't understand how her father could wear those heavy cloaks all day and not overheat. When she pried the crown from his frozen corpse, those cloaks would be the first thing to go.

"Why are you still up?"

Modesty turned at the sound of her brother's voice. Clement was standing several metres behind her, away from the edge of the roof. He wasn't like Modesty. He was round and kind and soft. His ears were fat and his horns curved downwards. His pale blue-green skin looked like ice in the moonlight.

"I'm enjoying the cold," Modesty said, turning back to look at the view of the Calndom. "And planning my next move."

Clement sighed. "This again, Modesty? Evelyn's betrothed now. She just came back with her new bodyguard earlier tonight. You might've had a chance before, but it's gone now."

"You think so little of my abilities," Modesty said. She froze her claws until the ice was creeping up her legs. "I have spent years preparing for this. Do you really think I would give up just because they're making it harder for me?"

"Why don't you forget about becoming High Caln and talk to the nobles?" Clement suggested. "You'd really like them if you gave them a chance. Maybe you'd even find someone to marry."

Modesty snorted. A cloud of icy mist flew out on her breath. "You think I care about any of that? Don't you know me at all? I'm not like you; prancing around after a dragon who'll never show any interest."

Clement sighed again. "Just go to bed, Modesty. It's the middle of the night."

"I will sleep when I'm ready," Modesty said simply.

"Alright." Clement turned to leave. "Goodnight, Modesty."

Modesty listened to his footsteps as he walked back to the stairs. She allowed the ice on her legs to melt and shook away the water droplets. Her brother didn't understand her. She never liked that Griffin could just choose who his heir would be. The stories of the old Calndoms from thousands of years ago spoke of bloodlines and inheriting the crown. That was how it should be. That was how Modesty would get the crown for herself. She just had to remove the right dragons from the equation.

Chapter 7

Alita woke to someone prodding her in the side. She opened her eyes groggily to see Heather standing over her.

"Time to get up," she said.

Alita looked around the room. Only a few dragons were still asleep. Most of the blanket piles were empty. There was a large window near where Alita was lying. The world outside was still dark, perhaps darker than when she'd gone to sleep.

"It's still dark outside," Alita said, turning back to Heather.

"The High Caln and Prinze get up at sunrise," Heather explained. "As Prinze Evelyn's bodyguard, you must be awake and ready before she leaves her room."

"Oh, okay." Alita got up with a deep breath. She felt like she needed more sleep. Sleeping late and waking early didn't make for the best night's rest.

Heather picked up a dark grey vest and placed it in front of Alita. "This is what you'll be wearin' while servin' the Prinze."

Alita looked at the vest for a moment. "How do I put it on?"

Heather looked like she was trying not to roll her eyes. "Step into it and I'll zip it up."

Alita nodded and stepped into the two large holes in the vest. Heather pulled the vest up her legs, wrapped it around her shoulders, and did up the zipper on the back. Alita fidgeted a bit, feeling the squeeze of the vest's padding.

"It's a bit tight," she muttered.

"It's meant to be," Heather said, turning to the door. "Come on, Prinze Evelyn will be up soon."

Alita followed Heather out of the guardroom and through the castle. She noticed they were heading in the same direction that Evelyn had taken her last night. Heather walked with her head high and wings folded. Her ears twitched as though she were listening for every sound in the castle. Alita followed her with her head a bit lower. Heather glanced at her with narrow, purple-grey eyes.

"Keep your head up, Alita," Heather instructed. "Don't drag your tail. Walk with purpose. You must radiate confidence and instil fear in those who threaten Prinze Evelyn or yourself."

Alita took a breath and straightened her neck. She did her best to mimic Heather's posture. It felt rigid and stiff. She looked back for approval. Heather smiled and nodded.

"You'll get used to it before long," she said.

They reached the top floor of the castle and Heather led Alita across the hallway, past the library. There was a door at the very end with a single armoured guard sitting in front of it. The guard dipped her head to Heather.

"Is Prinze Evelyn awake yet?" Heather asked.

"Lily just went in to wake her," the guard said.

"Good. This is Alita." Heather tipped her head to Alita. "She is Prinze Evelyn's new bodyguard. You are relieved of your post, Crystal, go get some rest."

The guard, Crystal, nodded and headed down the hallway. Heather turned back to Alita.

"You will wait here until Prinze Evelyn comes out," she instructed. "Then you are expected to stay at her side until she returns here for the night."

"What about food?" Alita asked. She hadn't even had breakfast yet. Was she supposed to go all day without a meal?

"You will be allowed to eat lunch with the Prinze at midday. But you must stay on your guard," Heather said. "Dinner will be served to you before you go to bed."

"What about breakfast?" Alita asked.

"The guards only eat two meals a day," Heather explained. "You have been allocated lunch and dinner."

"Oh." Alita dropped her gaze to the floor.

"You'll get used to it quickly," Heather said, turning to leave. "Just wait 'til you see the meals."

Heather headed back down the hall and disappeared around the corner. Alita stood by Evelyn's door, trying to maintain the stiff posture Heather had taught her. When she looked to her right, she saw another guard sitting in front of two more doors. Despite the large amounts of armour covering his body, Alita recognised the curve of his ear fins and lack of horns as Water Dragon traits. The guard watched her silently.

"Um... hey," Alita said.

"You're new," the guard said.

"Yeah. I arrived last night," Alita explained.

"It's about time they got Prinze Evelyn a bodyguard," the guard muttered. "Maybe that means I can stop doing night shifts here."

"Who are you guarding?" Alita asked.

"The same dragon as everyone else," the guard said. "But I'm responsible for tracking the Duchies' movements in the night. If either of them leaves their rooms, I report it."

"Right." Alita stared at the ground. She remembered Evelyn mentioning the Duchies being a danger. But they wouldn't really do anything violent, right?

While Alita was pondering the question, the door beside her opened. Alita turned to see Evelyn, dressed in her cloak and crown, emerge with a small turquoise Water Dragon beside her.

Evelyn noticed Alita and a smile crossed her face. "Good morning,

Alita."

"Morning, Evelyn," Alita said.

Evelyn nodded slightly and started down the hall. The Water Dragon followed close behind her, head down. Alita trailed after them, trying her best to maintain the uncomfortable bodyguard posture.

Chapter 8

Evelyn went straight down to the great hall on the ground floor for breakfast. She hadn't eaten dinner last night and was hungry. She was acutely aware of Alita following her. She wondered what Lily thought of her new bodyguard. Alita seemed more rigid than the night before. She figured Heather had taught her the basics of bodyguard posture.

The great hall was a large room. Not quite as spacious as the main room of the ground floor, but still big enough for at least a hundred dragons to eat at once. There was the crown table at the far side of the room, where Griffin was already seated, and several rows of tables spanning the length of the room for others to eat. It seemed strange that Griffin's wife, Misti, was nowhere to be seen, nor the Duchies, Modesty and Clement. The royal family usually always ate together, but perhaps a schedule change meant they'd be dining later.

Evelyn made her way up to the crown table and sat on Griffin's left. Lily sat next to Griffin's servant, Snowcloud, who was seated a few metres behind Griffin. Alita followed suit, sitting on Lily's left. Griffin snuck a glance back at Alita, then looked at Evelyn.

"Have you informed your bodyguard of the conditions to her employment?" he asked.

Evelyn's jaw tensed and she shot a look at him through narrow eyes. "I haven't had the chance yet. We got back quite late last night."

"Perhaps you should tell her now then," Griffin said. His voice was firm. There was an edge to it that suggested he would do it himself if

Evelyn refused.

Evelyn sighed and turned to look at Alita, who noticed her gaze in an instant.

"Come up here for a moment, Alita," Evelyn said.

Alita obeyed, cautiously stepping up to the table. "Have I done something wrong already?"

"No, you've been great," Evelyn reassured her. "However, Griffin just reminded me of a condition to you being my bodyguard."

"Condition?" Alita glanced at Griffin, then back at Evelyn.

"The condition is that you have a week-long trial. At the end of the week, Griffin and I assess your work and determine whether you stay my bodyguard, get employed elsewhere, or go back home," Evelyn explained. Then she smiled and added, "I think you'll do just fine though. We won't be sending you back to Tribe-Ali."

"Don't be so sure, Evelyn," Griffin said. He eyed Alita a moment. "If you ignore your duties or do not sufficiently protect Prinze Evelyn, I will see you removed from your position no matter what she says."

Evelyn spotted a flash fear in Alita's face and glared at Griffin. "There is no other dragon I would trust more with my life than Alita. Don't give her a hard time just because you don't approve of my decision."

Griffin narrowed his eyes at Evelyn. Then he let out a long, slow breath through his nostrils. She pretended not to notice the thin mist that escaped with it.

"Very well, Evelyn," Griffin said, turning back to his meal. "But believe me when I say trusting your friends too much can be dangerous."

With that, he took another bite of his food. Evelyn turned back to Alita and gave her a small smile. Alita smiled back weakly. A small growl emerged from her stomach and she suddenly looked very ashamed.

"Don't worry Alita," Evelyn said, holding back a giggle. She grabbed a plum from her plate and gave it to Alita. "Have this. It's not much, but it'll help you get through to lunch. Just be sure to eat it quietly so it doesn't bother Griffin too much."

"Oh, uh, thanks," Alita muttered. She went back to where she was sitting, stuffing half the plum in her mouth before she sat down.

"You should not be feeding the workers," Griffin said in a low, warning voice. "They are assigned meals for a reason."

Evelyn glared at him. Ice formed along her claws before she could stop it. "I'm not controlling like you. Besides, Alita and I didn't have dinner last night. It would be unfair of me to expect her to go so long without eating after all the flying we did yesterday."

Griffin narrowed his eyes at her. "I will pretend you did not just insult me. However, if you do it again, I will have to organise repercussions."

Evelyn bit back a remark and turned to her plate. She was sick of his authoritarian attitude but there was nothing she could do about it. She couldn't wait to be rid of it.

Chapter 9

The rest of breakfast went by in silence. Evelyn managed to subtly shake off the ice on her claws and eat like a perfect Prinze. Afterwards, she wordlessly followed Griffin to the throne room. Lily scurried away to clean Evelyn's room, though Alita followed Evelyn diligently. Evelyn decided to explain to her what they were doing next.

"This is the throne room," Evelyn said as they entered the room. "This is where Griffin oversees requests, messages, and courts in the morning. I sit with him to learn and give input."

"It's a big room." Alita's amber eyes were wide as she took in the sight.

Evelyn looked around the room with a hum of agreement. Several dragons were already in the room, preparing for the courts. Near the door sat a set of thrones carved from stone. Griffin's was the largest and most extravagantly designed. It had remained unchanged for centuries. On one side, Caln Misti's throne sat smaller and noticeably less decorated. The other side had Evelyn's throne, which, despite being smaller than Griffin's, was more extravagant than his wife's.

Across the room, there was a large, mosaic, stained glass window. The pattern wasn't anything other than a mesh of colours from what Evelyn could see. But it had a colour for each of the elements on it. Red for fire, yellow for lightning, blue for water, green for nature, brown for rock, purple for ice, and orange for dragons with no element. Evelyn wasn't sure why ice was represented by purple, but guessed it looked better than two shades of blue.

"Don't worry," Evelyn said, turning back to Alita. "You just have to sit on my left and make sure no one tries to assassinate me. Which won't happen during the courts."

"Are you sure?" Alita asked. "What happens during the courts?"

"It depends on the day. I believe today is mostly requests and messages from around Hiza Calndom. But there is a court case later in the morning that Griffin has to pass judgement on," Evelyn explained.

"A court case?" Alita echoed. "What about?"

Evelyn shrugged her wings. "I'm not too sure. Griffin was up late studying the aw books to ensure he made a fair verdict. Don't worry though, you don't need to know anything for it."

Despite her attempt, it didn't seem to relax Alita much. Griffin grunted, getting Evelyn's attention. He was already seated at his throne, his tail wrapped neatly around his feet. Evelyn followed suit, sitting on her throne and wrapping her tail around herself. Alita sat a few metres to her left, still tensely surveying the room.

A red and grey dragon approached the thrones with his head held high. In his grasp was a rolled up scroll. He let it roll open as he stopped in front of the thrones.

"High Caln Griffin, Your Majesty." The dragon greeted Griffin with a slight bow. "Prinze Evelyn, Young Ruler. Today's courts will contain requests from throughout the Calndom as well as here, in the castle. All requests made are anonymous."

Griffin eyed the open scroll in the dragon's grip. "That is quite the list you have there, Alvar."

"Yes, High Caln. Today's list contains requests from over the weekend as well. It would seem the impending wedding of Prinze Evelyn to Laird Luana has raised some queries," Alvar explained.

"Very well. You may begin," Griffin said.

Alvar nodded and raised the scroll up so he could read off it. "From the Northern Farmlands, a request to increase compensation for the work and produce supplied. There are also concerns of drought after last summer. What does the crown say to these requests and concerns?"

Griffin straightened his posture, sitting a little taller as he spoke. "The Farmland districts already have enough money. They are paid well for their work. Their request is denied. As for the concerns, we have seen no evidence of drought so far this year. If there does happen to be a drought, we will send Water Dragons trained in water detection to find, collect, and supply fresh water. However, the Northern Farmlands have a lake nearby. They should be using that for their water."

Evelyn wasn't sure she agreed with Griffin. If she had final say, she would look into the payments the farmers were receiving. She decided to speak up.

"High Caln Griffin, not to be rude, but I disagree," Evelyn said, looking at Griffin. "Perhaps we should investigate the effects of inflation on the cost of farmer equipment and adjust their payments accordingly."

Griffin gave Evelyn a side on look. "That would require extra labour and cost far more than it would be worth. The request is still denied."

Evelyn squinted at Griffin but didn't say anything. Alvar waited in silence for a moment, before continuing to the next item on the list.

"Businesses all over the Calndom have made requests for subsidies and financial aid for the slow winter season," Alvar said, reading from the scroll. "Given the estimated costs of the wedding, many businesses believe there is room in the budget for this. They have signed a petition to have their income and expenses checked regularly to ensure a balance that allows them year round profit."

Griffin huffed. "Nonsense. The businesses are responsible for their own earnings and spendings. If a business cannot afford to stay open over the winter months, they should not be operating. Those who cannot survive must close down so that others can thrive."

Evelyn frowned at Griffin. His attitude in denying a request was outrageous.

"Hang on, Griffin. The businesses have made a petition. We cannot ignore them when they have a document requesting our attention," Evelyn said.

Griffin scowled at Evelyn for a long moment. "Very well. *You* can look into it, Prinze Evelyn. I will make that solely your responsibility."

Evelyn nodded slightly. She expected such a reaction. Griffin often put things on her to sort out when she objected to his decision.

After a long moment of silence, Griffin nodded to Alvar. "You may continue."

"Er, right." Alvar glanced over the scroll again. "From within the castle, staff are requesting greater pay and more days off. They say only having one day off is leading to burnout and they feel the castle's money should be utilised in a better way. A few of the staff are trying to find places to live outside of the castle and noble districts but are struggling because the pay is too low."

Alvar glanced up at Griffin with a hesitant, wide eyed look that told Evelyn he was one of those very dragons. Whether Griffin noticed she couldn't tell.

"An interesting request," Griffin said. His tone made Evelyn's skin crawl. "Prinze Evelyn, do you have any opinions before I make my ruling?"

Evelyn glanced at Griffin, feeling the iciness in his gaze. She guessed whatever she said that wasn't agreeing with Griffin's trend of denying requests would make her responsible for sorting it out. Unfortunately for Griffin, she knew more about this topic than he did after helping Misti look at staff conditions a few months back.

"I believe the castle staff do deserve a bit more money for their work," Evelyn said. "Even though they live in the castle, they make very little compared to those who work outside of the noble districts. There is absolutely room for higher wages. We don't need to put so much into the wedding after all. I also understand their need for more time off. Dragons around the Calndom typically work five days and have three days off, whereas staff within the castle only get one day off and must work seven days. Perhaps changing up their work week would be beneficial."

"A well formulated argument, Prinze Evelyn," Griffin said. "However, if we changed the standard work week within the castle, we would need to move shifts and hire extra staff to make up for the loss of labour. Even *if* you were correct about spending less on the wedding and more on staff, this is still something we simply cannot afford. Those dragons should be proud to work so much, considering they are working directly for the royal family."

Evelyn noticed Alvar duck his head. It seemed he saw the rejection about to happen. Evelyn, however, wasn't going to just let it end there.

"You say we can't afford that, but I disagree," Evelyn told Griffin. "I see what we pay out in expenses and what we make in profits. The castle is a business much like any other. Just because we collect taxes as a revenue doesn't mean we don't have profitability. We're even more responsible for our accountability than a standard business because we are *leading* these dragons. We are rulers and lawmakers. We have the money to do something for these dragons. It's not fair on them that we can afford a lavish wedding but can't spare a coin for those in need. I don't think I've seen you spend a single Drachmar on bettering the Calndom since I became Prinze."

"Silence!" Griffin snarled suddenly. His breath hit Evelyn with a freezing chill and ice coated his teeth. "I will not tolerate such insolence in the courts! Especially not from you."

Evelyn glared at Griffin. She wanted to argue back but one look at the ice creeping along the edges of Griffin's mouth told her to keep her mouth shut. Griffin turned back to Alvar

"The requests are denied," he said. "Move on to the next item."

Chapter 10

The rest of the courts went by uneventfully. Evelyn kept her mouth shut as Alvar read the rest of the requests and Griffin denied them all. By the end of it, Evelyn wondered if there had been any point to reading them in the first place.

Alvar rolled up the scroll with a barely masked look of defeat. As he stepped away from the thrones, Heather stepped forward.

"High Caln Griffin, Prinze Evelyn, today I will be overseein' the trial of Korbin. This dragon has caused much grief to the Northern Districts," Heather explained. "He has been deemed a danger to anyone near him. For this reason, he has been chained and immobilised. My guards are bringin' him in now."

Evelyn glanced to the side of the room, where several heavily armoured dragons were guiding a grey-brown dragon into the room. She squinted at him through the guards. There was something vaguely familiar about him. His horns curved down and inwards. His ears were short, with pointed tips. His brown eyes darted around the room despite his inability to move more than a slight shuffle. His gaze locked onto the corner of the room as the guards lined him up. Evelyn followed it to see Alita sitting stiffly, her amber eyes wide and staring back at him.

"Do you know him?" Evelyn asked quietly.

Alita glanced at Evelyn and nodded slightly. Evelyn turned back to the chained dragon. She squinted at him again and searched her memory for where she recognised him.

"This is the dragon that caused the Northern Districts so much trouble?" Griffin asked. He scowled at the dragon. "Remind me what this young drake has done to require *my* verdict."

Heather nodded. "His name is Korbin. Originally from Tribe-Ali, Korbin challenged his Chieftain, then fled his home only to end up on our northern borders. There, he stole food and money from businesses and civilians alike. When offered a home by a kind civilian, he lied and manipulated her until finally attackin' her during an argument. The victim in question reported his location and cooperated with the Protective Unit to have Korbin arrested. We have collected testimonies from other victims throughout the Northern Districts as this case escalated. However, now we must reach a verdict."

"That is quite a list of crimes," Griffin said. "Though I must ask why this case was escalated all the way up to me? Surely a lower court could have dealt with it."

"I thought so too, High Caln. But every time we allowed Korbin to testify his stance, each judge and jury was left unsure," Heather explained. "It seems he has a way of sweet talking those around him. He's been muzzled today for this very reason."

"Interesting. Please lay out all the information on Korbin's case so that I can make an informed decision," Griffin said. He glanced at Evelyn. "Prinze Evelyn, please do not interfere with this case. I alone will pass judgement today."

Evelyn nodded to Griffin, then looked at Korbin again. There was still something familiar about him. He was the most unremarkable Rock Dragon she had ever seen, yet she felt she had met him before.

Heather mentioned he was from the Tribe, Evelyn thought to herself. Perhaps she had seen him there before?

As Evelyn racked her brain, she remembered small snippets from the Tribe. Days she had thought were long forgotten.

She was only ten when she'd first met him. Korbin was an odd dragon. His mother had been welcomed into the Tribe after seeking protection for herself and her son. He was behind on his schooling and placed into a class with Evelyn and Alita.

"Hey, Evelyn. Have you heard about our new classmate?" Alita asked as they gathered on the beach with their classmates. Her excitement was barely contained behind her grin. "He's a Rock Dragon like me!"

"So? There are plenty of Rock Dragons in the Tribe," Evelyn said. "Like your brother, Liam, or that oddball friend of yours. What's his name? Matt?"

"Yeah but they're the only two close to my age," Alita explained. "This dragon is completely new. Besides, Rock Dragons are the rarest in the Tribe."

"So? They're one of the most common in the Calndom," Evelyn retorted.

Alita shook her head. "You don't get it. Imagine if the only dragons who shared your element were your family and a few others. You'd be excited too. Maybe he knows things we don't about how to control rocks."

"I doubt it. I heard he's behind in his schooling," Evelyn said, rolling her eyes. "Also, Alita, Clyde is my father so most of the Tribe are my family."

"That's different. You don't see Clyde as a parental figure," Alita said. She looked across the beach and suddenly spun around. "There he is! The new guy!"

Evelyn rolled her eyes at Alita's excitement and followed her gaze. Approaching them was a grey-brown dragon about a year older than them. He had unremarkable brown eyes and his horns were still rounded at the tips. He didn't look all that exciting but Alita seemed completely enraptured.

"Hello. My name is Korbin," The new dragon said. He dipped his head a little in an awkward bow.

"I'm Alita. I'm a Rock Dragon too," Alita said, grinning ear to ear.

Korbin smiled. It was a little crooked. Not quite right. It made Evelyn

47

uncomfortable.

"I hope we get lots of time to become friends," Korbin said.

Alita beamed. "Me too."

Evelyn squinted at Alita. It was hard not to feel left out when it seemed Alita had already forgotten about her. Evelyn shuffled away slightly, watching Alita and Korbin continue to chat happily.

Evelyn pulled herself out of her thoughts and back to the present moment. As she looked at Korbin again, she realised he was the same dragon she had met years ago. Though he was bigger, meaner looking, and chained to the point that he could barely move or speak. She also remembered not liking him back then and it looked like her gut feeling had been right.

"What is your ruling, High Caln Griffin?" Heather asked.

Griffin surveyed Korbin for a moment. "I rule Korbin guilty for all of which he has been accused. The appropriate sentencing in this case is five years in the castle dungeon."

Korbin growled, glaring up at Griffin. The guards around him tensed, ready to jump to action if he dared to move. But Korbin stayed still, continuing to glare at Griffin until the guards shuffled him out of the room.

"Despicable dragon," Griffin muttered. "So many crimes, and yet not enough to be worthy of my time. I should add another five years just for wasting it."

"I don't think the rest of the courts would agree with such a ruling," Evelyn said.

"I am aware," Griffin said. He stood up and stretched his legs until he stood on his toes. "That was the last of the courts. No need for a formal closing. I must go to the library and prepare for my afternoon meetings. Prinze Evelyn, do not forget to visit Laird Luana after lunch."

Evelyn refrained from rolling her eyes at his reminder. "Yes, High

Caln Griffin."

Griffin left the room with his head held high. Evelyn turned back to the rest of the room to see the staff of the courts already packing up.

Sure. Don't wait for your future ruler to leave before concluding your work, she thought bitterly as she got up and left the room.

Interlude II

Modesty entered the great hall and scanned the room for an empty spot to have lunch. Her cloak sat heavy on her wings, but Misti had insisted she had to wear it. She couldn't wait to get lunch finished and get back to the arena to practise her battle techniques without it.

As she looked around the room, Modesty spotted her brother, Clement, sitting at a table near the far end of the room. Out of all the dragons she could possibly sit next to, he was the one she best tolerated.

Just as she was about to join him, Modesty heard a quiet voice behind her.

"Um, Evelyn?"

Modesty paused, pretending to look like she was still surveying the room. Out of the corner of her eye, she spotted Evelyn and her bodyguard walk past.

"Yes, Alita?" Evelyn said.

"Do you remember Korbin?" Alita asked.

Evelyn nodded slightly. "I do. It's been a long time, and I didn't know him very well, but I do remember him."

Modesty noted the sudden change in Evelyn's tone from cheery to serious.

"He's changed quite a bit from when I last saw him," Alita said quietly.

"Don't worry Alita. He'll have plenty of time to himself in the dungeon," Evelyn said. "There aren't any other dragons down there right now. Most are either moved to prisons around Hiza Calndom or banished. Maybe he'll come out a changed dragon."

"Maybe," Alita muttered.

Modesty raised an eyebrow at the conversation and glanced over her shoulder. She spotted Heather emerging from the stairs that led underground. A collection of guards followed her. Modesty knew there was a court case happening today. How interesting that the Prinze and her bodyguard knew the defendant.

Modesty turned back to the tables and went to sit with her brother. Even if she wanted to do anything, she'd have to wait for the guards to calm down a little bit. But perhaps she could question the dragon later. It would be useful to know more about Alita from someone who knew her personally.

Chapter 11

After the morning courts, Alita didn't have much focus on her surroundings. Her mind was focused on seeing Korbin chained and muzzled, glaring at dragons around the room. When his eyes had locked with hers, Alita felt a cold chill run up her spine that told her he was not to be trusted. Would she have turned out the same if she had left the Tribe with him years ago?

Lunch was ready for them in the great hall when they arrived. Unlike the morning, Evelyn sat at the end of a table near the entrance of the room. Alita hesitated as she wondered where she should sit. She hadn't forgotten that Heather had allocated her lunch as one of her mealtimes.

"Just sit next to me, Alita," Evelyn said, nodding to the spot next to her.

Alita obeyed, sitting beside her and reaching out to grab some food from the table.

"Hold on," Evelyn said suddenly.

"What is it?" Alita asked, withdrawing her foreleg.

"There are dishes of water under the table," Evelyn explained. "You need to dip your feet in them to wash off any impurities before eating."

Alita leaned back and spotted the water dish. She dipped her front feet in one at a time and shook the water off.

"Now, you may eat," Evelyn said.

Alita immediately reached for the closest dish. It was a bowl of different breads stuffed with roasted meat. The meat smelled a bit like rabbit, but warm and musky. She promptly stuffed a roll into her mouth. Beside her, Evelyn giggled.

"Is something wrong?" Alita asked after swallowing her food.

"You just look so relieved to be eating something," Evelyn said. "The expression you made was kind of cute."

"I haven't eaten a full meal since lunch yesterday," Alita explained. "This is the longest I've gone without food."

"I guess I should have arranged something for you last night before bed," Evelyn said, looking a tiny bit remorseful.

"It's okay. I'll be fine now," Alita reassured her. She grabbed another roll. "I've never had cooked meat before. It's kind of good."

"It's pretty popular here in the castle. The heat involved in cooking it removes impurities, making it safer to eat," Evelyn explained. "Though, the meat can then be flavoured easily, which makes it harder to identify potential poisons."

"You really think someone would poison you?" Alita asked.

"No, I think if a certain someone were to kill me, they'd go about it pretty directly." Evelyn glared across the room to a pair of Ice Dragons eating alone. They wore heavy looking cloaks that were blue-grey in colour, though both were lighter shades than High Caln Griffin's cloak.

"Are those the Duchies?" Alita asked.

Evelyn nodded. "The stripey one is Duchy Modesty and the one with the big nose is Duchy Clement."

Alita eyed the two dragons closely. Modesty only had two stripes on her neck. Alita wouldn't have described her as stripey, though there could easily be more underneath her cloak. As for Clement, he did, in fact, have a large nose. It was definitely the most distinctive feature about him. His eyes were a similar cyan blue to Griffin's, though his skin was much lighter in colour. Modesty, however, had similar colours to Griffin, but with dark blue eyes. Modesty spotted Alita and glared at her. The icy look sent a chill down Alita's spine. This dragon wasn't to be trusted.

"Don't pay too much attention to them, Alita," Evelyn said.

"Isn't it part of my job to watch for dangers to your livelihood?" Alita asked.

"Yes, but you're having lunch right now. Just enjoy it with me." Evelyn frowned slightly. "After this we have to go spend the afternoon with Laird Luana."

"You don't sound too happy about that," Alita said.

Evelyn shook her head. "Don't worry about it. It's just part of the betrothal process. We have to get to know each other and spend time together before the wedding."

"When is the wedding anyway?" Alita asked.

"It's about a month away," Evelyn said. "There's a lot of planning to do and stuff to set up so it's the soonest they can do it."

"They?" Alita echoed.

"High Caln Griffin and Laird Adelaide, Luana's mother," Evelyn clarified. "Adelaide is in charge of setting everything up since Griffin has a whole Calndom to manage. They're meeting in the throne room this afternoon to discuss how it's going."

"Do you not get a say in the preparations?" Alita asked.

"I probably could if I wanted to..." Evelyn trailed off. Alita felt like there were things going unsaid, but she decided it'd be better not to push Evelyn for answers.

Chapter 12

Luana sat in the library of Everhart Manor as her mother fussed over her mane and cloak. Her brothers, Markos, Jakob, and Hamlet, were sitting nearby. Luana could hear the pages of the book Jakob was leafing through and Hamlet shifting from one foot to the next as he waited impatiently.

"Seriously, Luana, will you stop with the smoke?" Adelaide complained. "You're going to give yourself smoke lung."

Luana hissed quietly. She couldn't possibly cool down when she had an impending visit with Prinze Evelyn to get through. The anger she felt made the fire in her chest flare up.

Adelaide ran a comb through Luana's fringe and rearranged the way it sat on her head. Luana frowned at her.

"Can you stop doing that?" Luana asked. "You've redone my mane five times in the last half hour! I'm only meeting Evelyn. It doesn't need to look good."

"Luana!" Adelaide huffed. "Prinze Evelyn is your future wife. You must look perfect!"

Luana rolled her eyes and shook her head to resettle her mane the way it was supposed to sit.

"Seriously, Luana, I just got that right," Adelaide complained, straightening Luana's cloak. "Why must you make this so difficult?"

"Perhaps because my whole life is being decided for me and I'm not allowed to do a single thing by myself?" Luana suggested flatly.

"You might as well just accept it, Sis," Jakob said. "Mother's always going to be like this."

"Easy for you to say; you aren't being forced to marry someone against your will," Luana retorted.

"Luana, dear, you will be safe in the castle," Adelaide said. "You'll keep Prinze Evelyn safe too. With your hearing, you can detect an attack before she's in any real danger."

"While I stay far away from the threat you seem to think I'll be so safe from. Right. Amazing common sense there," Luana said. rolling her eyes again.

"Luana don't roll your eyes. It's disrespectful," Adelaide scolded.

"Maybe I wouldn't have to if you weren't saying and doing ridiculous things," Luana said.

She'd finally had enough and stood up, pushing past her mother. Adelaide called after her but Luana ignored her. She walked over to the edge of the second floor railing, which overlooked the main room of the ground floor, and leapt off the edge, gliding down neatly and pacing out the door.

The sun was warm on her skin. Luana felt better just being out in the fresh air. The heat in her chest cooled and she let out a sigh as the smoky taste in her mouth finally faded. She only had a minute to sit on the cobblestone by herself before the door opened and she recognised the sound of Markos's footsteps.

"Are you alright?" he asked.

"Better now that I'm outside," Luana said. "I still don't get why Mother is so protective and controlling when it comes to my life. I'm an adult now. She needs to accept that."

Markos sat beside her. "You know why she's like that, Luana. She worries about how you'll get by on your own. Having you marry Prinze Evelyn is her way of dealing with those worries."

"Yeah, yeah. She's terrified of what her blind, only daughter might do if no one's around to watch her constantly," Luana muttered bitterly. "She still could have consulted me before making the deal with High Caln Griffin."

"Don't worry, Luana. Things will turn around soon," Markos told her.

"I doubt it," Luana said.

Markos nudged her with his wing. Luana smiled at him. She knew he was trying to reassure her. He looked out for all his younger siblings.

Luana took another breath of the warm air that surrounded them. She was starting to feel properly relaxed.

"Hey! Luana!"

Luana jolted at the sound of Zina's voice piercing the air. In her frustrations of the betrothal and her mother, she'd completely missed the sound of dragons approaching.

Markos chuckled. "Looks like Zina and Victoria have stopped by for an unexpected visit."

Luana shook head with a small smile. "It's a better visit than the planned one happening later."

Zina trotted up to them and sat beside Luana. Victoria followed at a slower pace. Luana could already sense the overzealous grin on Zina's face.

"Hey Zina. Hey Victoria," Luana greeted them. "What brings you by?"

"I heard a rumour that Prinze Evelyn was meant to be visiting you today and thought you could use a little cheer up before she arrived," Zina said.

"I tagged along to keep Zina in check," Victoria added. "You know how she gets."

Luana smiled. "Thanks Victoria."

"Hey! No thanks for me?" Zina asked. She flared her wings dramatically, tossing her cloak onto her back.

Luana laughed. "Alright, Zina. Thank you for showing up. I'm already feeling better."

"Yes! Now we just have to keep it that way." Zina grinned.

"Prinze Evelyn will be here soon so you don't have much time," Markos said.

"Thanks for the reminder," Luana's ears drooped a little and she frowned at the thought. Did she really have to spend the entire afternoon with Evelyn? Why couldn't she just enjoy her life the way she wanted to? "I wish I didn't have to marry her."

"Just remember what I said: things are going to turn around soon," Markos said.

Luana turned to him with a slight frown. "You repeating that makes me worried. Are you having weird dreams again?"

Markos chuckled. "Of course not. I'm just trying to help you see the silver lining."

Chapter 13

Alita and Evelyn ate the rest of their lunch in relative silence. Alita found herself glancing at Clement and Modesty several times during her meal. From a distance, Clement seemed like a polite, clumsy dragon and Modesty looked like the least dangerous dragon on the island. She had no spikes on her head or neck and her cheeks and jawline were round and smooth. But whenever Modesty glared at Alita from across the room, Alita chilled to the bone. She didn't look dangerous, but Modesty was certainly a threat.

Alita kept her impression of Modesty in her mind as she followed Evelyn out of the castle. Any dragon could be a threat and her job was to watch out for dragons that were threats. Were any of the guards a threat? Alita eyed the armoured dragons at the gate between the castle and the Noble Districts. Were there any dragons in league with Modesty? Everyone was on high alert for an attack, but it would only take a few dragons who wished for someone else to be High Caln for an attack to be successful.

Evelyn stopped at the gate, bringing Alita's attention out of her thoughts.

"I am visiting the Everhart family," Evelyn told the guards firmly.

"Of course, Prinze Evelyn," one of the guards said. "Have a safe visit."

The guards opened the gates and Evelyn strode through with confidence. Alita followed, feeling the strain in her back from holding the bodyguard posture. The empty plaza they had walked through the previous night was now busy with dragons. Dragons in cloaks of various colours and materials strolled happily with their servants trailing behind them. Some dragons were armoured or wore vests similar to Alita's. Others wore nothing but were busy carrying food or cleaning the cobblestone streets. It was a much livelier scene than the night before.

Dragons noticed as Evelyn walked through the plaza. Some waved outstretched wings while others dipped their heads respectfully. A few of the older dragons cast narrow looks at Alita as she followed Evelyn. Alita did her best to look like she was supposed to be there.

Evelyn walked through the plaza and down several wide streets before arriving at a large building. It wasn't anywhere near the size of the castle, but it was certainly big. Alita recalled the word 'mansion' from when she was a fledgling. She hadn't been able to picture dragons even living in houses at all back then, but this seemed to fit the definition she was taught.

"This is Everhart Manor," Evelyn said as they approached the building. "Looks like Luana and Markos are already outside."

Alita followed Evelyn's gaze to the front door and spotted four dragons sitting in front of it. She felt a momentary pang of guilt that she hadn't noticed them sooner.

"Greetings, Prinze Evelyn," one of the dragons called. He was the tallest, with red-orange skin and a messy red mane. His cloak was translucent and the purple-red colour complemented his skin nicely.

"Since when do you use the word 'greetings' Markos?" Evelyn asked.

"Well, you are the Prinze right? I'm supposed to be formal with you," Markos said, cracking a smile.

"Is this going to be the rest of my life after the wedding?" Evelyn asked flatly.

"Perhaps," Markos said. "Got to keep things interesting somehow."

Evelyn closed her eyes and took a deep, slow breath. Alita wondered what emotions she was trying to subdue.

"I suppose you're here for the afternoon bonding with Luana," one of the other dragons said. She was short, almost as short as the green dragon beside her. She had the characteristic pale blue skin of an Ice Dragon and a blue cloak draped over her wings. She had a mane, which was pale in colour and draped over her right eye.

"Who's the dragon with you?" the green dragon asked.

Her voice was soft and was almost drowned out when the blue dragon exclaimed, "Whoa! You really got a bodyguard after all!"

"No need to be loud, Zina, I'm right here," Evelyn said. "This is Alita. She started this morning. Alita, this is Victoria Hooper, Zina Kahn, and Markos and Luana Everhart."

Alita finally looked at the last dragon of the group. She had orange skin, covered by a translucent lilac cloak, and a red-orange mane. Her ears were almost comically long and her horns were short. Her fringe draped over her face, somehow managing to outline her pale green eyes. Alita found herself drawn in by those eyes. The milky pupils moved to look at her as though they could see. Alita felt as though they were seeing her very soul.

"Alita? Alita!"

A tail flicked at Alita's nose. She flinched and looked at Evelyn.

"What's wrong with your face?" Evelyn's voice was harsh. Alita got the sense that it wasn't a question and ducked her head.

"Sorry," she apologised.

Alita dared a quick glance at the others. Victoria and Markos were exchanging looks while Zina had a smirk on her face.

"Just focus on your job," Evelyn muttered. "Come on, Luana."

Luana stood up with a sigh and followed Evelyn. Alita quickly resumed the bodyguard posture and followed them, trying her best to look at anything and everything that wasn't Luana. Her ear twitched as she heard Zina sputter out a giggle behind them.

Chapter 14

Evelyn, Luana, and Alita walked in silence for several minutes. Evelyn tried not to focus on what had just happened. But she couldn't get past the way that Alita had stared at Luana. There was something about it that made her heart twist. Evelyn flicked her ear in a subtle attempt to brush off the feeling.

"How's the manor been?" she asked, glancing at Luana. Perhaps a conversation would take her mind off it.

"Fine," Luana muttered.

"Did Adelaide tell you about the colours for your new cloak?" Evelyn asked.

Luana huffed out a plume of smoke. "She said it was 'blue like the sky at midday.' I wouldn't have a clue what that looks like."

"What's with the smoke Luana?" Evelyn asked. "We're betrothed; we need to get along."

Luana turned her head away. "You're only marrying me because of the Duchies. But once you're High Caln, they'll move out of the castle and you won't need me around."

"They can still be a threat from outside the castle as well," Evelyn said. "Besides, I won't be High Caln until Griffin dies. That won't be for a while yet."

Luana didn't respond. Evelyn suppressed an exasperated sigh and turned down a short street that opened out into a wide expanse of grass. Tall hedges lined the edges, hiding them from the view of other dragons. A tree sat in one corner of the field. Evelyn turned off the path to sit under it. The shade would be much nicer than the warm sunlight. Behind her, Evelyn heard Luana and Alita starting a conversation.

"So your name's Alita?" Luana asked.

"Uh, yeah," Alita said hesitantly.

"You don't sound so sure," Luana said. Evelyn saw a small smile on her face.

"I-it is my name," Alita stammered, still not sounding very confident. Her cheeks started to turn a dark red. Evelyn squinted at her. Why was Luana able to fluster her so easily?

"Are you from Hiza Calndom?" Luana asked.

"No, I'm from the Tribe," Alita replied.

"Evelyn flew all the way to Tribe-Ali just to choose a bodyguard?" Luana asked, raising an eyebrow. "Are you really strong or something?"

"I wouldn't call myself strong," Alita said. "But we were friends back before she became Prinze."

Evelyn scowled. Alita was dense as a rock but Luana had a good head on her shoulders. The expression on Luana's face when she turned towards Evelyn told her what Luana was thinking. How could she get out of this?

Luana sat in a small patch of sun a few metres away from Evelyn. Alita stood awkwardly near the base of the tree, glancing between them and around at their surroundings. At least she was still doing her job.

"Your bodyguard seems nice," Luana said to Evelyn.

"Why does that matter to you?" Evelyn asked harshly.

"If you're going to have a bodyguard follow you around the rest of your life, then I should at least get to know her," Luana said.

"It's only for the week. She's on a trial period," Evelyn muttered. "Who knows what'll happen after the wedding."

Luana pulled her long ears back and frowned. "What is that supposed to mean? Am I meant to be your sole protector after that?"

"You'll be able to hear anything coming long before it jumps out to attack me," Evelyn said.

"I'm not going to be your bodyguard," Luana snapped.

"I never asked you to be," Evelyn replied coldly.

Smoke started to rise from Luana's nostrils. She growled slightly as she said, "Clearly that's your intention if you don't intend on keeping your bodyguard around long term."

"You know what, I can't deal with this," Evelyn muttered. She got up and started pacing away.

"Where are you going?" Luana asked.

"Back to the castle," Evelyn snapped. She couldn't stand being around Luana any longer.

Evelyn stormed out of the field and back into the streets of the Noble District. She heard Alita hurrying to catch up to her as she stalked through the cobblestone streets with her head down.

"Are you okay?" Alita asked.

"Just fine," Evelyn growled. Icy mist came from her breath as she spoke.

"You don't look very fine," Alita said. "Your feet are covered in ice."

Evelyn stopped and sighed. The ice forming on her feet melted and she shook it off. She raised her head back up and resumed the posture she'd been taught by Griffin. She shut her anger out of her mind and continued walking as if nothing had happened.

Alita followed her in silence for a moment. "Can I ask you something?"

"If you must," Evelyn said.

"Why did you agree to marry someone you don't even like?" Alita asked.

Evelyn sighed. "Because it's the safest option. I could try to marry someone I actually like but there's no guarantee that she'll even want to marry me. Adelaide is always worried about her daughter and Griffin worries about what the Duchies might do as he gets older. Luana's hearing is an asset to me and marrying her gives Adelaide and Griffin peace of mind. Besides, I have to marry someone before I can become High Caln."

"Who do you want to marry?" Alita asked.

Unfortunately, it seemed Alita wasn't completely thick headed. Evelyn silently kicked herself for letting that clue slip out and stared at the ground as she thought of how to respond. "It doesn't matter. I don't think she's interested in me."

"You can't know if you don't ask," Alita said. "Maybe she is interested in you but doesn't want to get in the way of your wedding."

Evelyn shook her head. "I don't need to ask, Alita. She likes someone else. Can we stop talking about this now?"

"Okay," Alita said with a nod.

Evelyn appreciated Alita's willingness to drop the topic. She didn't want to focus on the situation she was stuck in now. She tucked the thoughts away in her mind and focused on going back to the castle.

Chapter 15

Luana sat in the field for a while after Evelyn and Alita left. The sun was warm and the quiet was comforting. In the distance, she could still hear Evelyn and Alita talking until they reached the edge of her hearing's ability.

Her exceptional hearing could be a curse sometimes, so she chose instead to focus on the bird singing in the tree behind her. It was a sweet, beautiful tune. Perhaps in another life, Luana would sing along with the bird. But she hadn't been allowed to practise her singing since her dad died. Her mother seemed to dislike reminders of Gerold.

As she allowed her mind to drift, she found it snagging relentlessly on thoughts of Alita. Luana supposed others might find her awkward, but she had warmed up so quickly, and even after one meeting the pull to be near her again was undeniable.

As quickly as that thought came, it was whisked away. Alita was on her way back to the castle with Evelyn, sworn to protect her. How could Luana possibly get to know her when she couldn't stand to be around Evelyn? Not to mention the issue of her betrothal.

Luana finally got to her feet with a sigh and started walking home. She didn't need to see to find the way back to the manor. She knew the streets well and her senses were good enough to navigate on her own. With any luck, her mother would've left for her meeting with High Caln Griffin already.

Luana reached the manor without any trouble and pushed her way inside. The door hinges squeaked, drowning out the sound of her footsteps.

As the door swung closed behind her, she heard a horrified shriek fill the air. "Luana! What are you doing home?"

Luana winced, drawing back her ears. Adelaide frantically hurried up to her and pressed her wings into Luana's shoulders.

"You're supposed to be with Prinze Evelyn for the afternoon," Adelaide said.

"I know that, Mother," Luana muttered. She didn't bother trying to pull out of Adelaide's grip. "She left so I came home."

"She did *what!* She can't just leave you on your own. What if you got lost or hurt?" Adelaide released Luana and began pacing the floor. "This is unacceptable! I must report it to High Caln Griffin."

Luana rolled her eyes. "Mother, I'm fine. I'm going to go to my room for a bit."

Adelaide continued to pace in circles, muttering to herself. Luana pushed past her and started for the stairs that led to the second floor. She paused at the first step. Evelyn would be in trouble with Griffin for this. Luana didn't want to marry her, but she certainly didn't hate Evelyn.

"Mother," Luana said quietly, "don't get Evelyn in trouble. She's going through a lot right now."

Adelaide murmured an acknowledgement. Luana wondered if she had even registered the words or just heard her speak. She pushed the thought from her mind and headed upstairs to her room.

Her bedroom smelled like lavender and cedarwood. She knew there was a jar on her nightstand filled with wood shavings and flowers to scent the room. Luana wasn't big on floral scents but the added woody smell made her feel at home.

Luana went straight to her bed, tucked into the corner of the room. It was soft and warm. She sunk into the mattress and felt a few pillows slide into her side. Her cloak caught on one of her hind feet and she heard a distinct rip as the fragile fabric tore apart. She didn't care though. She ruined her cloaks every other week. Her mother wouldn't be happy but they had extras available for this very reason.

Luana collapsed into the bed with a sigh and ripped the button of her cloak away from her. She tossed it half-heartedly and heard it hit the wall just as the door opened.

"Hey Luana." It was Markos. "I heard what Mother said. Are you alright?"

"I'm fine," Luana muttered. She rolled onto her side and tilted her head so her fringe fell away from her eyes.

"You destroyed another cloak already? Mother's going to be furious," Markos said.

"I know. But it caught on my foot as I got into bed. I didn't do it intentionally this time," Luana explained.

"I'm not sure she'll believe that," Markos said. After a moment of silence he asked, "How was the walk with Evelyn?"

"She ditched me after we reached the nearby field," Luana said. "She was much quicker to anger today. We barely talked at all."

"What did you talk about?" Markos asked.

"The wedding and her new bodyguard." Luana remembered Alita and let out another sigh. "Alita's much nicer than Evelyn."

"You only just met her today. How can you be so sure when you've known Evelyn for seven years?" Markos asked.

Luana sat up and faced her brother. "She didn't treat me differently because of my title or blindness. She was nervous at first but she became comfortable really quickly." Luana couldn't help the small smile that crossed her face. "I thought she was cute."

"Wait. You have a crush on Evelyn's bodyguard?" Markos asked teasingly. "You've never liked anyone before. How did that happen so suddenly?"

Luana shrugged her wings. "She feels different from everyone else

I've encountered; even Victoria and Zina, and they respect me despite my disability."

"So what are you going to do?" Markos asked. "You're still betrothed to Prinze Evelyn."

Luana rolled her eyes. "Do you really think I care about that? I don't even want to marry her. I'd much rather spend some time with Alita and get to know her a bit more."

Luana let herself fall backwards on the bed and closed her eyes. She could still smell the hints of salt and sand that Alita had on her.

"Perhaps you'll get the chance for that soon," Markos said after a moment.

Chapter 16

Alita and Evelyn walked back to the castle in silence. High Caln Griffin was not too happy to see Evelyn back so soon, but he had to hurry away to a meeting with Laird Adelaide, so he didn't tell her off for long. After the meeting, he and Evelyn spent the rest of the day in the throne room, overseeing the many duties of being High Caln. Alita did her best to stay alert, but her mind kept going back to Luana. Had she gotten home alright? Was she safe? What if the Duchies were secretly planning to remove Luana? She was a threat to their goal, after all.

Alita pondered these questions in her mind as the day drew to a close. She followed Evelyn and Griffin to the great hall, where the two ate dinner. This time, the two Duchies were also present, along with another Ice Dragon who sat on Griffin's right. Alita guessed she was Griffin's wife.

After the family had eaten dinner, Alita followed Evelyn back up to her room. Crystal and Lily were already waiting by the door. Evelyn nodded to them and entered her room with Lily close behind. Alita went to follow but was stopped when Crystal stuck out her wing.

"We don't go into the Prinze's room unless absolutely necessary," Crystal explained.

"Oh. Right." Alita stepped back. "Why does Lily go in there?"

"She's the Prinze's personal servant. In the mornings, she puts on Prinze Evelyn's cloak and crown, and in the evenings, she removes them and lays out a clean cloak for tomorrow," Crystal explained.

"Okay, I guess that makes sense," Alita said.

"You can go downstairs and have dinner. I'm assigned to guarding Evelyn at night," Crystal said.

"Thanks," Alita muttered.

She turned and headed back downstairs. The great hall still had several dragons in it. Most were guards eating dinner. Alita recognised the Water Dragon guard from that morning and sat next to him.

"Hey Alita," the Water Dragon said.

"Hey. I don't recall telling you my name," Alita said.

"Prinze Evelyn used your name this morning," the Water Dragon explained. "Also, everyone's been gossiping all day about you. Made it hard to sleep."

"Gossiping?" Alita felt a stab of horror at the thought that others were talking about her.

"Don't worry about it. It's mostly just because you're new. We don't get many new dragons in the castle and the Prinze went all the way to Tribe-Ali to get you. Dragons are just curious as to why she'd do that," he explained. After a moment, he added, "I'm Lucas, by the way."

"We were friends several years ago," Alita said.

"Really?" Lucas stared at her. "That makes a lot more sense than some of the things the others were saying."

"Do I want to know?" Alita asked.

"No, you do not," Lucas said. "Don't worry though, I'm not one to gossip."

"Thanks... I guess," Alita muttered.

Alita turned her attention to the plates of food in front of her. There were vastly different options than at lunch. She noticed that only a few meats were cooked, none of which were in easy reach. She found herself reaching for a plate of raw fish. It had been a long day, and she wanted a taste of home.

"You like fish?" Lucas asked, noticing her choice.

"It's a staple in the Tribe," Alita said. "Why? Is it weird?"

Lucas shrugged his wings. "I just don't know any Rock Dragons who like fish."

"I guess it's not as common here, since the Calndom is inland," Alita said.

She took a bite of her fish. It tasted salty and fresh. It must have been brought from the ocean that day. She wondered what her brother would be doing at that moment. If Alita were still on the beach with him, they'd probably be sharing a fish together.

"Are you alright?" Lucas asked.

Alita sighed. "Just missing home a bit."

"It's hard to move into the castle and away from your old life," Lucas said. "I did the same thing with my friend, Tanner."

"At least you had a friend," Alita pointed out.

"Well, yeah, but I got assigned guard duty while Tanner works in heating bathwater," Lucas explained. "And you said Evelyn was your friend, so it's not that different."

Alita shook her head. "Evelyn's changed a lot since we were fledglings."

"She is the Prinze," Lucas said. "She would've had to learn a lot about how to act and talk and walk. She represents the future of Hiza Calndom. That's not an easy burden."

"I suppose not. But that's not even the worst part," Alita muttered.

Lucas watched her for a moment. "Do you want me to ask? Or should I just pretend you didn't say anything?"

"I met Luana today," Alita said, staring down at her fish, "She's... the most beautiful dragon I've ever seen."

"Oh." Lucas was quiet for a moment. "I'm not sure what advice or reassurance I can give you there. But I guess I know what it's like to be in that position."

"How so?" Alita asked.

Lucas nodded his head to a yellow and blue dragon across the room. "That's Priscila. She's amazing and giggly and smart and everything I want but..."

Alita watched as Priscila's ear twitched and she looked up at a Fire Dragon that had just entered the room. She grinned and rushed over to touch noses with him.

"That's Tanner," Lucas said.

"Oh..." Alita breathed as realisation washed over her. She turned to look at Lucas.

"I never told either of them how I felt," Lucas explained. "I saw Tanner's face the day we met Priscila and I knew I couldn't tell him. It didn't take long for Priscila to tell him how she felt."

"I'm sorry you had to go through that," Alita said.

Lucas shook his head and rubbed the edge of his wing across his face. "Don't worry about it. I'm working on getting over it. That's how the rain falls."

Alita reached out and brushed his wing with her own. Lucas gave her a sad smile before standing up.

"I need to get to my post," he said, picking up his helmet and putting it on. "I'll see you in the morning."

Alita watched him go, then turned back to her food. As she stared down at her half eaten fish, she wondered again if Luana had gotten home alright.

Interlude III

Modesty paced circles in her room. She'd been in the castle all day. The guards' rosters were the same and Evelyn and Griffin were never alone for a moment. Griffin had taken to having his servant, Snowcloud, follow him around everywhere. Unless Modesty could get Griffin alone for long enough, she'd have to kill her too.

Meanwhile, Evelyn's new bodyguard didn't leave her side from dawn to dusk. Modesty had seen the Rock Dragon for the first time during lunch. Her skin was a boring brown but her eyes were vividly amber. They caught in the light whenever she had glanced her way.

Modesty didn't like her. That dragon had seen right through her in a heartbeat. She had to find a way to get rid of her.

Modesty stopped pacing to look out the window. Her room was at the front of the castle, allowing her to see any dragons who went through the gates. It was a prime spot for watching the guards as well. But as Modesty glared out the window, she noticed the Rock Dragon talking to the guards at the gate. She watched as the guards opened the gates, allowing for her to go out into the Noble Districts.

"Well, well, well. Where might you be going at this hour?" Modesty pondered aloud as she watched the Rock Dragon walk into the plaza and take a right.

Modesty hummed with interest. There were only two manors in that direction, the Everhart Manor and the Kahn Manor. Curiosity took over her. She had to see where that dragon was going.

Modesty turned and pushed the door to her room open. The guard on the other side turned and looked at her.

"Where are you going so late?" he asked.

His ear fins twitched and his big nostrils flared a little. Modesty squinted at him. She hated Water Dragons. They were so useless. They could only move water, not freeze it into terrifying weapons like she could. She found it insulting that Griffin thought a single Water Dragon would be enough to stop her.

"Just for a walk," she said. "I need some fresh air."

The guard nodded, though he eyed her closely as she walked past.

Modesty went straight to the rooftop. She wasn't stupid, she knew all the guards were tracking and reporting her movements. If she tried to leave the castle at night, an urgent warning would be sent to Griffin in the castle and Adelaide in Everhart Manor. If she wanted to follow the Rock Dragon with no interruptions, she needed to start by flying to clouds. Luckily for her, the clouds had returned thicker than the previous night.

Chapter 17

Luana rested her head on the sloped bench in the library as her younger brother, Jakob, leafed through a book. Luana hadn't been a big fan of books since her father died. Being blind meant she always needed someone to read for her and no one could capture her attention the way Gerold used to. Now days, it was a frustration at the best of times, especially when she had something specific she was hoping to find here. Her ears drooped as the waiting continued and she felt the world beginning to drift away.

"Stay awake, Sis," Jakob said, nudging her with his wing. "I thought you wanted me to help you with this."

"I do." Luana lifted her head off the bench. "But this really is so dull. I don't even know what book you're going through."

"I told you finding a legal loophole to get you out of this betrothal was going to be hard, Luana," Jakob said. "I have to read and understand law. Do you know how hard it is to understand the law when you're fourteen? It's not easy."

"Keep looking. What if one day I meet someone I really want to marry instead?" Luana suggested.

"Someone, huh?" Jakob said. There was a teasing edge to his tone. "Not like a certain new bodyguard?"

Luana rolled her eyes. "I know it's not all in my head, Jakob. We definitely had a moment." she sighed. "I guess I could just run away instead. That would work."

"What would you do then? You'd struggle to find food on your own," Jakob said.

Luana frowned at him. She didn't actually plan on running away, but she didn't appreciate his comment. "I'm not that helpless."

Her ear twitched as she heard voices coming from the entrance on the ground floor. The library door was propped open so the voices carried faintly up to her ears.

"There's a visitor downstairs." Luana angled her ears to better hear the voices. "Lance is talking to someone."

Jakob was quiet for a moment. "Who's here this late at night?"

Luana squinted, focusing her hearing on the voices. She heard Lance calling for her, though not very loudly. Everyone in the manor knew how well she could hear. The visitor then spoke to Lance and Luana recognised Alita's voice. She turned and grinned at Jakob.

"It's Alita" she said smugly.

Jakob sighed. "I should have known. Fine, maybe she does like you. Go see her."

Luana nodded and trotted for the door. She exited the library and went over to the railing that overlooked the ground floor. She turned to the source of the voices with a smile.

"Who is it, Lance?" she asked to be polite.

Lance sighed before saying, "It is Alita, Prinze Evelyn's bodyguard."

Luana spread her wings and leapt over the railing, gliding neatly down to the ground floor. She felt Alita's wide eyes locked on her as she landed and tucked her wings close to her sides again.

"It's nice to meet you again, Alita," Luana said before turning to Lance. "Thank you, Lance, you may go."

Lance dipped his head, an action Luana picked up on based on the sound of his movements, then walked over to the front doors and sat down.

"Has he had any sleep?" Alita asked quietly. "He looks exhausted."

"He will. His shift is almost over," Luana said. "Why did you want to see me?"

"I, uh..." Alita hesitated, her words dropping off.

Luana couldn't help but smile at Alita's nervousness. "You wanted to make sure I got home safely. I heard your conversation with Lance."

"Then why did you ask?" Alita asked.

"It's more polite to ask." Luana turned for the doors to the gardens. "Come with me."

Alita followed her without hesitation. Luana pushed open the doors and led the way into the night air. Gravel crunched beneath their feet as they walked along the path. Luana heard the bubbling water from the fountain up ahead. She was glad to have Alita in her company. She doubted that Alita's reason for visiting was solely to make sure she got home safe, but she couldn't shake the 'what if' thought in her head.

"I appreciate that you're concerned about my safety, but you shouldn't worry," Luana said as they walked. "I might be blind, but I can still navigate just fine."

"I-I wasn't worried because you were blind," Alita said. "I was worried because there's threats to Evelyn's life. I thought maybe you might be a target as well."

"I'm not on Modesty's hitlist," Luana said. "She doesn't care if I live or die, just that I don't move into the castle."

"You know it's Modesty?" Alita asked.

"Everyone knows it's Modesty," Luana said. "She's not exactly subtle about her hatred for Evelyn. A few years back, there were rumours of things she might be doing. Manipulation and potential death threats, stuff like that."

"Why hasn't anyone done anything yet then?" Alita asked.

Luana reached the fountain and sat down in front of it. Alita sat beside her.

"Because they don't have proof that she's done anything. They were just rumours among the castle staff," Luana explained. "Imagine how it would look to the citizens, who don't know this is going on, if Griffin were to banish or lock up his own daughter."

"Yeah, I get that," Alita said.

"Let's not talk about that though," Luana said. "Tell me about yourself. You grew up in Tribe-Ali right? What's that like?"

"Uh, well, it's very different from here," Alita said slowly. "The Tribe is led by the Chieftain. He's responsible for managing everyone and making sure they're contributing to the tribe. Most of us are self-sufficient. We gather food and help look after and teach the young without much direction from him. Which gives him more time to worry about the future of the Tribe."

"Is it true that only the Chieftain has eggs?" Luana asked. She had heard of it during her younger years but even with her extensive schooling no one had officially confirmed it for her.

"Yeah. Though exceptions can and have been made in the past," Alita said. "For example, before Clyde became Chieftain, there was Jomo. He was a good Chieftain but a bit more loyal to the idea of a soulmate. He got challenged by a dragon called Elliott. Instead of fighting, he negotiated to let Elliott be Chieftain while he stayed with one dragon of his choice."

"And that worked?" Luana asked.

"Of course it did. Elliott was only interested in a few dragons anyway. He only hung on to the position for the power. But Clyde challenged him soon after and has been Chieftain ever since," Alita said, then she added, "My family wasn't even from the Tribe originally."

"Oh?" Luana tilted her head with interest. Was Alita from Hiza Calndom? Why would her family move to Tribe-Ali if that were the case?

"My parents were wanderers. They had no home and just roamed the uninhabited areas of the island," Alita explained. "When my brother and I hatched, they realised they wanted a safe, stable home and asked to join the Tribe. I don't have any memories from before the Tribe, so it's the only thing I've ever known."

"Are there many families like that in Tribe-Ali?" Luana asked.

"There's a few. The only dragon my age with a similar past is Matthias, but he's made an effort to be an asset to the tribe since his family joined years ago," Alita said. "He's one of the most respected dragons there."

"It sounds like a nice place," Luana said quietly. She tried to imagine what living there might be like. Helping others and contributing equally. It sounded much nicer than being told what to do with her life.

Alita was quiet for a moment. She then sighed and said, "It's not all great. Before I left, Chieftain Clyde asked me to give him eggs. I'm not ready for eggs yet and... it's kind of weird. He's been around as long as I can remember."

Luana lowered her head a little. She had overlooked that part. The responsibility to bear eggs to the Chieftain was one no female dragon could ignore. "I guess nowhere is perfect. Everyone has responsibilities they don't want."

Chapter 18

"What's it like living as a noble?" Alita asked.

"It's boring," Luana said. "All my mother cares about is our status and keeping me under constant supervision. She almost always has someone follow me around. Hiza forbid, I go anywhere by myself. I stay up late just so I can roam the manor in solitude after she's gone to bed. It's not much, but it's something."

"Has she always been like that?" Alita asked, remembering that the Everhart's used to be the royal family.

"Yes. But Dad was good at keeping her in check when he was around. He always said, 'Luana has a good life ahead of her, don't try to control it.'" Luana lifted her head to the sky. "I miss him."

Alita was quiet for a moment, unsure what to say. Luana sighed and lowered her head again.

"Markos says something similar sometimes too. But not to Mother, to me," she said. "I find it harder to believe him with each passing day."

"I'm sorry you feel like that," Alita said. "I wish I could make life better for you."

Luana smiled at her. "Coming to visit and talking to me is helping a lot."

Alita smiled back sheepishly. Her face heated up and she ducked her head. She heard footsteps approaching from behind them and turned to see a red-orange Fire Dragon approaching. She recognised

Markos from earlier that day.

"Lovely little setting here," he said, sitting beside Luana. "What are we talking about?"

"Just our lives. Nothing special," Luana said. "Why are you up so late?"

"Bad dream," Markos said with a shrug of his wings.

"So you *are* having weird dreams again," Luana said. She sighed and asked, "Do you have any words of wisdom?"

Markos looked up at the sky. His messy mane and fringe obscured his eyes. After a long moment, he said, "Nothing is set in stone. Keep your mind open and your heart true and you can set the world on fire."

Alita tilted her head in confusion. Luana snorted a laugh.

"That's cryptic. What on Laili are you going on about?" Luana asked.

"You wanted words of wisdom," Markos said. He turned and smiled at her. "Sounds pretty wise, right?"

Alita gave Markos a look. He grinned at her. His dark green eyes seemed to shine in the low light.

"That sounds like my cue to leave," Alita said, getting up.

"Alright," Luana said with a nod. "I'll see you tomorrow then."

"Tomorrow?" Alita echoed.

"Evelyn's required to meet with me almost every day this week. It's part of the requirement for being betrothed. We have to spend time together," Luana explained.

"Oh. I guess I'll see you tomorrow then," Alita said.

As she turned to leave, Alita felt her face heat up again. She would get to see Luana tomorrow too. Her heart felt light as she thought about it. But then she remembered that Evelyn would be with them too. Another argument seemed inevitable.

Lance let Alita out of the manor with a few grumbles and she began her walk back to the castle. Somehow, it felt even darker than when she'd left. There were no dragons on the streets. Alita felt a sense of dread crawl up her spine. Someone was watching her. Where were they?

Alita heard a pebble roll across the ground behind her and spun around. From the shadows, a blue Ice Dragon with dark eyes emerged. Alita lowered into an aggressive stance and raised her wings, ready to fight.

"Oh, please, I'm not going to kill you," Modesty said, rolling her eyes.

"What do you want then?" Alita asked, glaring at Modesty.

"I couldn't help but notice you have a thing for Luana," Modesty said casually, coming a step closer.

"How would you know?" Alita asked coldly.

"There's a lot of things you can learn from the roof of someone's home," Modesty said. "Your body language during your little chat screamed love and affection."

Modesty grimaced for a moment, perhaps at her own words. Alita watched her closely.

"Too bad she's betrothed to Prinze Evelyn," Modesty said with a sinister grin.

Alita took a step back as Modesty took another step forward.

"But perhaps there's something you can do about it," Modesty said.

"There isn't," Alita said. "I-I want to, but I have no say here."

"Think about it, Alita. That's your name, right?" Modesty continued without waiting for an answer. "Luana doesn't want to marry Evelyn. She doesn't even want to live here. Why don't you take her away from here? Perhaps the Northern Forest? I doubt anyone would look for you two there."

Alita shook her head. "I can't do that to Evelyn. I know you'd kill her the moment we leave."

Modesty looked shocked. "When did I ever say I wanted to *kill* our dear Prinze? You think so little of me." Her expression shifted. "Then again, you don't know me at all. Do you even know anyone here?"

"I know Evelyn," Alita defended.

"But do you really?" Modesty asked quietly. "It's been seven years since she became Prinze, hasn't it? Dragons change a lot in that time. Are you sure you even know who she is anymore? Is your life really worth risking for her?"

Alita was quiet for a moment. Modesty's questions stabbed at her and echoed some of her own thoughts. Evelyn *had* changed a lot from how Alita remembered her. She was a lot more refined. But that was a trait of being raised as a Prinze. Alita stood straight and locked her eyes on Modesty.

"I can't do that to her. She's still my friend, even if she's changed," Alita said.

"Hm, it's your funeral then," Modesty said.

Alita braced herself for an attack but Modesty turned and walked away, disappearing into the shadows again. Alita shivered and shook out her wings. Modesty was short for a dragon, but she was absolutely terrifying. Alita wasn't sure she'd be able to sleep at all that night.

Chapter 19

Luana and Markos sat by the fountain for a few minutes after Alita had left. Luana enjoyed the peace of the night air and the lingering scent of Alita's skin. But her brother's words worried her.

"Markos," she said, breaking the silence, "what exactly did you mean earlier?"

"About setting the world on fire? Who could say?" Markos said nonchalantly. "I say a lot of crazy things."

"You choose to do so. Why?" Luana asked.

"Bad dreams do crazy things to a dragon like me, Luana," Markos said. "I can't always explain them."

Luana sighed. She clearly wasn't going to get answers out of him tonight.

"So... Alita showed up for a visit," Markos said after a moment. "What did you think of that?"

Luana smiled. She wished Alita had stayed longer, but everyone had to sleep at some point. "She was nice. We talked about our lives and enjoyed each other's company. I'm looking forward to seeing her again."

"So you're still going to get Jakob to find you a legal out to the betrothal?" Markos asked.

"What else am I supposed to do, Markos? I can't just run away, even if I did have someone to go with. There'll be search parties, Modesty will put Evelyn in danger, perhaps even kill her." Luana sighed. "We used to be so close, the Silver's and us. I know Modesty always wanted to be High Caln, but I don't understand how she can be so ruthless to get her way."

"I know what you mean. Sometimes the best thing for everyone is the hardest thing for our hearts," Markos said. "But it's late. You should get some sleep for tomorrow."

Luana sighed. "I know. Just... give me a few minutes alone. I want to clear my head a little."

"Alright. Good night, Sis," Markos said.

Luana listened to Markos's footsteps as he got up and headed back inside. Once the doors closed behind him, Luana lifted her head to the sky. What did the stars look like at night? Were they big or small? What about the moon? Were there clouds covering its light or was it shining brightly down on her?

Luana silently cursed her blindness. Without it, she wouldn't be fretted over by her mother so much. She could live a life she wanted instead of being betrothed to a dragon she had no interest in.

Of course, her lack of sight meant that her other senses were heightened. Her hearing was better than average and her sense of smell was pretty good when she wasn't filling her own nose up with smoke. Her sense of touch was especially sensitive, allowing her to figure out what an object was by feeling it.

Wings flapped nearby and Luana turned sharply. Her ears pricked as she heard a dragon land on the grass.

"Don't look so startled, it's just me," Modesty said.

Luana frowned slightly. "What are you doing here? I thought you weren't allowed out of the castle."

"Technically, no, I'm not. But I know a little trick for getting past the gate guards," Modesty said. Luana didn't like the hint of malice in her tone.

"What did you do?" Luana asked.

"Not your concern," Modesty said, walking up to sit beside Luana.

"What we should be talking about is you and your new friend. What's her name again? Alita?"

Luana frowned at Modesty. "What about her?"

"Don't make that face, Luana. I'm just trying to help you," Modesty said. Her tone wasn't quite sincere. "I know you don't want to marry Evelyn. I also know Evelyn doesn't want to marry you. Perhaps you'd benefit from a little more freedom to be whoever, and with whomever, you choose. I hear the Northern Forest is lovely this time of year, and well out of the public eye."

Luana shook her head. "No, I'm not going to run away. I have to stay here or you'll do something horrible to Evelyn."

"What makes you say that? Do you really want to spend the rest of your life in the castle, sitting around with nothing to do and nowhere to go?" Modesty asked. "We both know your mother will find some way to control you and keep you from doing anything worthwhile."

Luana felt heat flare in her chest. The smell of a woodfire began to taint the air as smoke wisped out of her nostrils.

"Just think about it, Luana," Modesty said. "I know what you want to do. Perhaps it'll be good for you to finally take hold of your own life."

With that, Modesty got up and took to the air once more. Luana fumed on the grass, listening to Modesty's wingbeats. She couldn't tell if she was angry at Modesty for trying to manipulate her, or if she was mad because she knew Modesty was right.

Chapter 20

Evelyn woke to a gentle shaking. She raised her head and saw Lily nudging her awake. The curtains were already pulled open and the early morning light was drifting in.

"Good morning, Prinze Evelyn," Lily said with a smile. "Time to get up."

"Good morning, Lily." Evelyn pulled herself up and out of the bed and stretched.

"I trust you slept well," Lily said.

"Yeah, it was great." Evelyn remembered with a small smile that Alita would be waiting just outside her room for another day of work.

Lily grabbed Evelyn's cloak off its rack. "You seem extra happy today. Any reason why?"

"Lily, my best friend is my bodyguard," Evelyn explained. "I know I haven't seen her in seven years, but she's really here now. I'm excited to get to know her again."

Lily wrapped the cloak around her shoulders and did up the button.

"Maybe you can," she suggested. "The mid-week market is tomorrow. You won't be required to see Laird Luana then. Perhaps the two of you could enjoy the day together."

Lily carefully lifted Evelyn's crown from its stand by the bed.

"Tomorrow seems so far away though," Evelyn muttered. She dipped her head so Lily could slide the crown over her horns.

Lily lifted the crown, then paused. After a moment she said, "Maybe there's something you could do today."

Evelyn glanced up at Lily. "What do you mean?"

Lily lowered the crown onto Evelyn's head and stepped back to look at her. "Prinze Evelyn, I've known you a long time. I know you want to follow the letter of the law, but you're young. Perhaps you could take the day off to do something just for you. The Flight Range isn't too far away."

Evelyn stared at Lily. "Are you suggesting I take Alita to the Flight Range for the day and completely ignore all my responsibilities?"

A grin spread across Evelyn's face as she spoke. She couldn't help it. Her own personal servant was encouraging her to abandon her duties for the day.

Lily smiled back at her. "I won't tell anyone, I promise."

"Thank you Lily." Evelyn wrapped her wings around Lily and pulled her into a hug. "I'll find a way to repay you."

"Don't worry about it," Lily said. "Just enjoy your day out."

Chapter 21

Alita met Evelyn outside her room, then followed her down to the great hall for breakfast. Evelyn seemed much happier than she had the night before. Alita was glad for that and didn't think much of it until after breakfast, when Evelyn led her up to the roof of the castle.

"What are we doing up here?" Alita asked, looking around. She could see the to the edges of the Calndom in every direction.

"We're going to the Flight Range today," Evelyn said. She took off her crown and placed it down beside her. "No titles, no responsibilities, just two friends playing games."

"What?" Alita stared at Evelyn, baffled, as she took off her cloak and placed it next to the crown. "What about Griffin? Or Luana?"

"Nope! They don't matter today," Evelyn said, spinning to look at Alita. Her wings flared freely. "Today is just you and me being friends and getting to know each other again. Now, take off your vest."

"My vest?" Alita looked down at the vest she was wearing. "It zips between my shoulders. I can't take it off on my own."

"Then I'll take it off for you," Evelyn said. In an instant, she was beside Alita and undoing the zip.

Alita felt the vest come loose and slide off her shoulders. Hesitantly, she stepped out of it and turned to look at Evelyn.

"Great." Evelyn grinned. "Now let's go!"

Evelyn leapt into the air and beat her wings, rising high into the sky. Alita followed quickly, beating her wings hard to keep up. They rose and rose until they were near the clouds. The air was thin. Alita breathed heavily with each wingbeat, hoping that she wouldn't pass out this high up.

"We won't be this high up for long," Evelyn said, turning to fly east. "It's just so we can leave the Calndom without being spotted."

"The Calndom!" Alita gasped, hurrying after Evelyn. "We're leaving the Calndom?"

"Yeah! The Flight Range is right between the quarry, mountains, and Southern Forest," Evelyn explained. "It's quiet most days. No one really goes out there because it's so far. But it's the best place on Laili Island for flying."

Alita was too busy focusing on her breathing to respond. She followed Evelyn as they flew. Far below them, the Calndom passed by. The buildings seemed so much smaller from up there. She couldn't even make out any dragons on the streets.

Evelyn led the way to the Flight Range. After a few minutes, they dropped their altitude and Alita found it easier to breathe. They continued to fly for a while longer as the sun rose steadily through the sky. It was midmorning by the time they finally arrived.

The Flight Range wasn't much, just a mostly flat stretch of grass. There were trees nearby where the Southern Forest began. The mountains loomed ahead of them and a solid breeze swept down the slopes towards them.

Evelyn landed first, swooping low and tilting up at the last moment for a smooth and graceful landing. Alita followed, landing on the ground with a solid thud.

Evelyn giggled. "Looks like you need some flying practice."

"I flew a lot back at the Tribe," Alita said. "It wasn't my preferred mode of travel but I did it a lot."

"Well, you're going to do it a lot more today." Evelyn grinned and raised her wings dramatically.

"Aren't you still worn down from flying across the island the other day?" Alita asked.

Evelyn shook her head. "Not today. There's too much to look forward to for me to mope about aches and pains."

"Like what?" Alita asked.

Evelyn smiled. She whipped around and her tail whacked Alita in the shoulder. "Tag! You're it!"

Alita stood baffled for a moment as Evelyn took flight and winged away from her. She gathered her senses quickly and raced after Evelyn. If Evelyn wanted to forget about being Prinze for a day, Alita would happily comply.

Evelyn flew gracefully, but she wasn't very fast. Alita beat her wings hard and easily caught up with her. She sailed over Evelyn's head and tapped her nose with her tail.

"Now you're it!" Alita said with a laugh. She raced past and flew away.

Evelyn gave chase. When Alita peeked over her shoulder, Evelyn had dropped her graceful wingbeats in favour of faster flaps to catch up with her.

Alita rose into the sky, slowing slightly in the climb. Evelyn was right behind her when Alita dipped suddenly and dove back down to the ground. In an attempt to show off, Alita tucked in her wings and spun. She stopped her descent shortly before she reached the ground and flew just above the grass.

"Show off!" Evelyn yelled after her. Alita could hear the smile in her voice and flipped onto her back to grin at Evelyn.

"I told you I could fly!" she called back.

Evelyn laughed and sped after her. Alita tried to flip back over so she could flee, but her wing clipped the grass and sent her tumbling to the ground.

"Alita! Are you alright?" Evelyn asked. She swooped down and landed next to Alita.

"Yeah, just a little miscalculation," Alita grunted. She pushed herself up and tested her wings. "I'll be fine."

"That's a relief." Evelyn grinned and tapped Alita with her tail. "You're it again."

Alita laughed as Evelyn raced away, on foot this time. Alita folded her wings tight to her sides and chased after her. Playing with Evelyn reminded her of when they were fledglings. Back when nothing stood between them as they played in the sand. Evelyn seemed more like her old self today.

Chapter 22

Evelyn and Alita continued their games until midday. By then, they were both breathing too heavily to continue and stopped by a small pond near the foothills of the mountains. Evelyn lay down, stretched out across the grass, and tried to catch her breath. Alita sat beside her, also breathing heavily. They stayed quiet for several minutes, focusing solely on catching their breaths.

"This is nice," Evelyn said when she finally stopped gasping for air.

"Yeah," Alita agreed with a sigh. "It's like we're fledglings again."

Evelyn hummed in agreement and rolled onto her back. They were in the shade of a small cluster of trees. The sun shone through the leaves, giving the gaps a golden yellow hue and casting a dappled shadow across Evelyn's skin.

"So much has changed since then," Evelyn said quietly.

"Yeah. You've changed a lot," Alita said.

"I know. You've changed a bit too though," Evelyn said.

"Me? How?" Alita asked.

"Well, for starters you're taller than me now. I remember being taller than you seven years ago." Evelyn rolled onto her side and propped herself up so she could look at Alita. "For another, I thought nothing could shake you but the way you froze up yesterday during Korbin's trial... you two seemed to know each other quite well."

Alita ducked her head. At first, she didn't say anything. Evelyn started to wonder if she'd hit a sore spot.

Finally, Alita said, "We did. Back in the Tribe. Korbin and I... we dated for a little bit."

Evelyn sat up, eyes wide. "What! You dated a male dragon while Clyde was Chieftain? You know that's illegal!"

"I know. I knew it then too..." Alita paused, sighed, then continued, "Korbin wanted to move to the Calndom so we could be together properly. But I wasn't ready to leave the Tribe. One day, we got into an argument about it and Clyde overheard us. He was furious and banished Korbin. I thought he might try to come back for me, but he never did."

"I see." Evelyn stared at her own feet for a moment. "I guess that didn't feel very good."

Alita shook her head. "It was awful. But I never realised he had become a criminal in the Calndom after that."

"It happens sometimes," Evelyn said. "Some dragons just don't make it."

A silence settled over them as the conversation died. Evelyn briefly wondered if Alita felt a similar pain when the two of them were forced apart seven years ago. Evelyn had been distraught that she couldn't visit her friend. She hoped Alita had felt the same way.

"What was that?" Alita was suddenly up on her feet, scanning the trees and bushes around them.

"I didn't hear anything," Evelyn said.

"I think there's something nearby," Alita said.

Her voice became hushed and she crouched with her wings out. Evelyn sniffed the air and realised there was a new scent on the wind. The smell of wild boar.

Before she could say anything, the boar leapt out of the bushes and rushed at them. Evelyn jumped to her feet, ready to run, but she froze when she saw Alita charge at the boar. Wild boars were about half the size of most dragons, but they were extremely territorial and vicious to intruders. Every dragon in Hiza Calndom knew to run if a boar attacked.

Evelyn couldn't move. Alita had pinned the boar down by the tusks and was ripping into the back of its neck. Blood streamed down the boar's neck and it shrieked in pain and fury. But Alita didn't stop until she had a strong enough bite to break the boar's neck, leaving it dead on the grass.

When Alita turned back to Evelyn, her mouth, chest, and legs were covered in blood. Evelyn was too shocked to speak.

"Evelyn? Are you okay?" Alita asked.

Evelyn blinked and shook her wings to rid the tension. "That was... amazing. No dragon ever fights a wild boar on their own. How did you manage to kill it?"

Alita shrugged. "Boars are only dangerous if they can move their tusks. I managed to grab its tusks and hold it still until I could break its neck. It's not actually that hard. Just... messy." Alita glanced down at her body with a frown.

"We can clean that up," Evelyn said. "But I'm amazed you managed to react and stop it. That requires quick thinking and skill. It seems I made a great choice with you as my bodyguard. I think you'll pass the one week trial just fine."

Alita ducked her head. "Thanks, but it really wasn't much. At least we have lunch now."

Evelyn laughed. "I suppose we do. Thank you, Alita."

Chapter 23

The afternoon went by quickly for Evelyn. After eating the boar for lunch, Alita cleaned herself up and they got back to playing like a pair of fledglings. Evelyn was delighted to spend time with Alita the way they used to, without the weight of responsibilities on her shoulders.

But soon the sun started to set and Evelyn knew they had to return to the castle. She dreaded returning, knowing that Griffin would be furious with her for disappearing all day. But it was all worth it just to have a day by herself with Alita.

Evelyn led the way back to the castle and they landed on the roof just before sunset. Her crown and cloak were sitting where she'd left them, along with Alita's vest. However, Griffin and Heather were sitting as well. They both looked rather unhappy.

"Prinze Evelyn! Where have you been?" Griffin demanded the moment Evelyn's feet touched the ground.

Evelyn mentally prepared herself for the confrontation and said, "I took Alita to the Flight Range."

"You've been gone all day!" Griffin snapped, glaring down at her.

"I had Alita with me the whole time. I just needed a day off from everything I do here," Evelyn explained.

"Prinzes and High Calns do not get the luxury of taking a day off," Griffin said in a low voice. A growl rumbled in his throat. "Disappearing without notice like that sent the entire castle into high alert. Do you have any idea how stressed I was?"

"How stressed you were?" Evelyn frowned at Griffin, biting back a growl. "I'm supposed to take over in the next few years when you finally kick the bucket! But you don't give me the chance to properly practise everything you've taught me without second guessing and overruling every thought I have! I'm forced to keep up the appearance that I truly know what I'm doing and am ready for the role when I don't feel that way at all!"

"Watch your tone with me, Prinze," Griffin growled.

"Hey!" Alita snapped, pushing her way in between Evelyn and Griffin, "Everyone needs a break sometime and I was there the whole time! Evelyn was safe in my company."

"Know your place, remora! I am the High Caln!" Griffin yelled.

"What did you just call me?" Alita's pitch went up and she glared at Griffin through narrow eyes.

Evelyn pushed in front of Alita again and glared up at Griffin. Even in the Tribe, everyone knew what he'd said was the worse of insults. "Leave her alone! I told her to come with me."

Griffin growled and turned. He began to walk away, then stopped. Without turning around, he said, "Do not rely on your emotions, Prinze Evelyn. Doing so will cloud your judgement."

Griffin then left, taking the spiral staircase down into the castle. Evelyn watched where he had disappeared for a moment before a voice distracted her.

"You're in a lot of trouble Alita," Heather growled.

Alita shrunk away from Heather slightly. Evelyn was quick to push herself between them.

"Don't punish Alita for something I made her do," she said.

"Oh, it's not for that, Prinze Evelyn," Heather said. "It's for yellin' at the High Caln."

Evelyn flared her wings and frowned at Heather. "As Prinze and the one who chose Alita for her job, I decree that you will not punish her in any way for what she said today."

Heather glared at Evelyn for a moment before dipping her head. "Very well, Prinze Evelyn. But remember, High Caln Griffin still has the power to overrule your demands. If he says to punish Alita, then I will do so accordingly."

With that, Heather turned and left as well, following the same path Griffin had taken. Evelyn lowered her wings and turned to Alita.

"Are you alright?" she asked.

"I will be. Being called a remora was insulting, but I'll survive," Alita said. "What about you though? Griffin was really mad at you for sneaking away today."

"He'll get over it," Evelyn said. She sighed and picked up her cloak and crown. "I'll be fine too. He gets angry more and more often these days. I think being High Caln and refusing aid is getting to him. I just have to remember that none of it is truly personal."

Alita picked up her bodyguard vest and slung it over her shoulders. Evelyn took the time to put her cloak and crown on, lest she suffer more of Griffin's anger.

"We won't see much of him tomorrow, though," Evelyn said as they headed for the stairs. "For now, let's go have dinner."

"Dinner sounds good," Alita agreed.

Chapter 24

Alita didn't get to eat dinner until after Evelyn had eaten and gone to bed. By then, her stomach had begun growling. The wild boar they'd eaten for lunch had been tough and stringy; not exactly a great meal. Alita sat at one of the dining tables in the great hall with a sigh and reached for a bowl full of apples. Lucas was sitting beside her, eye her with curiosity.

"Where have you been all day?" he asked. "The entire castle was in chaos, looking for you and Prinze Evelyn."

"Evelyn took me to the Flight Range," Alita explained before biting into the apple she'd chosen.

"The Flight Range? No one in the royal family visits there. Why did she go?" Lucas asked.

Alita shrugged. "I think she just needed some time off from being Prinze. We played some games and talked a bit. It was like we were fledglings again."

Lucas didn't say anything at first. Alita continued to eat her apple until she felt the pressure of his gaze. She turned to him with a confused look.

"What is it?" she asked.

Lucas blinked and shook his head. "It's nothing. I was just thinking about how Prinze Evelyn has never done anything like that in the years I've known her. She's usually very good at sticking to a schedule."

"I don't know where it came from," Alita explained as she reached for another apple. "I just know that's what happened. It was actually a good day. Though, Griffin and Heather were pretty mad."

"I'm not surprised. They were looking all through the castle for you two. I think High Caln Griffin was worried the Duchies finally got to Prinze Evelyn," Lucas said.

"She was fine. I was with her the whole day," Alita said. "I even protected her from a boar."

Lucas's eyes widened. "You took on a wild boar?"

"Yeah. Why is everyone so surprised by that?" Alita asked.

"Because wild boars are horrible, vicious creatures! They'll attack anything that moves, even birds!" Lucas lowered his voice and added, "Some dragons call the forest where the boars live the Silent Forest."

Alita shrugged. "The one that attacked us was stopped pretty easily. I pinned it by the tusks and broke its neck."

"You absolute lunatic." The sound of a new voice made Alita jump. She looked across the table to see the yellow and blue dragon she'd seen yesterday. Her name had already slipped Alita's mind.

"Hey, Priscila," Lucas greeted her. "Alita, this is Priscila. Priscila, this is-"

"Alita," Priscila said, finishing Lucas's sentence. "You've only been here two days and you've already stirred up the castle gossip."

Alita felt a twist of uneasiness in her chest at the mention of gossip. "What have dragons been saying about me?"

"Mostly, it was just speculation about why Prinze Evelyn hired you specifically," Priscila explained. "But ever since yesterday, everyone agrees that you two definitely know each other, though your opinions on each other might not be aligned."

"What is that supposed to mean?" Alita asked, tilting her head.

Priscila shook her head and smiled. "Don't worry about it. Tell me about this boar you defeated. I can't believe you managed to kill one!"

"Uh..." Alita hesitated on what to say next. She was concerned about what other dragons were saying about her. But Priscila didn't seem like she was going to tell her.

As Alita fumbled over what to say, a slender Ice Dragon with a blue-grey cloak and curved horns approached.

"Lucas. You're late for your shift," the dragon said.

Lucas yelped and ducked his head. "Apologies, Caln Misti. I'll head there now."

Lucas hurried to put his helmet on and raced out of the great hall. Caln Misti watched him go, then turned to Alita and Priscila. Alita felt a prickle of fear creeping up her neck.

"Priscila, aren't you meant to be working as well?" Misti asked, tilting her head towards the kitchen door.

"Yes, Caln Misti. My apologies." Priscila dipped her head to Misti and quickly left.

Alita ducked her head, worried that Misti would turn to her next. Was she here to punish Alita for yelling at Griffin earlier?

"Alita." Misti sat down beside her with a grace that rivalled Evelyn's. "I hear you and Evelyn snuck away from the castle this morning."

"Yes, Caln Misti," Alita said, consciously mimicking Priscila's line.

"Did you two have fun?" Misti asked.

Alita glanced up at Misti. She had a small smile on her face.

"My husband has been putting Evelyn through a lot of unneeded stress lately," Misti explained when Alita didn't speak. "Personally, I disagree with him and Laird Adelaide over the arranged marriage. But my opinion has minimal effect on such a decision. I do hope she had fun at the Flight Range today. Youth should not be wasted sitting in a throne room, listening to grumpy old dragons who refuse to listen."

"I... er, yeah. We... we did have fun," Alita said hesitantly.

"Good." Misti smiled. "I remember when I was your age. I lived in Tribe-Ali, just as you and Evelyn did. Griffin wasn't even Prinze then.

102

But he was best friends with Gerold Everhart. Those two were trouble makers on the beaches."

"Gerold Everhart? Is that Luana's father?" Alita asked.

"He was, before he died." Misti's smile disappeared. She stared, unblinkingly, across the room. "He always knew how to get out of any trouble he found himself in. He often saved Griffin's tail too."

Misti didn't speak for a long moment. Then she shook her head and turned back to Alita.

"Don't mind me, dear. I rarely get to talk to someone from home anymore," Misti said. "How is my brother-in-law doing? Is he still Chieftain?"

"Clyde is your brother-in-law?" Alita asked.

Misti nodded. "That he is. Griffin and Clyde were quite the pair when they were young. Very similar in appearance. But I'd say their personalities are quite different. Clyde suits his role as leader far better than Griffin ever has."

"Do you think Evelyn will be a good leader?" Alita asked.

Misti hummed in thought. "It's hard to say. I think she's a bit like Gerold. She never intended to become High Caln, but someone chose it for her. I think she'll step up to the role as best she can. Though I fear her unhappiness could get the better of her if she's forced to marry Laird Luana. Perhaps you can give her the joy she needs to face each day head on."

"I can try. She's always been my best friend," Alita said.

Misti outstretched a wing and placed it over Alita's back. "Keep an eye on my daughter too. I may have bias for my own offspring, but even I can see that Modesty has a heart filled with hate. I fear that she may act soon."

Before Alita could think to speak, Misti had removed her wing and stood back up. She exited the great hall with elegant strides. Alita watched her go until she was out of sight. She hadn't expected Misti to be so friendly when Griffin was so strict and grumpy.

Chapter 25

Alita went to bed shortly after dinner. She was too tired to visit Luana, though she did consider it. The next day began normally for her. She woke, put on her vest, met Evelyn outside her room, and followed her down to breakfast.

It was an uneventful meal for a change. Despite Griffin's narrow glare, Alita was starting to feel like she was getting used to her job. As she followed Evelyn out of the great hall after breakfast, Alita noticed the small satchel hanging from Evelyn's neck.

"So what are you doing today?" she asked curiously.

Evelyn smiled. *"We* are going to the mid-week market."

"The mid-week market? What is that?" Alita asked.

"It's exactly what it sounds like," Evelyn explained. "A two day market in the middle of the week. It happens once a month in the Noble Districts. Dragons from all over Hiza Calndom are carefully chosen to present their stuff to the nobles and royal family. You can find all sorts of things there."

Evelyn led Alita out of the castle and towards the gates. Alita could already see the tents and stalls filling the plaza and hear chatter and music as dragons weaved from stand to stand.

"That's a lot of dragons," Alita said out loud before she could stop herself. How was she supposed to be an effective bodyguard in such a crowd?

"Don't worry, there's only two dragons you need to keep an eye out for," Evelyn said. "The nobles, servants, and guards are the least of your worries. Just try to have fun."

"Fun?" Alita echoed. "I'm still working right?"

Evelyn rolled her eyes and smiled at Alita. "We'll be fine, Alita. Just relax."

The gates opened and Evelyn trotted into the crowd. Alita hurried to keep up with her. Evelyn wove between dragons and stalls with a sort of elegance that Alita couldn't quite understand. Then, she noticed many dragons were recognising her and actively moving out of her way, making it easier for Evelyn to traverse the crowd.

They eventually stopped at a stall made of dark wood and a cream and brown patterned fabric cover to shade its contents. The dragon behind the stall was unmistakably a Rock Dragon, with dark brown skin and short, rounded ears. The stall had several racks and bowls of jewellery and gems. Alita recognised several colours and precious metals, though she could barely name a few.

"Greetings, Prinze Evelyn," the Rock Dragon said, bowing his head.

Evelyn regarded him for a moment before saying, "You were here last month."

The dragon smiled. "Indeed I was. My stock sold so well that I was allowed to return. I used my increased profits to try and increase the size and value of my collection."

The dragon nodded down to the jewellery and gems. He then looked up at Alita. She saw something flicker in his brown eyes.

"You must be the Prinze's new bodyguard," he said. "The name's Trey. Prinze Evelyn told me on my last visit that I reminded her of you. I must say I don't see the resemblance, but it's good to know she decided to bring you here."

Alita tilted her head and looked at Evelyn. She was intensely staring at a rack of earrings, though her ears twitched in a way that suggested she was listening to the conversation.

"My name is Alita," Alita said hesitantly. "I didn't know Evelyn spoke to anyone about me."

Trey glanced at Evelyn before hurriedly saying, "Uh, I guess all Rock Dragons look alike. Anyway, what catches your eye?"

Alita glanced at Evelyn again. She had purposefully turned herself away so Alita couldn't see her face. Her ears still twitched intensely. Trey seemed to recognise this too and leaned over to Alita.

"If I were you, I'd really think about what you want most," he whispered, almost too quiet for even Alita to hear. "Find what matters to you, and go for it."

He winked at her, then turned to Evelyn, who had picked up a pair of silver hoop earrings.

"Those are a lovely choice, Prinze Evelyn," he said. "My father mined that himself. Purest silver we could find."

Evelyn eyed the earrings for a moment before putting them down and picking up a pair of silver earrings with translucent, blue, diamond shaped gems.

"Ah, the diamonds," Trey said. "I was hoping you'd see those before someone else bought them. They were a very lucky find, especially at that size. I made sure to make them into clip-on earrings so that anyone could enjoy them."

Evelyn smiled slightly and looked at Trey. "How much?"

"For you, my Prinze, 4,000 Drachmar," Trey said.

Alita's jaw almost hit the ground. That was a lot for a pair of earrings. Evelyn squinted at Trey. "1,000 Drachmar."

Trey grinned humorously. "Prinze, Evelyn, these are pure diamonds. If I let them go for only 1,000 Drachmar, I'd be a laughingstock."

"The castle can come by diamonds easily," Evelyn said. "We have the ultimate control over what gems found in the mines are sold to the general public and what gems stay among nobles and royals."

As Trey and Evelyn haggled back and forth over the earrings, Alita caught a glimpse of another pair of earrings next to her. They were much simpler than the diamond earrings. Each earring had a pale green, oval shaped stone rimmed with gold. Alita found herself drawn in by the earrings. Staring at the pale green stones she was reminded of looking into Luana's eyes.

"That's a fine choice," Trey said, turning his attention to her. "Jadeite is the rarest stone on this island. You'll be hard pressed to find another stone like it."

Alita glanced up at him before looking at the earrings again. "How much are they?"

"Far above your pay grade I'm afraid," Trey said with a wince. "5,000 Drachmar for each earring."

Alita blinked at him, eyes wide. "That's a lot of money for a single earring."

"It is," Trey agreed. "But jadeite *is* the rarest stone on the island. There was quite a nasty bidding war over the raw, unpolished stones when they were found. My family almost lost."

Alita looked at Evelyn, wondering if she could ask for the earrings. To her surprise, Evelyn was staring at the earrings with a defeated expression. She sighed and put down the diamond earrings she was holding.

"Let's just go," she said, turning to leave the stall.

Before Evelyn could leave, however, Markos and Luana came around a corner and approached the stall.

"Prinze Evelyn!" Markos grinned. "Fancy meeting you here."

Alita caught a dark expression on Evelyn's face before it was replaced with regal neutrality.

"I always make time for the mid-week market, Markos. You know that," she said firmly.

"That was a little cold," Markos said. "I'm just trying to be friendly to my future sister-in-law."

"How about respecting your future High Caln?" Evelyn suggested, narrowing her eyes.

Markos raised an eyebrow. "Alright, Your Greatness."

He bowed deeply, spreading his wings just slightly. He stood back up a moment later with a grin.

"How was that?" he asked.

Evelyn rolled her eyes, earning a barely stifled laugh from Markos.

"Why are you even here?" Evelyn asked.

"Well, it's just like you. We always come to the mid-week market," Markos shrugged.

Alita suddenly realised that Luana was standing next to her. She turned and smiled, feeling her ears heat up.

"Hey Alita," Luana said with a small smile.

"H-hey," Alita stammered.

"Anything interesting at Trey's stall?" Luana asked.

"You know Trey?" Alita questioned.

"Of course." Luana smiled in Trey's direction. "We met at the last market. He promised to set his stall up in the exact same place so I could visit again. He's got some great stories from outside the Noble Districts."

"Not many more this month, Laird Luana," Trey said. "Though the tale of the bidding war over jadeite is quite interesting if you ask me."

"Jadeite?" Luana's blind eyes widened slightly. "That's rare."

"It certainly is. But my father managed to win it, thanks to last month's profits," Trey explained. "I crafted it into a pair of earrings and a necklace."

"Have they sold yet?" Luana asked.

"Not yet," Trey said.

Luana stepped up to the stall and leaned her head forward. "How much for the lot?"

"I've priced them at 5,000 Drachmar per stone, for a total of 15,000 if you buy all three," Trey said.

"That's quite a lot of money. Last month your most expensive item was only 2,000 Drachmar," Luana said.

Alita thought she saw Trey fidget a bit. Luana's blind gaze was locked on him.

"Yes, that is true. But with the profits of last month, I managed to increase the quality and rarity of my stock," Trey explained, averting his gaze from hers.

Luana didn't blink for a long moment. Alita felt a tension rising. Was Luana about to haggle for the rarest stones on the island?

"I'll give you 20,000 for all three," Luana said suddenly.

Alita stared in disbelief. Trey's eyes widened and his jaw fell open. "Y-you... n-no. L-Laird Luana, that-that's too much."

Luana shrugged and opened the satchel hanging from her neck.

"Perhaps next month you'll have something even rarer," she said. In a quieter voice, she added, "Though I doubt there's anything rarer than this."

Luana's ear flicked and Trey glanced at Alita for a split second. He looked back at Luana and nodded.

"Very well, Laird Luana," he said, pulling out a necklace that matched the earrings.

He placed all three in a small box and passed it over to Luana. Luana put the box in her satchel and gave him a bag of gold coins. Trey took the bag shakily and started counting out the coins.

"What on Laili did I just watch?" Alita breathed.

Luana smiled at her. "Just a little generous trading."

Chapter 26

Evelyn pulled Alita away from the stand, where Markos and Luana were still talking to Trey. She didn't want to spend another moment in Luana's company when she could be having a good day with Alita instead.

Leading Alita through the market, she occasionally stopped to browse a stall, but nothing caught her eye. Soon, the delightfully sweet smell of hot honey filled her nose and Evelyn spotted a colourful stall.

"Alita, have you ever had cotton candy before?" Evelyn asked.

"I don't think so," Alita said. She looked at the stall ahead of them with slight confusion on her face. "What is it?"

"It's honey heated and spun to make it string-like. Often, dragons will put food colouring in it to make it look pretty too." Evelyn explained.

"That sounds... unhealthy," Alita said slowly.

"They're pretty good," Evelyn said, shrugging her wings. She reached for a bright blue cloud of cotton candy on a small cone. She reached into her pouch and gave the stall attendee a copper coin, then she offered the cotton candy to Alita. "Have some."

Alita regarded the giant cloud-like ball. For a moment, Evelyn worried that she might turn it down. But then Alita pulled off a small piece and put it in her mouth. Her skeptical expression suddenly morphed into surprise, then delight. Evelyn couldn't help the grin that spread across her face.

"It's good, right?" she asked, tearing off her own piece of cotton candy.

"Yeah, it is pretty good," Alita agreed. She reached out and grabbed a larger piece of the cotton candy.

Together, they finished off the cotton candy in just a few minutes. The dragon attending the stall looked rather pleased as she offered them a bowl of water to wash the sticky honey off their feet.

Once their feet were clean, Evelyn turned and dove back into the crowd with Alita close on her tail. Their day of fun was back on track and Evelyn knew exactly what she wanted to do next.

It only took a few minutes for the familiar music of the market's band to fill the air. Evelyn weaved through the crowd until she found herself on the edge of a ring of dragons. The band was on the far side and several dragons were dancing in pairs in the open space. Evelyn felt another grin spreading across her face.

"I've always wanted to dance with someone here," she said to Alita.

"Wh-what?" Alita stammered as Evelyn wrapped a wing around her and pulled her into the ring.

Everyone recognised Evelyn in a heartbeat. The pairs of dancing dragons sidled away, giving her and Alita the whole clearing. The band grew quiet as they waited for Evelyn to make the first move.

"Evelyn, I don't know how to dance," Alita said. Her eyes were wide and she had a look of fearful desperation as she glanced around at the crowd.

"It's easy enough," Evelyn said with a smile. "Do you remember the mimicking game we played as fledglings? Just copy what I do."

Evelyn put her forefoot forward and spread her wings slightly. Her cloak gathered on her back as she unfolded her wings carefully. Alita hesitantly copied her. Evelyn smiled, then nodded to the band. They began to play a slow paced song. Evelyn moved her forefoot out to the side, turning her body smoothly to follow it. Alita copied her, turning the opposite direction. Evelyn gave her a small nod, then stretched her wings up above her head. In a single, graceful motion, she pulled her wings down and forward while flicking her head back and raising one forefoot. Alita copied her movements, barely keeping up. She had far less grace than Evelyn. But Evelyn didn't care. She was dancing with Alita and that's all that mattered to her.

The two continued to dance, slowly building up speed with the music. Evelyn stepped and twirled with refined grace, built from years of practice. Alita was less graceful, but each step and spin and twist was more confident than the last. Evelyn wondered if she spotted a smile on Alita's face for a moment. She hoped Alita was enjoying this just as much as her.

As the dance ended, they both spread their wings, rearing up with the music. Evelyn was so wrapped up in the moment that she didn't notice Alita lose her balance and fall into the crowd until the song ended and she dropped back to her feet. She rushed over, carefully avoiding the nearby dragons who had moved to avoid being squashed.

"Alita! Are you alright? Any scratches?" she asked.

Alita rolled off her back with a groan. "I'm alright. I've taken harder falls than that in the Tribe."

"Are you sure you're not hurt?" Evelyn asked as Alita pushed herself up.

"Yeah. Yeah, I'm fine," Alita said.

"Well that was certainly exciting."

Evelyn looked up to see three dragons standing in front of them. Zina was grinning mischievously, her icy silver eyes glinting with amusement. Next to her Victoria was as poised and calm as ever. Evelyn quietly wondered why Victoria chose to hang out with Zina, but she supposed they balanced each other well. Finally, there was August. She stood tall and regal next to the others. Her sandy yellow skin seemed to shine under her translucent cloak.

"Nice dancing, Evelyn." Zina had a sly grin on her face. "You could give August a run for her money."

"Oh shush, Zina," August said.

Zina grinned at August, who just ignored her and turned to Evelyn and Alita.

"Is this your new bodyguard?" August asked. "I hadn't expected to see you dance with a guard."

"I can dance with whomever I like," Evelyn said. Her tone was harsher than she had intended.

"Ouch. That was mean." Zina winced. Then she grinned again. "Are you upset because August is calling you out on your disloyalty?"

Evelyn frowned at Zina. It took everything in her power to keep her ice abilities from flaring. "What disloyalty?"

"You're betrothed to Luana. Yet you're dancing with your personal bodyguard," Zina said, still grinning. "Or perhaps you're mad that August has a happy and loving relationship with an Everhart while you're seething in contempt?"

"That's enough Zina." August flared a wing in front of Zina's face, blocking her from Evelyn's view. "Sorry, Prinze Evelyn. How is your bodyguard doing? Is she taking to the job well?"

Evelyn inhaled slowly, calming the icy storm in her chest. She smiled, glad for the slight change in topic. "Alita is doing very well. She's alert, strong, and quick to react when necessary. I think she'll pass the trial week just fine."

"That's good to hear." August smiled at Alita, who had been silent for several minutes. "It's good to meet you, Alita. I'm August Waltz."

"Uh, good to meet you too," Alita said hesitantly. She ducked her head and glanced at Evelyn with questioning eyes.

"August is one of the last two family members for the Waltz family," Evelyn explained. "And you met Zina Kahn and Victoria Hooper the other day."

Each of the three dragons in question wore cloaks held together with a button, just like Evelyn's. Each of their cloak buttons were different, representing the families they came from; a dancing dragon for the Waltz, a crown for the Kahn, and a pair of intersecting rings for the Hooper.

Suddenly, Zina was in front of Alita, eyeing her suspiciously. Alita stepped back, clearly uncomfortable by the sudden invasion of her personal space.

"You don't look very strong or quick to react," Zina said, looking Alita up and down with narrow grey eyes. "Quick! Tackle me to the ground! Time's up!"

Zina darted away with a laugh before Alita could even blink. Evelyn frowned at Zina.

"That's enough, Zina," she said, stepping between Alita and the others. "Alita isn't going to tackle you in a public place just because you want to test her. She already proved herself yesterday."

"Oh? What did she do?" Zina asked.

"That's none of your concern. All you need to know is that she will protect me when the situation calls for it," Evelyn said. She turned to Alita and quietly said, "Come on, let's get out of here."

Evelyn wasn't in any sort of mood to deal with Zina's antics. She also didn't want word to get out that they had faced off against a wild boar. If that got back to Griffin, he'd be outraged. Evelyn was almost certain he would forbid her from ever leaving the castle again if he found out.

Interlude IV

Modesty hissed as she followed her brother through the mid-week market. The sky was clear and the sun was warm. Her blue-grey cloak was heavy on her wings. The warm material made her skin sweat, making her horribly uncomfortable. Icy mist laced her breath as she tried to turn the sweat to ice and cool herself down. It was torture.

Clement didn't seem to be bothered by the heat. His ears twitched and he scanned the crowd around them intensely. Modesty rolled her eyes. She knew who he was looking for and she knew it was a complete waste of time.

Suddenly, Clement turned and trotted up to a trio of dragons. Modesty followed him slowly, narrowing her eyes at August, Victoria, and Zina. August wore a thin, translucent cloak that complemented her skin with a peach tint. Victoria's cloak was brown and heavy, but as a Nature Dragon she enjoyed the warmth. Zina had a silvery-grey cloak made of silk, allowing her to stay cool in the sun. Not one of them was bothered by the heat. Modesty hated all of them for it.

"Hey guys." Clement smiled as he greeted them.

"Duchy Clement," August said politely, dipping her head. "Are you enjoying the market?"

"Of course," Clement said. "Though, it's a little better now."

Clement smiled bashfully at Zina. A sickening twist gripped Modesty's stomach from his dumb, sappy expression.

Zina raised an eyebrow at him. "What's so great about the market now?"

"It's more the company, than the market itself," Clement admitted, trying to sound nonchalant.

"You're pathetic, Clement," Modesty muttered.

August looked at her. "I see you're here too. I didn't expect you to be wandering the market on a day like this."

Modesty glared at August. She hated that August knew her so well. If there was one thing she hated almost as much as Water Dragons, it was dragons without an element at all. They were just as defenceless, yet so much more perceptive of the dragons around them. That made them a threat.

"If you *must* know, Mother sent us on an errand," Modesty told her. "I knew my lovestruck, idiot brother wouldn't be able to stay focused, so I had to come along."

"I'm right here, Modesty," Clement said.

"For once, I believe you," August said, ignoring Clement's comment. "But I suspect there's more lurking behind that reason in your mind."

Modesty snorted out a large cloud of icy mist at August, but Victoria stepped in between them.

"Don't pick a fight here," she said, watching Modesty carefully. "There's too many dragons around."

Too many witnesses, Modesty thought bitterly. Oh, how she would love to rip August apart then and there. But that would have to wait until she took the crown for herself.

"You know..." Zina started, with a crooked smile on her face, "Prinze Evelyn was here just a few minutes ago."

Modesty reacted with surprise before she could stop herself. Zina's satisfied smile made Modesty want to impale her and rip off her face.

"Perhaps you'd be interested in knowing where she went," Zina said, nodding to a gap in the stalls that led out of the plaza.

"And what makes you think that?" Modesty asked.

Zina didn't reply, opting to just smile up at her. Modesty glared at her and bit back a snarl.

"Perhaps we should go with you." Luana's voice was unmistakable. Modesty looked up to see her and Markos approaching them. Luana would have heard the entire conversation; Modesty knew that.

But try as she might, Modesty couldn't hate Luana. She hated Luana's powerful hearing, which threatened her plans at every turn. But she couldn't hate the dragon she had grown up alongside in the castle.

"Why don't you two go find Evelyn." Markos nudged Luana with a wing. "Make sure she's alright."

Luana raised an eyebrow but nodded. "Come on, Modesty. Let's go find Evelyn and Alita."

Modesty noticed the addition of Alita's name with intrigue. Luana and Alita had just met, and Luana was already actively thinking about her. Perhaps her plan to get them out of the way would work after all.

Chapter 27

Evelyn led Alita out of the market and away from the constant noise of music and talking. There was a small grassy area not too far from the market which was completely empty. A single, blooming, cherry tree sat in the centre of the space, offering shade from the midday heat. Evelyn sat down near the trunk and stared at the ground, which was a mix of green grass and pink petals.

Alita sat beside her and surveyed the area. "Why did we leave the market?"

"It was getting too noisy," Evelyn said. She didn't want to admit she just wanted to get away from the crowds for some more time alone with Alita.

"You said it was safe though. Surely you'd want to stay there or go back to the castle," Alita said.

Evelyn breathed a sign and flopped onto her back. Fallen flower petals sprung into the air around them before floating back down to the grass. Evelyn felt her crown slip on her horns, but she didn't care. The comfort she felt in lying on her back, exposing her belly to the sky, without the pressure of looking like the perfect picture of royalty was all she wanted. She could feel Alita watching her and wondered what she thought.

"You used to do that a lot back in the Tribe," Alita said.

"Back when we were young and had nothing to worry about." Evelyn sighed, feeling the weight of the crown pulling at her horns.

"Before crowns, before royalty. It was just you and me playing with sand and water."

"Yeah." Alita had a wistful smile on her face. "Do you remember how we used to put sand on each other's head spikes?"

"Yeah, I do," Evelyn said with a smile. She remembered her head spike and her smile fell. "I guess we can't do that anymore."

"Well, there's no sand here..." Alita trailed off. Evelyn glanced up at her just in time to see a swirl of pink petals fall on her face. She laughed and swatted the petals away.

"You absolute goof!" Evelyn giggled.

She swirled her wings so the petals flew up into Alita's face. Alita stood up and dodged out of the cloud of pink. Evelyn was quick to get to her feet and tackled Alita. They tumbled back on the grass in a flurry of brown and blue and giggles.

"Hey! You're heavy!" Alita exclaimed.

Evelyn grinned down at Alita. "You're a Rock Dragon. If you want me off your back, maybe you should do something about it."

Alita smirked up at Evelyn and smacked her tail on the ground. In an instant, Evelyn felt the dirt beneath her push up. Evelyn lost her footing and rolled over in the grass. Alita was up in a heartbeat and pinned Evelyn down with a forefoot.

"Is that better?" Alita asked.

In response, Evelyn breathed a small cloud of ice on Alita's foreleg. Alita yelped and pulled back. Evelyn got back to her feet and knocked Alita onto her back, pinning her down again.

"Much better." Evelyn grinned.

Alita laughed. "That was a mean trick!"

"You used to do stuff like that to me all the time." Evelyn giggled.

Alita smiled back at her. Evelyn felt a warmth in her chest at the look of genuine happiness on her face. She silently wished they could both be happy like that all the time.

But Alita's smile faded. Confusion and concern took its place.

"What happened to your head spike?"

Evelyn blinked. She hadn't expected that question. She sat up, consciously touching the scar tissue on her head with her forefoot, realising that her crown had fallen off completely.

"It was removed," she explained. "Shortly after I became Prinze, Griffin was worried my head spike would get in the way of my crown. So he instructed that it be removed."

"That sounds horrible," Alita said. She rolled onto her side and sat next to Evelyn. "I didn't realise we could even remove our spikes."

"It was incredibly risky... and painful. But Griffin insisted it was for the best," Evelyn screwed her eyes shut as she remembered the unbearable pain, the blood, the screaming. She quickly reopened her eyes and focused on Alita. "But, hey, you've got scars too. Like that one there."

Evelyn pointed to the long, pale line on Alita's foreleg. She saw Alita visibly wince. For a split second, she considered not continuing the conversation. But her desire to know what pain Alita had endured overtook the hesitation.

"You didn't have that one seven years ago. What happened there?" Evelyn asked.

Alita hesitated, clearly reluctant to share. Finally, she said, "It may have been caused by a fight... with Chieftain Clyde."

"You *fought* Chieftain Clyde?" Evelyn's eyes widened. She hadn't expected that at all.

"Sort of." Alita took a deep breath. "Okay, so you know how yesterday I told you that Clyde banished Korbin when he found out we were dating? Well, I sort of left a bit out. Korbin was angry that we couldn't just be together and challenged Clyde. Clyde took on the challenge but I tried to stop the fight. In all the commotion, Clyde sliced my leg with one of his horns."

"That sounds painful." Evelyn scrunched up her face as she imagined it.

"It was," Alita agreed. "Anyway, I needed medical attention and couldn't leave the Tribe because of it, so Clyde forced Korbin to leave and took me to get treated. While I was recovering, I was hoping he might come back for me. Seems I dodged a rockslide though."

"Yeah, he turned out to be a horrible dragon," Evelyn said. They were both quiet for a moment before she added, "At least it all worked out. You got to escape the life you had in Tribe-Ali and I got my best friend to be my bodyguard."

Alita smiled slightly and nodded. Evelyn felt a flutter in her chest as she smiled back. But then the crunching of feet on grass made her look up. She saw Luana and Modesty approaching and her mood instantly soured.

"What do *they* want?" she hissed as she grabbed her crown and put it back on.

"Looks like they're fine, Luana," Modesty said loudly enough for Evelyn to hear them clearly. "They're just hanging out in a field of cherry blossoms."

Luana shot a blind glare at Modesty but didn't say anything. Evelyn pushed herself to her feet and glanced at Alita. She was still sitting, her eyes darting from Modesty to Luana. But then Luana sneezed when a stray petal landed on her nose and Alita's face melted into a saccharine sweet expression. Evelyn felt as though the icy storm her chest was stabbing at her very heart. She turned and glared at Modesty.

"What are you two doing here?" she asked coldly.

"We came to check up on you," Modesty said. Her tone was carefully trained into innocence but Evelyn didn't believe a word of it.

"I have Alita, I'm fine," Evelyn said. "I certainly don't need either of you trailing after me."

Modesty's expression twisted into a smirk. "And yet, here we are."

Evelyn glared at Modesty, a growl rising in her throat. Alita quickly stepped between them to break the eye contact.

"I think it'd be best if you left," Alita said to Modesty.

"Just me? Not your blind little lovebird as well?" Modesty asked, sounding innocent before smirking again.

"Hey!" Luana snapped. "Watch your mouth, Modesty!"

Modesty rolled her eyes. "Fine. I'll leave. But I think whatever precious mood you had is gone now."

Modesty turned and left, head held high. Evelyn watched her go, knowing in her heart the Modesty had seen through her. There were no secrets that Modesty couldn't find out.

Chapter 28

After Modesty left, Alita noticed a shift in the atmosphere. While she enjoyed getting a chance to talk to Luana, Evelyn became oddly quiet for the rest of the day. Eventually, Evelyn went back to the castle and Alita had no choice but to follow her. But even as they went through the rest of the evening, Evelyn stayed quiet.

Once Evelyn went to bed for the night and Alita sat down for dinner, she found herself thinking of Luana. She wanted to visit Everhart Manor again and talk to her. Seeing her at the market had been great, but it wasn't enough.

"Hey there Alita," Heather said, sitting down next to her. "How you likin' the job so far?"

"It's not bad," Alita said. "I guess I kind of like it. Though having to keep an eye on Duchy Modesty all the time is kind of stressful."

"But you are, so that's good. Your trial is goin' well," Heather said. "What's important is that our Prinze stays alive and well until the weddin'. But don't worry, you'll still have a job after that. Lots of thin's to do in the castle. If guard work gets too much or too borin' for you, then there's always other jobs you can try. Just don't go yellin' at the High Caln again."

"Thanks, Heather," Alita said. "I'll see how I go."

Heather nodded and got up again. Alita watched her walk down the table and sit next to a familiar yellow dragon. What was his name again? Right, Henry. Heather seemed awfully fond of him, based on how close they were sitting.

"Hello again Alita."

Alita jumped at the new voice. She turned to see Jai sitting across the table from her.

"Sorry, I didn't mean to scare you," Jai apologised. "How is your job going?"

"It's fine." Alita took a breath to calm the jolt of adrenaline running through her body.

"I couldn't help but notice you were watching Heather and Henry down there," Jai said. "They don't make it very subtle how much they mean to each other."

"Is it supposed to be a secret?" Alita asked.

"Of course. Heather is the head of the guards," Jai explained. "She takes great pride in the perception of her strength and dedication to her job. She doesn't want others to know that she has a soft spot for another dragon."

"Is everyone here focused on how they're perceived?" Alita asked. "That seems to be a theme with the nobles and their... regalness."

"Not everyone, no," Jai said. "But many dragons focus on it as part of keeping their job. If it got out that they weren't an unmoving rock or gentle artist, they might feel as though their world were crumbling around them. The royal family's focal point is on their perception. Those who are privy to their unguarded selves should feel blessed and trusted like none other."

Alita remembered her playfight with Evelyn earlier and realised she was in the tiny group of dragons trusted by a royal in that way. But that was just because she and Evelyn used to be friends. She knew Evelyn from before perception meant anything to either of them. They were able to feel comfortable with each other simply because of that previous familiarity, right?

Alita finished her dinner and left the great hall. She remembered Luana again and felt another pang of longing in her chest. Before she knew it, she had left the castle and started for Everhart Manor. The plaza was an open space once again. Alita wondered where the stall attendees stayed when the market closed for the night. Did they have somewhere to stay nearby so they could make an early start for tomorrow's market? Or did they have to go all the way back to their homes with all their stuff? That sounded like a long and tiresome journey for dragons who would just come back to set up their stalls for the second day of the market.

Unable to answer her own question, Alita pushed it out of her mind and continued to Everhart Manor. She knocked on the door when she arrived and was met by Lance's tired face. He recognised her and sighed heavily, allowing her to enter.

"Laird Luana, you have a visitor," Lance said. Much like the last time, he wasn't very loud when he said it.

Alita looked around, wondering where Luana was at that moment. Then she heard a flurry of footsteps and looked up in time to see Luana leap over the second floor railing and dive to the ground floor. Alita blinked several times, trying to understand what she'd just witnessed.

"Hey Alita." Luana smiled. "I was hoping you'd stop by."

Chapter 29

Alita followed Luana out into the gardens and they sat next to the water fountain like they had the other night. The sky was clear, allowing all the stars to shine, though the full moon was brighter than all of them.

"How's Evelyn doing?" Luana asked.

"She's fine, I think. She was pretty quiet after the market this morning," Alita said.

"I think that's got to do with me. Sorry about that," Luana apologised.

"Why would you have anything to do with it?" Alita asked.

"I could hear you guys long before Modesty and I actually showed up," Luana explained. "It sounded like you two were having fun."

Alita smiled a little. "It was like we were back on the beach, running around like reckless fledglings. Wait... does that mean you heard us talking about our scar stories?"

"Yeah." Luana ducked her head. "Sorry, sometimes my hearing is a curse."

"I guess there's no secrets with you," Alita said.

"Only if they're spoken out loud. Sometimes I can also piece it together from tone," Luana explained. "That's how I figured Evelyn wasn't so happy after I showed up today."

Alita felt a pang of guilt. She had been so delighted to see Luana earlier she'd completely ignored Evelyn. Her job was to protect the

Prinze. She shouldn't be getting distracted while on the job.

"And now you've gone quiet," Luana said. "What's going on in your mind?"

"Just thinking about earlier," Alita admitted. "I should've noticed Evelyn's change in behaviour the way you did. I am her bodyguard after all. I shouldn't be letting myself get distracted."

"Aw, do you find me distracting?" Luana teased.

Alita felt her ears heat up. "I-I guess. In-in a way."

"It's okay, Alita. I find you distracting too." Luana smiled.

Alita ducked her head as her face heated up even more. What was she supposed to say now?

Before she could think of anything, Luana said, "I wanted to give you something. Wait here a moment."

Luana hurried back inside the manor. She came out a minute later with her satchel around her neck. She sat down next to Alita, closer than before. In fact, they were close enough that their wings touched. Luana dug around her satchel and pulled something out of it.

"Hold out your forefoot." she said.

Alita obeyed, sticking out her forefoot with her palm up. Luana put the item in her palm. Alita exhaled in awe when she recognised the Jadeite earrings Luana had bought earlier.

"I wanted you to have them," Luana explained. "I think you were quite fond of them."

"I... I don't know what to say. You spent so much on these and you're giving them to me? Ar-are you sure? Don't you want them for yourself?" Alita asked.

Luana shrugged. "I'm not a big fan of earrings. I don't like things that pull on my ears."

"Why did you buy them then?" Alita asked.

"Because I wanted to give them to you," Luana said.

"That's... are you really sure? These were 5,000 Drachmar *each*. I'm not worth that much," Alita insisted.

"Alita." Luana leaned closer to her. Her wing was warm as it pressed against Alita's. "I want you to have it. I like you, okay? I've never liked anyone as much as you. And I only just met you. Take the earrings. Wear them. Enjoy them. They're a gift from me."

Alita stared into Luana's pale green eyes for a long time. When she finally spoke, she could only think of one thing to say. "I really like you too."

Luana smiled and rested her head on Alita's neck. "I'm glad."

Alita wrapped a wing around Luana and pulled her closer. Something about it just felt right. She sighed blissfully.

But then her mind started to swim with thoughts.

"You're betrothed to Evelyn," Alita said. "Isn't this wrong?"

"Evelyn and I don't even want to marry each other," Luana explained. "To be completely honest, this feels right to me. We can make it work."

Alita thought for a moment, then nodded. "Yeah. You're right. This is right."

Alita put the earrings on her ears. Thankfully, they were clip-ons. They were heavy on Alita's ears but she didn't care. They were a gift from Luana and that's all that mattered.

Interlude V

Modesty stalked down the spiral staircase and into the dungeons. It had been two days since she'd learned of the prisoner, Korbin. That was enough time for the guards to start a routine of guarding him. She had noticed Heather going down the stairs a lot, but she was currently preoccupied with a meeting with Griffin. Modesty would be able to question Korbin and leave before she came back to the dungeon.

When Modesty approached the cell, she was surprised to see a Nature Dragon sitting by the wooden bars. His armour was loose. The helmet sat crooked on his head. Modesty knew the castle guard didn't have any Nature Dragons. Whoever this was, he wasn't a guard.

The dragon froze up when he spotted Modesty. He trembled slightly and his limbs were tense.

"You're not a guard," Modesty said.

"N-no, I'm not," the dragon stuttered. "I'm Koa. I'm the garden caretaker. Heather needed a Nature Dragon to guard the prisoner so I'm filling in until they hire someone."

Modesty scowled at him. "Get out of here."

"Uh..." Koa hesitated, not moving from his spot by the cell.

"Now! Go! Get out of here!" Modesty snapped.

Koa yelped and scurried past Modesty for the door. He tripped on his own feet in his hurry to flee the room.

Modesty smiled, revelling in the thrill of scaring such a pathetic dragon. Once she was High Caln, she would be sure to do that more often.

"Nice work. I couldn't get him to leave no matter what I said."

Modesty looked at Korbin as he chuckled. Despite being in the only wooden cell in the dungeon, his legs were still chained together. He shuffled over to the bars of the cell and grinned at Modesty.

"I'm not here to let you out," Modesty told him, grimacing at his expression.

"So mean." Korbin pouted. Modesty wanted to gag at the fakeness of it.

"You're a criminal. Why would I do anything for you?" Modesty said.

"Well, you came down here and scared off the guard. You must have wanted to talk to me in private for a reason." Korbin's brown eyes were locked on Modesty in a way that made her skin crawl.

In a flash, Modesty grabbed Korbin by his throat, ice-sharpened claws gripping his skin. Korbin's eyes went wide. Modesty held back a grin of satisfaction. This was much better.

"I won't be intimidated or manipulated. I've been doing that sort of thing long enough to recognise when someone is attempting it on me," she warned, a growl on the edge of her voice. "I need information that you have, so you are going to tell me what I want to know."

Korbin's expression relaxed. He looked Modesty up and down, then smiled. "You're clearly a very smart hen. Perhaps I'll cooperate. After all, I find hens like you extremely attractive."

Modesty narrowed her eyes in a hardened glare. "You're disgusting."

Korbin simply smiled back at her. Modesty released her grip on his throat and stepped back from the bars. Korbin felt his throat before looking back up at her.

"So what information do you need?" he asked, grinning crookedly at her.

"Don't look so pleased with yourself," Modesty growled. "I need to know about Alita. I understand you two have a past."

Korbin pulled his head high as he hummed with thought. "It's been a long time since that past. What could I possibly tell you that would be helpful in any way?"

"What is she like? Is she dangerous?" Modesty asked.

Korbin laughed. "Dangerous? She's the least dangerous Rock Dragon I've ever met. She always tried to break up fights and arguments between her friends. Even between me and Chieftain Clyde. She never tried to hurt anyone."

Modesty squinted at him. That description didn't match up with the dragon that was ready to fight her two nights prior.

Korbin raised an eyebrow. "What? You don't believe me?"

"Of course not. I have information that goes against what you just said," Modesty told him.

"I see. Perhaps she's changed since I last saw her two years ago," Korbin muttered. "But that's what she was like when I knew her."

"What is her elemental skill like?" Modesty asked.

Korbin shrugged. "She can control sand and dirt and rock like any other Rock Dragon. Some of the teachers in the Tribe saw great potential in her. I doubt she's professionally trained in her element though."

"If someone were to fight her, how do you think she'd hold up?" Modesty asked.

Korbin narrowed his eyes. "These are oddly specific questions you're asking. What are you planning?"

"That's none of your business. Answer my question," Modesty said.

Korbin sighed and rolled his eyes. "If she's anything like she used to be, she's not much use in a fight. But who knows, maybe she's had combat training or something since then."

Modesty growled at the impractical answer. This was turning into a waste of her time. Without another word, she turned and marched out of the room. She would just have to keep practising her own techniques in case she couldn't get Alita out of the way.

Chapter 30

Evelyn awoke slowly. Her memories of the previous day replayed in her mind on repeat. She wished she had dreamed it all, but there was no changing the fact that it happened. Her day with Alita had been going great until Luana and Modesty just *had* to show up.

As Lily prepared Evelyn for the day, she tried her best not to think about it. It was just one day. The way Alita's attention shifted was just an outlier. It wouldn't happen again, would it?

Evelyn exited her bedroom and saw Alita talking to Crystal and Lucas. But the world grew quiet around her as Evelyn recognised the gold rimmed jadeite earrings on Alita's ears. How had she gotten those? Luana had bought them. Did Luana give her the earrings? How? And when?

"Good morning, Evelyn." Alita smiled.

Evelyn forced a small smile. "Good morning, Alita. I see you have some new earrings."

"Er, yeah. Luana gave them to me last night," Alita admitted.

That explained the when. But Evelyn wasn't sure how they'd even found themselves in the same place to begin with. Perhaps Luana had visited the castle to drop them off. That would mean Luana had a crush on Alita.

Of course she does, Evelyn thought bitterly. *Why wouldn't she want someone like Alita?*

Evelyn shoved the pang of jealousy down and forced a smile back onto her face.

"Let's go to breakfast," she said. She didn't give Alita the time to respond before heading for the stairs.

Once at the great hall, Evelyn sat beside Griffin and dipped her feet into the cleansing bowl beneath the table.

"You are late," Griffin said.

"Apologies, Griffin. I must have overslept slightly," Evelyn lied. She didn't want him to know that she had taken her time getting up and ready for the day.

"How is that possible when you have a servant to wake you on time?" Griffin asked.

Oops. She was about to get Lily in trouble. How could she fix this?

"Lily did come on time. I just took a while to be roused," Evelyn explained, doing her best to sound honest. "My drowsiness caused a delay in getting ready."

Griffin hummed quietly. Evelyn guessed he wasn't convinced.

"As Prinze, you must wake on time every day," Griffin said. "If you are tardy again, I may have to reconsider your right to the crown."

"Please do," Evelyn muttered before she could stop herself.

"Prinze Evelyn." Griffin's voice was suddenly cold and firm. "I will not tolerate such statements. You cannot get out of the wedding just by acting like you do not wish to be High Caln."

Evelyn shot him a glare. She had called his bluff. It was too risky for him to revoke her crown now. Modesty would surely jump at the opportunity.

"Speaking of the wedding, you must visit Everhart Manor today," Griffin continued. "Laird Adelaide and I have agreed that a day with the Everhart family will be good for you. You must get to know your future in-laws, after all."

Evelyn felt ice begin to form on her claws as anger cooled her chest dramatically. She didn't want to spend the day with anyone from the Everhart family! But she forced herself to calm down before letting out a breath. Thankfully, the icy mist was thin enough to go unnoticed.

"Very well. I will go to Everhart Manor after breakfast," Evelyn said.

Griffin didn't say anything in response, which Evelyn took to mean he was satisfied with her choice of words. They continued with breakfast in silence. Evelyn could only hope that the rest of the day went by quickly.

Chapter 31

"Come on, everyone, move faster!" Adelaide's voice was even higher pitched than usual. Luana could tell she was stressed. "The Prinze will be here any minute. The floors must be shiny, the windows spotless! Lance, don't let the door squeak when you open it!"

Luana's ear twitched as she felt her mother's gaze fall on her. She didn't want to be here. Why did Evelyn have to come over at all? And she was going to be there all day! Luana wasn't sure she was up to a full day of pretending to get along.

"Luana, darling, don't make that face," Adelaide said. "You're going to spoil our dear Prinze's day."

Luana scowled at her mother. Surely Adelaide knew by now that she and Evelyn didn't even want to marry each other. What difference would it make if Luana wasn't happy to see Evelyn?

"Don't give me that look, Luana," Adelaide scolded her. "The Prinze is spending the day here whether you like it or not."

Adelaide rushed off to check on a pair of servants scrubbing the windows. Luana pulled her ears back and frowned at the ground.

"Cheer up, Luana," Markos said, coming up beside her. "Alita's going to be here too."

Luana turned to her brother. "Alita's coming?"

Luana couldn't help the wistful smile that spread across her face. Perhaps the day wouldn't be so bad after all.

There was a knock at the door and suddenly Adelaide was in a panic. "That's the Prinze! Everyone on their best behaviour. This day needs to go perfectly!"

Adelaide stood next to Luana and Markos. Luana sensed her younger brothers joining them. The whole family was together, almost. For a brief moment, Luana wondered if her father could see them from the afterlife.

Lance pulled the door open in a smooth motion. Miraculously, the door didn't squeak once. Luana recognised Evelyn's footsteps as she entered the manor. Alita's footsteps were newer to Luana and harder to recognise, but she heard the distinct sound of a second set of feet on the floor.

"Prinze Evelyn," Adelaide said, bowing deeply, "welcome to our home."

Luana dipped her head slightly, knowing her mother expected some form of respect to be shown to Evelyn.

"Thank you for letting me visit," Evelyn said. Her voice was the pinnacle of politeness.

Adelaide stood upright. "I have planned for you to spend time with each of my sons individually. First will be Jakob. He has planned to give you a tour of the library."

"Thank you, Laird Adelaide," Evelyn said. "I look forward to getting to know you all better."

Luana could tell right away that Evelyn was lying through her teeth. It wasn't just the hint of forced politeness in her tone. Luana already knew in her gut that Evelyn never wanted to be there in the first place.

"As do we, Prinze Evelyn," Adelaide said. "Jakob, Luana, please escort Prinze Evelyn up to the library."

"Yes Mother," Jakob said politely.

Luana stayed silent, only giving a small nod as she joined her brother. Jakob happily led the way, with Evelyn walking beside him. Luana was more than happy to walk in step with Alita behind both of them. She could already feel Alita's nervous joy. She was probably glancing at Luana every few steps.

"We meet again," Luana said to her with a small smile.

"Uh, yeah," Alita mumbled. Luana wondered if she was smiling or blushing at all.

Jakob did most of the talking while they were in the library. He talked about the Everhart collection, which didn't impress Evelyn at all. He also talked about some of the history books he'd been going through. Evelyn didn't seem impressed by that either. Luana understood why. Even though she was blind, she'd heard all about the castle's book collection, which was never allowed to leave the castle. The collection had some of the rarest and oldest books in the Calndom, so it was by far more valuable.

"This is what I'm reading at the moment," Jakob said as he pulled a book off one of the many shelves. "It's so old that it's written in the Original Language. It's hard to translate but I'm slowly transcribing it."

He opened the book and leafed through a few pages for Evelyn to look at.

"That's the Original Language?" Evelyn asked. "It looks like bird scratch."

"I know!" Jakob said excitedly. "The castle may have old books, but this is one of the only ones found from the time of the Original Language. I'm translating it a little bit at a time and I think it actually *is* a bird language."

"Oh? But it's supposed to be a dragon language, isn't it? What makes you think it's a bird language?" Evelyn asked.

"Well, from what I've pieced together, the writing is rather melodic," Jakob explained. "If I try to pronounce words using the phonetic base of our language, it makes no sense and sounds awful. However, ancient bird and gryphon languages have clicks and whistles built into their speech. Using their base sounds, the words suddenly make some sense and sound song-like."

"That... that's incredible," Alita said suddenly.

Luana raised her head and turned to Alita. She sensed Evelyn and Jakob turning to look at her as well.

"What's the book about?" Alita asked.

"That's the most interesting part," Jakob said. Luana could hear the grin on his face. "It's all about the dragons of the time. Their elements, their cultures, even descriptions of the land they lived in and their naming systems."

"Why would a bird species be writing so much about dragons?" Alita asked. "And why is it called the Original Language if it's not even dragon?"

"That's what I've been trying to figure out. See, this book was one of the few brought to Laili Island when our ancestors migrated here. They lived in a much bigger land with many other species. Equines, Draconids, Gryphids, and even Aves – birds – were on the land. It's possible that a bird species learned to live among dragons of the time and studied them," Jakob explained.

"Our ancestors already had a written word," Evelyn said blandly. "The Original Language is from long before that time."

"I know, but perhaps the dragons that lived with birds didn't have a written word," Jakob suggested. "So the bird species wrote everything down and that became the writing system adopted by our ancestors."

"Jakob, you're missing a very important thing," Evelyn said. "Our language is phonetic and has no clicks. We don't even try to sound melodic when we speak."

"Languages change and adapt over time, Prinze Evelyn," Jakob said. "I think there's a connection I'm missing between our ancestors' written word and the Original Language. There has to be a gap where the language evolved drastically."

Luana sighed. This conversation could go back and forth for hours now that Jakob was on the topic. Although she hadn't expected Alita to take interest in language and history. She seemed more of an outdoorsy dragon than one who would sit in a library all day, but hearing her excitement over these old books was enough to brighten Luana's mood.

Chapter 32

Alita listened to Jakob and Evelyn go back and forth on the history of their language for the rest of the hour. She was fascinated that Jakob knew how to translate such an old language. When she looked at the pages of the book in question, she could only see scratch-like lines on incredibly well preserved pages. Evelyn's description of 'bird-scratch' certainly made sense.

As the hour came to an end, Alita heard a knock from the library entrance and turned to see Markos coming in. He seemed to notice Jakob and Evelyn's in depth conversation as he approached.

"Sorry to interrupt you two, but I believe it's my turn to bond with Evelyn," he said.

Evelyn blinked at Markos, then looked at the window across the room. "I hadn't realised we were talking for that long."

Markos cracked a smile. "Yeah, that happens when you engage with Jakob's studies. He's very passionate."

"I can tell," Evelyn said. She turned to Jakob and dipped her head. "Thank you, Jakob. Perhaps we can continue this discussion another time."

"I'd love that, Prinze Evelyn." Jakob smiled. "Perhaps your bodyguard could even take part next time."

Alita stiffened as Jakob looked at her. She had been the first one to take interest after all. She couldn't help but smile at the thought of learning more about dragon history.

"I'd love to," she said.

Evelyn smiled, then nodded to Markos. "Alright, Markos, lead the way."

"Great. I think you'll like the gardens," Markos said. He turned and headed for the library exit. "We've got a fountain and lots of flowers and trees."

"Sounds intriguing," Evelyn said.

Alita couldn't help but notice that Evelyn's mood seemed better than it had when they'd arrived at the manor. She was glad that Evelyn was enjoying herself.

Markos led the way down the stairs and out the door that led to the gardens, Alita found herself in step with Luana once again. She couldn't help but smile and gave Luana a small nudge with her wing. Luana smiled back at her.

"Hey," Luana said quietly.

"Hey." Alita smiled. "I like the earrings."

"I'm glad," Luana said. "Are you wearing them today?"

"Yeah." Alita leaned her head over just enough to tap Luana's cheek with her ear. Luana's face reddened slightly and she ducked her head.

"I wish I could see them," Luana muttered after a moment.

"Does being blind bother you?" Alita asked.

"Sometimes," Luana said. She raised her head back up and turned her face to Alita. "I'm used to it but sometimes I wish I knew what colours are or what the faces of the dragons around me look like."

"Maybe I could try to describe that stuff to you," Alita suggested.

Luana smiled. "Thanks, but my brothers have already tried multiple times."

"I'll keep the offer open in case you change your mind," Alita said.

"Keep up you two!" Markos called.

He and Evelyn were already standing by the fountain in the garden. Alita realised she and Luana had slowed a bit during their conversation.

"Sorry!" Alita apologised.

She trotted over and stood beside Evelyn. Luana was slower to join them. Once they were all gathered in front of the fountain, Markos turned his attention to the garden around them.

"Welcome to the Everhart Manor gardens, Prinze Evelyn," he said, sweeping his wings wide in a gesture of grandeur.

"It's smaller than the castle gardens," Evelyn said. Her tone was flat again, almost sour, Alita noticed.

"I know. But you have to admit that there's nothing quite as unique as a manor's own garden," Markos said. "The castle has a hedge and a gazebo, but here you will find flowers of every colour and scent. Well, every good scent that is."

Markos laughed at his own joke while Evelyn surveyed the surrounding area. Alita looked around too, realising she had only been here during the night. It was hard to appreciate flowers when the darkness made them so much harder to see.

"This is truly amazing," Alita breathed.

"It certainly is," Markos agreed. "Nothing will ever match it."

Markos tilted his head and grinned at Alita. For a moment, she could have sworn she saw a glint in his eyes. That glint was starting to become familiar. What was it about Markos that made his eyes glisten like that so much?

"You know, I'm surprised you even need a tour, Alita," Luana said with a small giggle.

Alita smiled at her, feeling a light feeling in her chest. She'd probably be visiting Luana again that evening, just like she had before.

"What is that supposed to mean?" Evelyn asked.

"Just that Alita already knows the gardens a bit," Luana said.

"Well, to be fair, we only sit by the fountain," Alita added.

"We?" Evelyn echoed. "Alita, have you been visiting Everhart Manor?"

"Only a couple times," Alita explained. "The day you ran off and left Luana in a field, I visited the manor to check that she got home safe."

"And the other time?" Evelyn asked. Alita got the feeling it was more of a demand.

"Last night," Alita said. "I, uh, wanted to check she was alright again because Duchy Modesty is a threat."

Evelyn stared at Alita for a moment. Alita couldn't read her expression, but she knew they'd be discussing this when they got back to the castle.

Chapter 33

Markos continued to show off the garden like it was made of gold. Evelyn had lost interest in it entirely. Instead, her mind was focused on what Alita had said earlier. She had been visiting Luana at the manor. That was how she got the earrings.

It was unacceptable. Evelyn couldn't have her bodyguard visiting her future wife outside of work. Dragons would talk, and gossip was bad for any ruler. What would she look like to the Calndom if her wife and bodyguard were potentially romantically involved with one another? She didn't want to, but she would have to tell Alita to stop visiting Luana on her own.

"Here we have the wonderful and rare Winter Star," Markos said, pulling Evelyn out of her thoughts. He was dramatically waving a wing at a tiny plant growing under a tree.

"It doesn't look like much," Evelyn said.

"Not at the moment, no. The flowers only bloom in winter. But when they do, it's the most beautiful thing. Its petals are stark white in the centre and turn to blue on the edges. The petals even take the shape of a four point star," Markos paused for a moment to watch the flower, before adding, "It's my favourite flower."

"I'm sure it's amazing," Evelyn said. She didn't care to put effort into sounding interested. Her mind still dwelled on the fact that Alita had been visiting Luana.

"We had one of these in the castle gardens back when Dad was High

145

Caln," Markos said. "The day he died, the whole plant shrivelled up and turned black. We couldn't do anything to save it."

Evelyn looked at Markos. "That's an odd coincidence."

"It seemed so at the time," Markos said with a small nod. His dark green eyes were still trained on the plant. "Perhaps one day this plant will die with me too."

"That's morbid, Markos," Luana said.

Markos jolted and took a few steps back. "Sorry. I got carried away."

"Shall we head back inside?" Evelyn suggested. With all that she had learned from Alita and Markos, she wanted to get out of this garden as fast as possible.

"Good idea," Luana said. "I think lunch is ready anyway."

Luana was the first to head for the door back into the manor. Evelyn was close behind her, with Alita walking beside her. Markos lingered by the Winter Star a bit longer before following them.

Evelyn considered talking to Alita about what had happened earlier, but she decided against it. They could discuss it later, back at the castle. Or perhaps she could tell Heather to pass on the message. She really didn't want to say anything directly to Alita.

They all filed inside just as Adelaide came trotting down the stairs. She spotted them and hurried over.

"Good timing, Prinze Evelyn," Adelaide said. "The cooks just finished preparing lunch. Come and eat."

Adelaide led Evelyn and the others to the dining room. It was a grand room, with a table large enough to fit more than ten dragons. There was already food served up on one half of the table. Too much for seven dragons, but Evelyn had grown accustomed to that. There were paintings on the walls of the Everhart family. She couldn't help but notice the lack of paintings of Gerold.

"Prinze Evelyn, please sit at the head of the table as our honoured guest," Adelaide said, indicating to the end of the table.

Evelyn nodded and sat at the end of the table. Adelaide sat on her left and directed for Luana to sit on Evelyn's right. Markos and Jakob sat on Luana's other side while Hamlet sat next to his mother. After some hesitation, Alita went to sit next to Hamlet.

"Excuse me, bodyguard," Adelaide said suddenly. "What do you think you're doing?"

Alita blinked at Adelaide a few times, glanced at Evelyn, then back at Adelaide. "Uh... having lunch?"

"You most certainly are not," Adelaide told her. "You are working. You will sit by the door and supervise."

"That won't be necessary, Laird Adelaide," Evelyn said. "Alita is assigned to eat lunch with me. She may sit with us."

"That- that-" Adelaide seemed to be stuck on how to respond.

"Do not question my word, Laird Adelaide," Evelyn said, lowering her tone slightly.

Adelaide closed her mouth and nodded. "My apologies, Prinze Evelyn. I will not give orders to your bodyguard."

"Thank you," Evelyn said.

Evelyn glanced at Alita and spotted the grateful smile on her face as she made herself comfortable. Evelyn dipped her feet in the rinsing bowl underneath the table and reached for some charred fish near her plate. Cooked meat wasn't her favourite, but she was craving a taste of home after her time in the manor's gardens. She took a delicate bite of the fish, ensuring that she remembered her table manners.

"Perhaps, Prinze Evelyn, we could discuss the plans for the wedding," Adelaide said.

Evelyn coughed, nearly choking on her fish. A servant was at her side in an instant with a bucket of water. Evelyn gratefully drank from it and forced herself to ignore the newfound pain in her chest.

"My apologies, Laird Adelaide. You caught me off guard." Evelyn had to resist the urge to cough more. "What did you have in mind?"

"I thought we ought to go over the colours High Caln Griffin and I have been discussing," Adelaide said.

"Very well. Go on," Evelyn said.

Adelaide smiled. "Thank you, Prinze Evelyn. We have been discussing using shades of white, blue, and purple to accentuate your own colours and symbolise the unity of you and my daughter. As for fabrics, I believe thin silks would complement the day nicely. I believe High Caln Griffin also suggested velvet to drape over your horns, though I wasn't too sure. I respect our High Caln greatly, but his eye is not made for outfit designs."

"The colours sound just fine, Laird Adelaide," Evelyn said. "As for the velvet, perhaps I can try a sample to see how it will look."

"A marvellous idea, Prinze Evelyn," Adelaide agreed. "I will begin arrangements for samples after lunch."

"Speaking of after lunch, I believe Hamlet is the only one of your sons left for me to spend time with. Do you have any plans for what we should do?" Evelyn asked.

"That is something I have left up to each of my sons," Adelaide said. "I believe Hamlet will want to play a game after lunch, though he hasn't told me what he wants to do."

Evelyn looked at Hamlet, who was busy stuffing his face with bread. He was only seven. Evelyn rarely spoke to fledglings his age anymore. She wasn't sure how to approach a conversation with him.

"What would you like to do after lunch, Hamlet?" Evelyn asked.

Hamlet paused with his teeth sunken into a piece of bread. He pulled off the bite and swallowed it whole before replying.

"I want to go to the market again," Hamlet said.

"Oh, dear Hamlet. You just went to the mid-week market yesterday," Adelaide said.

"I know, Mother. But I want to go again," Hamlet insisted. "It's so big. I know I missed something."

"Very well, then that's what we'll do," Evelyn said. Perhaps it would be a good thing to get out of the manor for a few hours.

Chapter 34

After lunch, Hamlet happily led the way out of the Manor with Evelyn, Alita, and Luana close behind. Alita found herself wondering if she would see Trey's stall again. But as Hamlet took the lead, it became clear that he was taking a very different path through the market than what Evelyn had led the day before. His first stop was a colourful stall filled with toys.

"Evelyn! Look!" Hamlet said with a wide grin. His eyes were locked on a small object that looked a bit like a spinning top.

"Surely you've outgrown toys by now," Evelyn said.

"He's seven, Evelyn," Luana said. "He always wants new toys."

Alita didn't pay too much attention to the conversation as she looked at the various types of toys at the stall. Most were made of wood or stone and were carved into shapes to resemble dragons, birds, fish, or mammals. There were a few toy sets intended for games such as knucklebones and pick up sticks.

"I remember some of these toys from when I was young," Alita muttered to no one in particular.

"Anything specific that stands out?" Luana asked.

"Not really. I just remember stone toys carved into fish or dragons. There were also some games we played in the Tribe that I can see here," Alita explained.

"Did you ever break any toys?" Luana asked.

Alita glanced at her. "I was a Rock Dragon with stone toys.

Anything I broke I could put back together."

"I suppose that's better than giving a Fire Dragon wooden toys." Luana giggled. "I destroyed a few toys in my young years."

Alita smiled. "I can imagine that."

"Hey! You broke toys too," Luana shot back.

She frowned at Alita but her laugh betrayed her. Alita laughed along with her, but quickly remembered that she was meant to be working and turned her attention back to Evelyn. It seemed she and Hamlet were still talking about the spinning top toy.

"Come on, Evelyn. *Please?*" Hamlet begged. His eyes grew wide and he drooped his ears, putting on his cutest face.

Evelyn rolled her eyes and sighed. "Fine. I'll buy it for you."

"Yay! Thank you!" Hamlet exclaimed.

As Evelyn paid the stall attendee, Hamlet was beaming from ear to ear. The attendee handed Evelyn the toy and she promptly passed it on to Hamlet. He grabbed it and put it on the ground, where he puffed a small flame onto it. Alita watched in awe as the flame circled around the spinning top, making it spin and glow. The toy spun for several seconds before the flame dissipated. It then began to wobble and soon stopped spinning. Hamlet grinned up at Evelyn.

"Impressive," Evelyn said. "But don't lose it."

"Of course not. I'll tuck it under my wing until we get back home," Hamlet said, picking up the toy.

"Can *you* do that?" Alita asked Luana quietly.

"Do what?" Luana asked.

"Make a spinning top spin by breathing fire on it," Alita said.

"No. Not all Fire Dragons can learn to do that," Luana explained. "Hamlet is the only one in my family who can do it. He'll be a skilled Fire Dragon one day."

"It's amazing," Alita muttered.

"It definitely is," Luana agreed. "Our mother will probably push for him to become an elemental teacher for noble Fire Dragons. Though

I think he'll want to pursue something less academic."

"What makes you say that?" Alita asked.

"He's too athletic," Luana said. "He doesn't have much interest in books or studying. He just likes to run, fly, and control fire."

"Maybe he could join the castle guard. Or even – what are they called – the Protective Unit?" Alita suggested.

"Perhaps. Mother would never allow it though. Not if he isn't working near the castle," Luana said.

"Sounds like she's controlling with everyone, not just you," Alita pointed out.

"You're not wrong," Luana said. "But Hamlet and I have it worse than Markos and Jakob. I hope she calms down before Hamlet is old enough to fight for his own decisions."

Chapter 35

Hamlet continued to drag Evelyn through the market while Luana and Alita followed behind. Evelyn was beginning to zone out as Hamlet went from one stall to the next, looking at toys, games, and snacks. Hamlet glanced at a stand filled with toffee apples and cotton candy, but quickly went to the very next stand, which had various flavours of fudge on display.

"Look at this, Evelyn!" Hamlet grinned at her.

Evelyn suppressed a sigh and ducked her head to Hamlet's height to get a better look at the fudge. The displays were simple, yet elegant, with sets of five of each flavour arranged into little stacks. The fudge was stored in little glass cabinets as an extra protection measure.

"They've got pecan fudge," Hamlet said excitedly.

"Oh, I suppose you're going to convince me to buy you some fudge now." Evelyn couldn't help a little smile.

"It would be nice," Hamlet said. "Think of it as bonding with your future brother."

Hamlet tried his cute face again. Evelyn rolled her eyes. "It's brother-in-law, not brother."

Her ear twitched as she picked up on Luana and Alita talking behind her. They were still standing by the previous stall.

"Have you ever had cotton candy before?" Luana asked.

"I had some yesterday," Alita replied. "Evelyn convinced me to try some."

"What about toffee apples?" Luana asked.

"They sound vaguely familiar, but no, I don't think I've tried them," Alita said.

Evelyn glanced over her shoulder and saw Luana pay for two toffee apples and offer one to Alita.

"Try it," Luana said. "They're a little bit better than cotton candy since the apple is real. Just be careful with your teeth. The coating is a bit hard."

Alita took the toffee apple and carefully sunk her teeth into it, pulling off a bite. Her amber eyes lit up as she chewed.

"It's good," she said before taking another bite.

Evelyn felt something within her ache. Watching Luana and Alita interact made her so uncomfortable. She wasn't able to dwell on it for long, though, as Hamlet tugged on her cloak.

"Come on, Evelyn. Please?" Hamlet asked.

Right. He wanted fudge. Evelyn decided not to fight it and paid for a box of fudge for Hamlet. She passed him the box almost immediately. Hamlet grinned and thanked her over and over again before opening the box and taking a small piece. His smile was pure joy and for a moment, Evelyn thought he might melt from happiness.

"Do you want some?" Hamlet asked, offering the box to her.

Evelyn shook her head and forced a smile. She didn't want to eat anything sweet anymore. "No thanks. You can have it."

Hamlet soon tucked the fudge under his wing along with his spinning top and continued on. Evelyn noticed how much more he was struggling to get around with two things to carry and bought him a pouch to hang around his neck. Hamlet was grateful for something to help him carry his stuff and joked about looking like Evelyn with her little pouch for money around her neck.

As they continued through the market, Evelyn realised Hamlet was leading them straight for the spot where she and Alita had danced yesterday. The same band as before was playing and the music was playful and upbeat. Hamlet pushed his way to the front of the crowd and grinned at the dancing dragons.

"We should all dance!" Hamlet declared.

"I'm good, thanks," Evelyn said, stepping back from the edge of the clearing.

"I think it would be quite fun," Luana said. "What do you think, Alita?"

Evelyn's head snapped to look at them at the sound of Alita's name. Alita smiled at Luana and said, "I'm not a great dancer, but yeah, I think it would be fun."

Evelyn frowned, then squashed it with an expression of indifference. "I don't think it would be wise for you two to dance together. The Prinze's bodyguard and future wife dancing in public could spread unnecessary gossip."

Alita looked at Evelyn, then ducked her head and gave a small nod. "You're right, Evelyn. Sorry."

"Come on, Evelyn!" Hamlet pouted. "Stop being such a buzzkill. You can dance with me!"

Evelyn opened her mouth to decline again but Hamlet pushed her shoulder until she had stumbled into the clearing of dancing dragons. She knew everyone would be watching from the moment the music grew quiet and decided to just go along with it. Hamlet started jumping from foot to foot in a classic but unofficial dance form that fledglings often used. Evelyn shook her head and copied him. The band returned to their upbeat song.

Evelyn allowed herself to get lost in the silliness of Hamlet's dance. He swung his wings around wildly and stamped his feet with youthful joy. Evelyn couldn't help but feel like she was dancing with a younger version of Alita, back when they lived in the Tribe.

They had danced like this a few times before Evelyn became Prinze. Neither Alita, nor herself tried for any real artform when dancing at holiday celebrations. Evelyn recalled her hatchdays back in Tribe-Ali. Being one of the first two offspring of the current Chieftain had its benefits, such as having her hatchday celebrated by the entire Tribe. Being able to play and dance with her friends, especially Alita, had been one of the highlights of each year.

Evelyn did a little spin, getting caught up in the joy of the memories. As she turned, she spotted Luana and Alita dancing in the clearing as well. She hadn't noticed them join in. The way they looked at each other as they danced, their faces so close, and their partially spread wings overlapping, it suddenly felt so much more real than before. They liked each other. It was clear to see. What was she supposed to do now?

Chapter 36

Eventually the sun began to set and the chill of the evening set in. Alita talked with Luana and Hamlet all the way back to Everhart Manor. Evelyn remained quiet, but Alita barely noticed.

"This was a good day," Luana said as they arrived at the entrance to the manor.

"Are you glad I suggested it now?" Hamlet asked.

"Definitely," Luana smiled.

"Agreed," Alita said. She looked at the door of the manor and realised it was time to part ways. "I guess Evelyn and I should head back to the castle now."

"Yeah, it's past dinner time for the royal family," Luana said. "I'm pretty worn out too. I might skip dinner and go straight to bed."

"Good idea, Sis," Hamlet said. "Markos was saying he wanted to take you on a trip tomorrow. He refused to explain what he meant though."

"A trip?" Luana smiled and shook her head. "I'm sure he has something in mind."

"Well, enjoy your evening. And whatever your brother has planned for tomorrow as well," Alita said.

"Thanks. You enjoy your day as well," Luana said, smiling at her.

Alita smiled back; her heart turned to mush. Luana's smile was even more amazing since their dance at the market. Alita wished she could see it every day.

"Goodnight, Alita, Evelyn." Luana dipped her head to Evelyn before leading her brother into the manor.

Alita turned to Evelyn, who was already walking away with her head down. Alita followed behind her quietly for a few minutes before deciding to start a conversation.

"Today was fun, wasn't it?" Alita asked.

"I suppose," Evelyn muttered so quietly that Alita almost couldn't hear her.

"Did you not have fun?" Alita asked.

"It was a fine day," Evelyn said. "I'm just... tired."

Alita sped up to walk beside Evelyn. "I thought you were having fun. I saw the smile on your face when you were dancing with Hamlet. You looked really happy."

Evelyn glanced at her before turning her gaze back to the ground. Something in her eyes was very sad, almost regretful.

"It was fine," Evelyn repeated. "Like I said, I'm tired. It's been a long day."

"Alright. Well, we'll be back at the castle soon," Alita said. Evelyn merely grunted a reply.

They ended up walking in silence back through the cobblestone streets and past the plaza, where dragons were packing up their stalls now that the market had ended. Alita idly wondered about Trey's stall again. She couldn't see him among the dragons in the plaza, but perhaps he had already finished packing and returned home. Perhaps she could look for his shop if she ever got a day off.

Evelyn and Alita entered the castle in silence. Alita followed Evelyn up to her bedroom before going back down to the great hall to eat some dinner. She wasn't as hungry as the past few days, since she'd been snacking on sweet treats at the market all day. But she was craving something hearty after and ended up choosing raw rabbit and a couple of carrots.

As she exited the great hall, Alita spotted Heather and a Nature

Dragon guard in loose fitting armour entering the spiral staircase. She remembered the trial of Korbin from the other day and wondered if she could or should talk to him. Perhaps she could find out why he never came back for her. As she pondered, she found herself turning towards the staircase.

Chapter 37

Alita went down the spiral staircase to the dungeon. She was surprised to see that it didn't open directly into the dungeon. Instead, she found herself in a small room with two doors. She poked her head through the first door and found a large room with various training dummies set up in it. It looked like some sort of training room for the castle guards.

Alita stepped back from the door and turned to the second one. When she pushed it open, she was greeted with a long stone and brick hallway lined with bars. Behind each set of bars was a small space, barely large enough for a dragon to pace around in. Most of the bars were made of metal, but one, Alita noticed, was made of wood. Heather and the Nature Dragon were standing next to the wooden cell. Heather looked up as Alita entered the hallway.

"What are you doin' here?" she asked.

"Uh, I was wondering if I could talk to Korbin," Alita managed to say despite the shake in her voice.

Heather regarded Alita for a moment. "Very well. But only with our supervision. We've already had someone scare Koa out of here. We don't need a repeat of that."

Alita nodded. Hesitantly, she approached the wooden cell. It looked much newer and cleaner than the rest of the dungeon. The bars were perfectly round and the walls and floor were all smooth. Evidence of Korbin's stay in the cell existed in the dirty footprints and scrapes in the floor. He didn't look like he could move much in the small space, thanks to the chains around his legs. Korbin watched Alita with guarded eyes as she approached.

"Korbin." Alita gave a tiny nod of her head.

"Interesting that you would come here at all," Korbin said slowly. His words were smoothed, almost practised. Alita recognised the ease with which he spoke, but he was much more calculating than she remembered.

"I just wanted to ask you something," Alita said.

Korbin dipped his head in a bow-like motion. "Ask away."

"Why didn't you come back for me when Clyde banished you?" Alita asked.

Korbin raised his head and met her with a level stare. After several seconds, he finally spoke. "You proved your loyalties on that day. You tried to stop me from fighting for our future. If you had really cared about me and what we had, you would have let me fight Clyde without getting in the way. And if I had lost, you would have come with me to the Calndom."

"You knew I didn't like conflicts back then," Alita said. "But that experience taught me that I couldn't always avoid them. I know better now. Some fights are unavoidable. And I *will* fight them. But the fight you chose that day wasn't necessary. I got injured because of it. I won't let that happen again."

Korbin smiled. "So you have changed since then. Impressive."

Alita frowned at him. "I'm glad things worked out the way they did. After hearing what you've done, seeing what you became, I'm glad I didn't leave with you. I've got a much better life now than what I ever could have had with you."

"For now, at least." Korbin chuckled.

Alita turned back to Heather, trying her best to act like his laugh didn't send a chill up her spine.

"I'm done now," she told Heather before leaving the dungeon.

Chapter 38

Alita woke the next morning feeling good. She prepared for the day and went up to Evelyn's room to wait for her. To her surprise, Evelyn was already up and standing outside her room. She was talking to Caln Misti, who turned to Alita with a confused look as she approached.

"Alita, why are you here? Did Heather not inform you of your day off?" Misti asked.

"Day off?" Alita echoed.

Evelyn smiled at her. "Everyone needs a day off sometime. All castle staff get one day off per week."

"Yes, and today Evelyn will be spending time with my family," Misti explained. "She will have myself and Griffin with her at all times."

"Oh. Alright. If you're okay with it then." Alita hesitated. "Am I allowed to leave the castle for the day?"

"Of course," Misti said. "Many dragons use their day off to visit their family or friends. You can go wherever you like as long as you're back for your shift tomorrow."

Alita chuckled. "I don't think I could fly all the way to the Tribe and back just for a one day visit to my family there. But I'd love to explore the Calndom."

Misti smiled and nodded. "Of course, Alita. Go take off your vest and explore the Calndom."

Alita smiled, dipped her head, and went back downstairs to the guardroom. She noticed Lucas, Priscila, and Tanner in one corner and nodded to them, nearly walking into Heather in the process.

"Alita, there you are," Heather said. "I've been lookin' for you. Caln Misti informed me that you are to take a day off today."

"She just told me," Alita said. "Are you able to help me get my vest off?"

"Of course." Heather nodded.

Alita turned and sat in a clear spot, away from her friends and colleagues getting ready for their own days. Heather easily pulled down the zip on her back, allowing the vest to drop off Alita's shoulders.

"Do you know anything about where dragons from the market live?" Alita asked as she folded up the vest.

"I don't have their exact addresses, no. But I can point you in the direction of a particular shop for some of them," Heather said. "I helped High Caln Griffin choose the dragons for the market."

"Great. I want to visit a Rock Dragon named Trey," Alita explained. "He had a jewellery stand and mentioned having a shop."

"Yes, I remember him. One of the few dragons to get back to back requests at the mid-week market," Heather said. "His shop is in the Northern Districts, though I don't know where exactly."

"Oh...uh... thanks Heather." It wasn't anywhere near as helpful as she'd hoped. Alita could spend all day searching the Northern Districts for his shop.

"You're looking for Trey's shop?" Priscila asked, jumping up from her spot with Lucas and Tanner. "I'm actually going there today!"

"Really?" Alita stared at Priscila with wide eyes.

"Yeah! My sister works there. I have a day off today too," Priscila said. "Come on, I'll take you."

"Thank you so much!" Alita said gratefully.

Priscila said a quick goodbye to Lucas and Tanner and led Alita out of the noble districts on foot before taking flight. Together, they flew over houses and streets of varying cleanliness and quality. Alita noticed that the noble districts were far cleaner and tidier than the rest of the Calndom.

After flying for a while, Priscila tilted her wings and landed smoothly on a field of grass. Alita had a heavier and noisier landing as she flapped erratically until she was close enough to the ground to drop.

"Wow, Rock Dragons really are heavy on their landings," Priscila said with a small giggle. "Why don't you try a swooping landing like I did? Get close to the ground before tilting your wings up. They'll catch in the wind and stop your momentum."

"I'll have to remember to try it," Alita said. "Which way now?"

"Trey's shop is just a bit west of here," Priscila said, already trotting out of the field.

Alita followed her quietly. The streets here were different. Instead of cobblestone, it was just trampled dirt and dust. The buildings around them were worn down. Some were built of clay and stone, as if a Rock Dragon had simply pulled the ground up in the shape of a house. Others were made of timber and bricks, but they were patchy, with holes, cracks, rot, and newer panels overlapping the old. It was clearly a poorer district.

"The dragons around here don't get paid very well," Priscila explained. "And some of the houses have been around for generations. Many dragons stay with their family or their partner's family because it's easier to sustain everyone that way. Tanner's family is from around here."

"It's strange that something like this is just a short flight from the castle," Alita said.

"It is a bit sad to see," Priscila agreed, "But Trey's shop isn't quite as bad on the inside."

They rounded one last corner and the shop came into view. To any other dragon it would look just like the other shops on the street, with its nondescript clay walls and tiny glassless windows framed with timber posts. But as Alita neared the entrance she felt the difference in the ground beneath her feet. It was moved regularly. She presumed it must be shifted to block the entrance at night, and wondered how other dragons protected their stores without the benefits of a Rock Dragon on site.

Priscila was right about the interior; it was much nicer inside. Although the walls in here were still clay, the shelves and pedestals that displayed the jewellery were made of stone and timber, and the light hitting the various gems threw beautiful patterns around the room.

As Alita was looking around the room, a shrill voice filled the air. "Priscila!"

Turning to find the sound of the voice, Alita spotted a yellow and blue dragon come pouncing over to her and Priscila. Unlike Priscila, her colours were duller and the blue markings took up a larger portion of her body. She also had a curly mane in stark contrast to Priscila.

"Darlene, it's good to see you!" Priscila was grinning as she wrapped her wings around Darlene in a hug.

"You almost never leave that stuffy castle anymore," Darlene said. "How are you?"

"I'm good." Priscila stepped back from the hug and waved a wing to Alita. "Darlene, this is Alita. She's Prinze Evelyn's personal bodyguard. Alita, this is my sister, Darlene."

"Wow, I'd heard the Prinze got a bodyguard but I wasn't sure if it was true," Darlene said. "With all the gossip that goes around out here, I was sure you were made up!"

"I am definitely real," Alita said stiffly.

"Clearly!" Darlene laughed. "But now I have to wonder how much of the gossip about you is real."

Alita awkwardly shifted from one foot to another. Dragons all over the Calndom were talking about her? Surely there was nothing good about that.

"Darlene? What's all the noise for?"

Trey appeared from an archway that Alita hadn't noticed before. His eyes brightened as he recognised the dragons in the room.

"Priscila! Hi. And Alita. I didn't think I'd see you again so soon," Trey said. "What a coincidence for you to visit the same day as three nobles."

"What?" Alita looked around the room for the nobles she had apparently missed. To her surprise, Markos, Luana, and August were standing near one of the tiny windows.

"It's good to see you again so soon, Alita," Markos said in a rather dramatic tone.

"What are you all doing out here?" Alita asked, still confused by their presence.

"I thought I'd bring Luana out here to visit Trey's shop," Markos explained. "Then I thought August might like to meet Trey as well."

"You definitely surprised me," August said. "Not sure yet if it's a good surprise or not."

"You'll learn to love it," Markos said with a grin.

Luana walked up close to Alita's side. "Hey Alita."

"Hey Luana," Alita greeted her quietly. Her chest fluttered at their closeness.

"Did you come to visit Trey as well?" Luana asked.

"Yeah," Alita said simply.

"Aw, aren't you two cute," Darlene cooed.

Alita ducked her head and shuffled away from Luana when she realised Darlene had been watching them.

"And here I thought you were betrothed to the Prinze," Darlene said to Luana.

"Darlene, don't be rude to the nobles," Priscila hissed. "What if I lose my job?"

"We won't tell anyone, Priscila," Markos said. "We're not like most of the others. Just talk to us like we're normal dragons."

"Speaking of cute together, you and the Waltz hen look like a lovely couple," Darlene said with a grin.

"Please don't call me a hen," August said. "My name is August."

"Sorry. I forgot that terms like hen and drake are condemned by nobles," Darlene said casually.

"Darlene, please don't start with that," Trey said quietly.

Darlene shrugged and continued, "They're just normal terms for female and male dragons."

"Yes, but I'm not a bird sitting on eggs all day," August said. "I'd appreciate it if you didn't call me or Markos by those terms."

As the conversation continued, Alita felt a nudge on her shoulder. She looked at Luana, who smiled at her.

"Want to get out of here?" Luana asked quietly.

"Yes please," Alita whispered back. She didn't want to stick around if the conversation turned into an argument.

Luana nodded and slipped out the door. Alita followed wordlessly.

Chapter 39

The sunroom was warm. Evelyn wasn't a big fan of it. But Misti had suggested everyone sit in the sunroom for the day. No cloaks or crowns either. Those had been left by the door.

"Today we're just a family playing a game," Misti said as she and Clement set up the board.

Evelyn watched in silence. She was sitting between Griffin and Clement. She had made sure that Modesty wasn't too close to her. However, it meant watching her from across the board.

The board itself was a basic game, something they had all played since Evelyn had first joined them at the castle. She wouldn't be surprised if they'd been playing the game since Modesty and Clement were nestlings. It was such a basic game that nestlings could probably grasp it. Pick a wooden piece, roll the die with the cup, move the piece the correct number of steps until the game ended.

Evelyn didn't mind the simplicity too much. With everything that had been going on the past few days, playing such a simple game was a nice break. She only wished she could play it with Alita instead of the Silver family.

"Alright, who goes first?" Griffin asked.

"The youngest," Misti said. "So Clement."

"That's not fair. We're the same age," Modesty said.

"You hatched a whole day before me," Clement said. "That makes me the youngest."

"What if we let Evelyn go first?" Griffin suggested. "She hasn't been here as long as you two. That counts as the youngest in a way."

"She's older than us by two years!" Modesty growled.

"Don't shout, Modesty," Misti said. "Why don't we roll to see who goes first? Highest number wins."

Misti didn't give anyone the opportunity to object and chucked the die out of the cup. They went around in a circle until Modesty rolled last. Clement ended up with the highest number so he went first anyway.

As the game progressed, Evelyn did her best to focus, but Modesty was snapping and complaining and generally acting like a nestling. It was making Evelyn nervous.

"Two," Griffin mumbled after rolling the die. He moved his piece forward two spaces and landed on a card space. Griffin picked a card off the top of the deck and read it quietly. Then he said, "Look at that, I get to move two more spaces."

"What? No way! You're cheating!" Modesty snapped.

"Daughter, I'm looking at the card. It says I can move two spaces," Griffin said.

Modesty growled. "I don't believe you. Give me that card!"

She snatched the card out of Griffin's grip before he could respond and read it with furious narrow eyes, which only narrowed more. Finally, Modesty slammed down the card with a huff.

"Fine. You're not cheating," she muttered. "But it's not fair that you always get the good cards."

"Modesty, dear, you know that's not true," Misti said calmly. "Your father has the same chances with the deck as the rest of us. It's just bad luck that you got a bad card on your turn."

"He never gets bad cards though!" Modesty yelled.

"Modesty, calm down," Clement said. "We're meant to be having a fun day."

Modesty shot an icy glare at Clement but said nothing. It was her turn again and she snatched up the dice cup. She tossed the die from the cup with excessive force, causing it to knock over Griffin's and Clement's pieces in the process.

"Now, now, Modesty. No need for such violence," Misti said. "Look, you rolled a six, that's a good number."

Modesty said nothing. Instead, she snatched up her piece and moved it along the board. She reached a barrier space and was forced to stop when she didn't have enough remaining moves to go past it. She growled quietly.

"Looks like it's your turn again, Mum," Clement said, placing the die back in the cup and giving it to Misti.

"Thank you, Clement," Misti said, gently taking the cup and rolling the die. She moved her piece according to the number on the die, easily overtaking Modesty and passing the barrier space.

Evelyn managed to pull her eyes off Modesty's dark expression for a moment and looked at the board. Griffin was in the lead. In fact, he was almost at the end. Clement was a few spaces behind him. Evelyn was next, with Misti now one space behind her. Modesty was in last place, three spaces behind Misti.

Clement took his turn to roll the die and was able to move his piece up in front of Griffin. However, Evelyn doubted he would win if Griffin got a good roll on his next turn. Clement passed the cup to Evelyn and she rolled the die.

The die landed with the three side face up. Evelyn moved her piece forward and landed on a card space.

She picked a card off the deck and read it out loud. "You find some good food on your journey and it re-energises you. Take a second turn."

Evelyn could already hear Modesty growling as she finished reading the card. Evelyn pretended not to hear it and rolled the die again. This time she got a five, bringing her all the way up to Clement's space.

"That's not fair!" Modesty snapped. "Anything more than a three should be disqualified on a reroll! It's an unfair advantage!"

"Modesty, that's how the game works," Misti said. Her tone was calm, but firm. "We've been playing this since you and Clement were four years old. You've even had that card a few times."

While Misti and Modesty were talking, Evelyn handed the dice cup to Griffin, who took his turn.

"It's still not fair. How come she can just show up and start winning the game? She's not even part of our family!" Modesty complained.

"Modesty! That is not polite," Misti scolded her. "Evelyn is your cousin and future High Caln. She has a right to be in our family."

"She's not even from Hiza Calndom!" Modesty yelled. "Why should she get anything here?"

"Hey, look at that," Griffin said suddenly. "I won."

Evelyn looked down at the board, along with the others. He was right. He had rolled a six, which was just enough to get to the end of the game. Modesty growled, icy mist lacing her breath. She got up and spun around, aggressively swinging her tail across the board and sending pieces flying, before storming out of the room.

Interlude VI

Modesty stormed out of the sunroom and through the castle. Dragons actively avoided her as she made her way to the arena. She had to destroy something. It would be too easy to simply kill Griffin and Evelyn while in the sunroom. But she didn't want any witnesses and she couldn't kill her mother.

Misti had raised her with so much care and compassion that it was impossible to hate her. No matter how much Griffin had wronged her, Misti always helped her feel better. Though it felt like she had started to pull back on that unconditional love lately.

Modesty burst into the arena and immediately turned for the dummies stacked in the corner of the room. A pair of guards stopped their battle training and watched her with wide, fearful eyes. Modesty shot them a glare and yanked one of the dummies out of the pile. Their shudders gave her satisfaction.

The guards quickly abandoned their training and scurried out of the room, leaving Modesty alone. She took the opportunity to set up the dummies around the room. Once done, she pounced on the closest one and ripped into it with her teeth and claws. She willed ice to grow from her feet, making her claws longer and sharper. The dummy was torn to shreds within seconds.

"That really is quite vicious."

Modesty turned and saw her mother standing near the entrance. Misti's expression was unreadable, though Modesty was sure she could see a hint of regret.

"It's what I do," Modesty said in a low tone, turning back to the dummies. She shot an ice blast at the next closest one.

"Modesty, we need to talk about your behaviour," Misti said.

"You can talk," Modesty said. "I won't listen."

"Modesty Silver, stop attacking things and look at me," Misti demanded.

Modesty rolled her eyes and frowned at Misti. She hated that her instinct told her to listen to her mother. Perhaps one day she would stop listening, but for now she would simply make do.

"Thank you," Misti said. "Darling, I know you want things, but we can't all have what we want. We can't always win a game, and we can't always be the first choice."

Modesty scowled, barely biting back a growl. "This isn't just about the game. This is about my entire life! When I was young, Griffin paid attention to me and listened and cared. He never had to worry about the Calndom over his daughter because Gerold was managing everything. But then Gerold had to go and die and within *months* Griffin chose a Prinze."

Modesty started pacing in circles, glaring at the ground. Her claws had iced over and her tail twitched angrily.

"No other High Caln chose a Prinze as quickly as he did," Modesty continued, no longer holding back her growl. "And, to make it worse, he chose Evelyn! My cousin! A Tribe-Alian with no knowledge of, nor desire for the crown! If he wanted someone related to him so badly, why didn't he just choose me?"

"Modesty, that's not how it works," Misti said. "You're a Duchy. You can't be Prinze as long as you have that title. And your father didn't choose Evelyn because of blood relation. He chose her because he feared the sudden mortality that Gerold succumbed to and wanted a Prinze in case something happened to him as well."

"Great. So she was convenient," Modesty huffed. "But he had a

172

family. I could have been his backup plan. He didn't need to name me Prinze or teach me anything. I already know everything I need for being High Caln."

"Modesty, we have laws for a reason. Our law states that a High Caln's offspring can only take the crown if the High Caln dies with no Prinze. Furthermore, a Prinze must be selected by the High Caln within five years of taking the crown," Misti explained. "Your father broke no law. He's following it perfectly."

"It's a stupid law," Modesty said. "Our ancestors passed the crown to their offspring. Why do we have to do it differently? What's so wrong with keeping the power with the family?"

"For exactly the reason you just said," Misti said. Her expression had turned to a frown. "If the power stays in one family alone, that family will only get richer and greedier while everyone else gets poorer. Hiza Calndom's founders set the law to what it is so that everyone gets a turn. It promotes fairness and equal distribution of power."

Modesty snarled and slashed her ice covered tail across a nearby dummy. The gash that remained caused one of its legs to fall off and the dummy tipped over.

"I suggest you leave before I do something we'll both regret," Modesty growled darkly.

Misti took a slow breath, then turned to leave. As she elegantly strode out of the room, Modesty could tell how much she was trying to hide her trembling fear.

Chapter 40

"I never realised how different the rest of the Calndom would be compared to the noble districts," Alita said.

Luana nodded. She had never seen anything, but smell and sound alone told her that she might as well be in a different world. She could feel every clump of dirt and every loose stone on the dusty path beneath her feet.

"My mother never wanted any of us to see the world outside the noble districts," Luana explained. "But Dad took us out often, so I've been to many places around the Caldnom."

"Do you have any favourites?" Alita asked.

"As a fledgling, I really liked going to the Flight Range," Luana said. "Dad would teach me and my brothers how to fly and do cool tricks. If there was little or no breeze, he would coach us on our fire usage. I think he'd be proud of what Hamlet's achieved."

"Hamlet must have been very young when you lost your father," Alita said.

"He was only an egg," Luana said. "They never got to meet."

"Oh. I'm so sorry," Alita apologised.

"Don't be. You didn't know." Luana smiled. "Why don't we talk about something happier?"

"Good idea. Have you ever been to the Tribe?" Alita asked.

"No. That was one of the few places Mother convinced Dad not to take us," Luana said. "Another was the lake."

"The lake? Oh, right, there's a lake nearby isn't there?" Alita said.

"Yeah. I'd love to visit it one day," Luana said.

"Well, why don't we go now?" Alita suggested. "I mean, we should probably eat lunch first. But then we could go."

Luana smiled. "I like that idea. What do you want to eat?"

"Uh... I'm not sure what's even sold around here," Alita said. "And I don't have any money."

"I do," Luana tapped the pouch around her neck with one forefoot. "I can smell bread nearby. It's not exactly filling by itself but it is what most dragons in the area eat on a daily basis."

"Alright. Let's eat bread," Alita said.

Luana led the way, letting her nose guide her. The nearest bakery was only a few minutes away. Along with the savoury scent of fresh bread, Luana also smelled something sweeter. It resembled strawberries and honey and Luana guessed it was icing on some of the sweeter buns.

After she and Alita picked out some fruit bread, Luana paid and they tucked into a quick meal. Luana's small loaf was gone in just a few bites, though she noticed Alita ate hers even faster.

"Shall we go to the lake now?" Alita asked as Luana rinsed off her feet in a bowl of water by the bakery entrance.

"Yes," Luana said. "Can you lead the way?"

"No problem," Alita said.

Luana heard Alita spread her wings suddenly and leap into the air. She hurried to follow, pretending not to hear the angry shouts of dragons in the street. She beat her wings hard and quickly caught up to Alita.

"Hey, Alita, you know you're not supposed to just take flight like that in the middle of the street, right?" Luana asked.

"Really? Oops," Alita said. "I'll keep that in mind for next time."

Chapter 41

The flight to the lake was short. Luana enjoyed feeling the air in her wings. She rarely got to fly, but she loved the feeling of freedom it gave her. If only she didn't need someone to guide her, then she would take long trips across the island by herself. Although having Alita as her guide was just as good.

Alita picked out a spot to land and directed Luana towards it. Luana heard Alita's heavy thump as she landed and tilted her wings to land nearby. The grass that touched her feet was soft and long. She dug her claws into the ground a little, feeling the squish of muddy dirt between her toes. It was a little gross, but Luana enjoyed the feeling of real nature, rather than the tamed perfection of the gardens at the manor.

"It's beautiful out here," Alita said quietly.

Luana took a deep breath, inhaling the scents of water, plants, and dirt. She could hear the gentle ripple of the lake just a few metres away. Birds were singing in the trees of the forest somewhere off to her right. Even further away, a large waterfall rumbled and churned.

"There's a waterfall across the lake," she said.

"You can hear that?" Alita asked. "I can't even *see* a waterfall. Just water and trees and grass."

"It's so nice to be outside the Calndom for a change," Luana said. "It's much more peaceful... quieter."

"Do you get overwhelmed by all the sounds in the Calndom?" Alita asked.

"Sometimes," Luana said. "I think my hearing reaches further out here because of the lack of noise. Most of the time I can't hear too far outside the walls of the manor."

"Well, let's make the most of it," Alita suggested. "Why don't we go find that waterfall?"

Luana smiled and stretched her wings. "I'll race you."

She took off before Alita could respond. Luana beat her wings hard and climbed into the sky above the lake. She heard Alita laughing as she gave chase. Luana couldn't help her silly grin. She stopped climbing and tilted her wings downward to start a dive. Then she tucked in her wings and angled them just right to get a spin going. The rushing wind filled her ears, completely shutting out all other sounds. She adjusted her wings after only a second so that her spin carried her steadily out of the dive. When she stretched out her wings again, Luana tilted into a hard turn. She circled as she listened for the sound of Alita's wingbeats.

"That was amazing!" Alita called from somewhere above her.

Luana beat her wings so that she rose higher. "Thanks. It's not often I get the airspace for a move like that."

"Maybe I can bring you out here every time I get a day off," Alita suggested. "Then you can fly like that more often."

Luana couldn't help but smile at the thought of spending more time with just Alita. She heard Alita's wingbeats get closer and started to feel the gusts of wind from each flap.

"Can you see the waterfall from up here?" Luana asked.

"No, we're pretty high up," Alita said. "Can you hear it?"

Luana twitched her ears around in different directions. She detected the rumbling sound coming from somewhere north of them. She turned and started flying that way.

"It's this way," she called back to Alita.

They were so high up that Luana felt safe swooping downward. She didn't want to completely miss the waterfall and fly into or over the mountains that rimmed the northern parts of the island.

"I think I can hear it now," Alita said. "There! On the left!"

Luana dipped to the left and swooped low. She wanted to get as close to the waterfall as possible. As she passed it, she felt the spray of the water against her wings and belly. An excited shiver spread across her wings. As Luana circled away, she heard Alita grunt, then yelp.

Luana quickly stopped and turned mid-air. "Alita? Are you alright?"

The only sound in response was the rumbling of the waterfall. Then, somewhere below her, Luana heard a faint splash, barely audible over the churning water. Her stomach dropped.

"Alita!" she called. "Alita, are you there?"

Luana dove towards the water. Did Alita just fall in? Was she alright? If she hit the water too close to the waterfall, she could be caught in an underwater spiral and drown.

"Alita!" Luana called again as panic rose in her chest.

"I'm okay!" Alita gasped from below her. "I just lost my balance!"

Luana slowed her descent. "Did you fall all the way into the lake?"

"Yeah, sort of," Alita admitted. "I think I got caught by a gust of wind as I turned. I'm okay."

Luana sighed as relief loosened the knot in her chest. "I thought you might get caught in the waterfall's hydraulics."

"The what?" Alita asked. There was a splashing, flapping sound with her question as she hauled herself out of the lake.

"The water currents," Luana explained as they rose back into the sky to continue their flight, "It's easy to get caught up in the churning of the water and not be able to resurface."

"I'm a strong swimmer, Luana. It'll take a little more than a circular current to drown me," Alita joked. "How do you even know that term anyway?"

"How do you *not* know?" Luana asked. "I would have thought every dragon in the Tribe would know terminology for water currents."

"Well... maybe I didn't pay complete attention in classes growing up," Alita said.

Luana laughed and swooped down to the water's surface. She felt her wingtips touch the surface of the lake. The cool feeling of the water joined with her relief that Alita was alright. She continued to fly above the water for a few seconds, then tucked her wings and dipped into the lake. The sudden resistance from the water slowed her to a stop. She swam back up and raised her head out of the water.

"You absolute nutcase!" Alita said through a laugh.

"You should join me!" Luana called back.

"I just fell in the water a moment ago!" Alita said.

"It's not dangerous here. The water's calm!" Luana told her.

"Fine!" Luana could practically hear the grin in her voice.

A moment later, Alita plunged into the lake with a massive splash. Luana yelped and giggled as the wave rocked her. Alita burst out of the water a second later.

"It's still cold!" She exclaimed.

Luana was laughing too much to reply. Instead, she pushed her wing through the water, causing a small wave to splash into Alita.

"Hey!" Alita yelped before splashing her back.

Luana tried to shield herself with her wings but the movement caused her to tip backwards. Her head was under the water for a moment before she corrected herself and resurfaced. Alita was laughing and splashing more water at her. Luana grinned and returned the favour.

Chapter 42

Alita and Luana played in the lake for a while before going to shore. Alita pulled herself onto the gravel and stone bank, then turned to check that Luana made it out of the water too. They were both breathing heavily from the workout.

"I wish this day would never end," Luana said, collapsing into the pebbles. She had a small smile on her face.

"We'll have to go back eventually," Alita looked at the sky. "Judging by the sun, I'd say it's about mid-afternoon."

Luana sighed. "Not yet. I want to enjoy this a little longer."

"The freedom of doing whatever you want?" Alita asked.

"Yeah. Doing whatever I want. Talking to you. It's nice to have time alone," Luana said.

Alita felt her heartbeat speed up. They were finally having some time to get to know each other. Alita hadn't thought about whether Luana felt the same way, but knowing she did made her giddy.

Luana stood up and shook the pebbles off skin. "The good thing about being a Fire Dragon is that I can dry off just by heating my body."

"That sounds so nice," Alita said. She could see the steam rising from Luana's skin. A small wisp of smoke was rising from her nostrils. "I wish I could do that."

"Do you want me to dry you off?" Luana asked, raising one of her wings.

Alita blinked a few times as she tried to wrap her head around the mental image. Her face heated up until she was sure it was bright red.

"I-I mean, if y-you want-want to," Alita stammered.

Luana giggled and smiled at her. "You're so cute when you're flustered."

Alita tried to frown but a silly little smile at Luana calling her cute took over.

"Don't worry, I won't burn you," Luana walked over and lay down beside Alita.

"I mean, it's not like you can set me on fire," Alita said.

"Well, I could," Luana said.

She stretched her wing across Alita's back. Alita relaxed into the warm feeling.

"Fire Dragons can set themselves on fire for short periods of time," Luana said.

"Really? You tell me this now? Right after you encase me in your little fire trap?" Alita said with a grin.

Luana giggled. "It's extremely dehydrating, so we don't like to do it. Most Fire Dragons go their entire lives without doing it. Did you not know that?"

Alita tried to remember if she had heard of it before at any point in her life. She couldn't.

"I guess I never paid attention to fire classes as a fledgling either," she said bashfully.

"Well, now you know," Luana said.

Luana pressed her body against Alita's side and squeezed her in closer with her wing. Alita felt herself heat up from more than just the heat coming from Luana. She found herself wrapping her tail around Luana's and leaning her head on Luana's neck. Luana rested her head on top of Alita's and sighed quietly.

"This is nice," Alita said. She liked not having to think about anything and be fully in the moment.

"Yeah," Luana agreed quietly. After a moment, she asked, "Have you ever been in love before, Alita?"

"Sort of, maybe. It's hard to say for sure anymore," Alita said. "I've dated dragons before, when I was in the Tribe. But nothing felt... well none of it felt the same as how it feels to just talk to you."

Alita raised her head to look at Luana. Her pale green eyes were calm and loving.

"I feel the same," Luana said. "I've never been in love before. But it feels amazing."

"Really? Never?" Alita asked. "Not even a crush or something?"

Luana shook her head. "No. I've never felt like this before. It's like a constant tugging to be next to you. You don't make me feel less important or incapable because I'm blind, and you don't act submissive because of my title. You treat me like an ordinary dragon; one you just want to be with. I never thought I'd feel anything like that myself. Until now."

Luana smiled at her. Alita felt her face heat up, but she couldn't look away from Luana's pale green eyes.

"You're amazing," Alita breathed.

"So are you," Luana said.

Alita felt her ears burn from embarrassment and ducked her head. "I said that out loud?"

"You did." Luana laughed. "And I'd love to hear it again every day."

"Why would you even want to be with someone like me?" Alita asked. "I'm just-"

"The kindest and sweetest dragon I've ever met," Luana said, interrupting her.

Alita smiled, though she was certain her face was on fire. But then she remembered Evelyn.

"What about your betrothal?" Alita asked. "You have to marry Evelyn and be her Caln."

"I never cared for the betrothal," Luana said. "I was only doing it because I wasn't given a choice. But now, I'd rather run away with you than go back and be Evelyn's future wife."

Alita smiled slightly, but then she sighed and said, "We can't do that. If we leave, Modesty will kill Evelyn. I can't leave when I know my best friend will die because of it."

Luana's ears drooped a little, but she nodded. "I understand. Perhaps we can work out another way to keep me from marrying Evelyn."

"Like what?" Alita asked.

Luana was quiet for a moment, looking thoughtful.

"Perhaps I could ask Markos," she said. "He's always had an uncanny sense of what others should do."

"He is a bit of a weirdo, isn't he?" Alita joked.

Luana smiled. "He can come across that way. He's actually pretty normal if you get to know him."

"I'll have to take your word for it," Alita said.

Luana leaned into Alita's side with a hum. Alita sighed and nuzzled into her neck. It was so nice to be just the two of them.

Suddenly Luana's ear twitched and she raised her head with a small hiss.

"Markos and August are looking for us," she said.

Alita looked around. She spotted two small dots in the distance and guessed it was Markos and August flying towards them.

"I guess we have to go now," Alita said with a sigh.

"Yeah." Luana stood up and stretched her wings. "Are you dry?"

Alita got up, feeling cold without Luana's body heat. She checked the skin on her wings, legs, and chest.

"A little damp, but dry enough," she said. "Let's go."

Luana nodded and took to the air. Together, they flew back to Markos and the Calndom.

Interlude VII

Modesty tossed the last of the now destroyed dummies across the arena. She was breathing heavily and coated with sweat, but her anger had subsided. She was ready for anything that might come her way. Almost anything, at least.

Modesty took a deep breath, allowing the sweat on her skin to freeze into ice. She then shook the ice off and turned for the exit. She felt the salt residue of the sweat across her skin as she walked and shuddered. She would have to take a bath to get rid of it.

But before she did that, she wanted to pay the prisoner another visit.

Modesty exited the arena and immediately turned to the dungeon. Upon entering the hallway, she spotted the same Nature Dragon guard as before. He idly glanced her way before freezing up.

"Get out of here," Modesty growled.

"I-I-I won't." Koa's voice shook as he spoke. "I'm n-not allowed to leave the prisoner unguarded."

"Too bad," Modesty snapped. "Either get out now, or stay and die."

Koa gulped and his skin paled. But he still hesitated. Modesty raised a forefoot, freezing it into an icy spear as she did so. Koa whimpered and scurried past her for the door. Modesty grinned, letting out a little cackle. Scaring weaker dragons was so much fun.

"You're back," Korbin said.

"I am." Modesty shook the ice melt off her foot and turned to him.

"She visited, you know," Korbin said.

"Who?" Modesty asked before she could stop herself. She scowled for letting her tongue slip.

"Alita," Korbin muttered, paying no mind to Modesty's expression. "She really has changed since I last knew her."

"How so?" Modesty asked, intentionally this time.

"She's not afraid of fights anymore," Korbin told her. "If you want to confront her for anything, she might just fight you on it."

Modesty growled. That didn't bode well for her. But it made this visit so much more important.

"Just as well I visited you again, then," Modesty said. "Because you're going to teach me how to stop a Rock Dragon."

Korbin laughed. "And why would I do that? I've got nothing to gain from helping you."

Modesty frowned at him. Clearly, he had gotten plenty of time to think since their last interaction. For now, she'd have to cooperate with him.

"If you help me, then when I become High Caln, I'll let you out," Modesty said.

"An intriguing offer," Korbin mused. "Let me out *and* give me a home in the richer districts. Then I'll help you."

Modesty refrained from the urge to roll her eyes. "Very well. Now tell me how to stop a Rock Dragon."

Korbin sighed and shuffled closer to the wooden bars. "The tricky part about stopping Rock Dragons is that we can control the very ground under our feet. Unless it's wood."

Korbin stopped and scowled at the wooden floor of his cell. Modesty rolled her eyes. She didn't care for his troubles.

"If you get pinned by a Rock Dragon, they could use the rocks in the ground to trap you on the floor. They could strangle you with a metal string that you can't pull off." Korbin shrugged as he spoke. "Anything made of rock or metal is a strength for Rock Dragons."

"Great," Modesty said flatly. "Now, how do I *stop* that from

185

happening?"

"I'm getting to that." Korbin paused for a moment. "If you're going up against Alita, she'll probably try to pin you. I'm not sure if she'll use her element. But she's definitely bigger than you. She'll probably use her size against you and try to hold you down. If she does, you'll want to get her off you as quickly as possible, before she thinks to hold you permanently."

"So, I kick her off? Shouldn't be too hard." Modesty flexed her legs, imagining the thrill of fighting another dragon. "I've been practising battle tactics for years."

"Don't get cocky," Korbin warned. "Alita is bigger and heavier than you. If you want to get her off you completely, you will need to kick her hard enough to *throw* her. If you don't succeed, you'll lose."

"And if I do succeed in throwing her off?" Modesty asked. "What do I do to actually stop her?"

"I say you turn the tactic back on her," Korbin said. "Pin her down. Use your wings to hold her down and use your ice to scratch her, lock her muscles, all that stuff. I'm sure you know better than me how to best use your element."

Modesty grinned. "That, I do."

She was already imagining all the ways she could make Alita suffer. Did she want a quick death or a slow, painful one? She was the main obstacle, and the newest one. Modesty's attempt to make Alita run away with Luana hadn't worked. It made her quite the nuisance. Slow and painful it would be.

"Well, you've been very useful," Modesty said, turning to leave. "I'll be sure to thank you when I'm High Caln."

"Don't forget our deal!" Korbin called after her. "When you take the crown, let me out and give me a good home!"

"Yeah, yeah, I will," Modesty said nonchalantly. She could decide later what she wanted to do with him.

Chapter 43

Evelyn woke slowly. The curtains in her room were already open, letting the early morning sun flood in. After the way the family game day had ended, she was hoping for a good day. At least Alita would be back on duty and with her all day.

Evelyn lifted her head after a few moments and looked across the room. Lily was making her way over from the window, as Evelyn expected. However, she was surprised to see Heather standing by the door.

"Good mornin', Prinze Evelyn," Heather said with a nod.

"Heather." Evelyn dipped her head in kind. "What are you doing here?"

"I came to discuss some news that made its way to me by the staff gossip," Heather explained. "It would seem that yesterday Alita spent her day off in the Northern Districts with Laird Luana."

Evelyn tilted her head and frowned slightly as she climbed off her bed. "What were they doing all the way out there?"

"If I recall correctly, Alita wished to visit one of the vendors from the mid-week market. However, I do not know why Laird Luana was out that way," Heather explained. "But the how and why is not the reason I'm bringin' it to your attention. I believe the amount of time they have spent together outside of your company is concernin'. It reflects poorly on you, Laird Luana, and your bodyguard if it continues."

"What do you recommend?" Evelyn asked. She lifted her head a little as Lily laid a clean cloak across her back and did up the button.

"I think Alita should be restricted from leavin' the castle without permission," Heather said. "This will also affect her record for her one week trial."

Evelyn considered the idea for a second. She didn't want to lose Alita if Heather and Griffin decided that she wasn't good enough or too troublesome to be a bodyguard.

Evelyn shook her head. "No. Don't do that. I'll talk to her about it."

Heather dipped her head. "Of course, Prinze Evelyn. I will leave it to you."

Heather turned and left the room. Evelyn turned to Lily, who was lifting Evelyn's crown carefully off its stand. As Lily turned, Evelyn dipped her head so it was easy to slide the crown onto her horns.

"You seem very fond of Alita," Lily said. Her voice was soft, clearly worried about offending Evelyn with her statement.

"She's my best friend," Evelyn said. "Or was, I guess. We still get along well though."

"That's not quite what I meant," Lily said. "From what I've seen and heard, you're fonder of Alita than of Laird Luana."

"Oh. I suppose so. I didn't think anyone really noticed that," Evelyn said. Then she frowned. "Fine, I like her. What should I do?"

Lily stared at Evelyn with a firm, unblinking gaze. "Tell her how you feel. If she reciprocates, you might be able to get out of your betrothal and marry someone you actually like."

"And if she doesn't feel the same way?" Evelyn asked.

"You'll just have to accept that," Lily said. "But it's better to know than do nothing and wish things could be different."

Evelyn sighed. "Alright, I'll gather the nerve to tell her today. Thanks, Lily."

Lily smiled and dipped her head in a small nod. With that, Evelyn headed out into the hallway. Alita was already outside, waiting with the two night guards. Evelyn realised with a mix of giddy joy and nervousness that she would be confessing to her today. For better or worse, their relationship would change forever. Evelyn wanted the day to be memorable.

"Morning Evelyn," Alita greeted her with a smile.

"Good morning, Alita," Evelyn said. She did her best to keep her smile even despite the swirling emotions in her chest.

Alita followed Evelyn as she led the way down to breakfast. Griffin was already at the head table, as usual. Evelyn took a seat on his left and dipped her feet into the cleansing bowl beneath the table.

Before Evelyn could even lift a forefoot above the table, Griffin said, "I've arranged for you to visit Laird Luana today. Take her for a walk around the Noble Districts."

Of course Griffin would have plans that would keep Evelyn busy all day. Evelyn held back a scowl and forced herself to remain calm.

"Of course," she said with a level tone.

Chapter 44

After breakfast, Evelyn left the castle and headed into the Noble Districts. As she came to the paved clearing, instead of turning for Everhart Manor, she continued straight and walked across the clearing.

"Evelyn? Luana's place is the other way," Alita pointed out.

"I know. We're not going there today," Evelyn said.

"But Griffin told you to visit Luana today," Alita reminded her.

"We're not doing that," Evelyn repeated. "I've got something else planned."

"Won't Griffin be mad?" Alita asked.

"Probably." Evelyn shrugged. "But I'm taking you to the Calndom Gardens regardless."

"Gardens? The castle already has gardens," Alita said.

"That's different. These gardens are publicly available to any dragon in the Calndom," Evelyn explained. "They're a bit like a public park, but there's plants everywhere and they're carefully planted and cared for."

"Sounds a little bit like a nature reserve," Alita said. "Like the one across the river from the Tribe."

Evelyn tilted her head as she thought about it. Then she nodded and said, "Yeah. It kind of is."

Evelyn continued on the path out of the Noble Districts. She was aware of Alita following from a few metres back. As they made their way through the Districts, Alita edged closer to Evelyn's side. Evelyn smiled to herself with the closeness.

Once they had cleared the Noble Districts, Evelyn turned for the streets that would lead to the Calndom Gardens. Dragons recognised her as they passed, mostly from her cloak and crown, and actively moved out of her way. Some dragons, especially the young fledglings, stared at Evelyn with wide eyes. The longer she walked, the more Evelyn felt the judgement and questioning gazes of the civilians around her. It wasn't every day that the Prinze left the Noble Districts entirely. Evelyn hated it. The feeling of being observed never got easier to stomach and made her skin crawl.

"Dragons are staring at us," Alita said quietly.

"They're staring at me, not you," Evelyn told her. "Many of the families around here used to be noble families in the past few generations. Some of them keep close tabs on the goings on of nobles and the royal family."

"So will you get in trouble for being out here?" Alita asked.

"Not from dragons around here," Evelyn said. "But Griffin will find out when Adelaide tells him I never visited Luana."

"What will he do?" Alita asked.

Evelyn shrugged her wings. "Not sure. I doubt it'll be much. It's surprising how much you can get away with when you're Prinze."

Alita didn't say anything in response. Evelyn didn't think much of it. She had been dealing with Griffin for seven years. At this point, Evelyn knew what she could get away with. After all, she knew he wouldn't revoke her crown. Not with the threat of Modesty hanging over their heads.

They made their way through the streets in silence for a while. Soon enough, Evelyn recognised the fencing and signs for the Calndom Gardens. A dragon stood near the gate, watching everyone who entered or exited the gardens. Evelyn knew he was watching for anyone that might bring in plant poisons or try to remove the plants from the gardens. The gardens were the largest area of greenery available to the general public in Hiza Calndom, after all. It was important that it stayed that way.

"So what exactly is the plan for today?" Alita asked as she and Evelyn entered the gardens.

"Walk around, talk, enjoy the sights," Evelyn said simply. "I just want to spend a day outside of the Noble Districts with you."

"Okay. But I don't know anything about plants," Alita said.

"You don't need to know anything about plants." Evelyn smiled and barely held back a giggle. "We can learn about them while we're here. Look, there's a map over there."

Evelyn nodded her head to a large map framed with wood and glass where the path split into two. There were multiple paths they could take through the gardens, and they would most certainly loop back around several times to see everything. Evelyn looked over the map for a moment, reading the names of the different areas in the gardens. She wanted to take Alita to see some of the more interesting plants. There were several that wouldn't grow near the Tribe.

"Let's go left here and go up the hills," Evelyn said. "We can circle back around to look at the rest afterwards."

"Alright. Lead the way," Alita said.

Evelyn smiled and turned for the steeper pathway. The plants growing on the hills were mostly low lying shrubs or grasses and flowers. Evelyn lingered near the informational signs to read about each plant before moving on to the next. She was keenly aware of Alita following along behind her, not too close but not too far.

Near the top of the hill, Evelyn spotted an array of colourful flowers. She recognised the petal shapes and colours of irises. Most of the flowers were various shades of purple with white and yellow accents to them. But some were pinker or bluer, some had more white or more yellow, some had frilly leaves while others were smooth. There was a lot of variety in the flower patch.

"What are these?" Alita asked. She leaned past Evelyn to read the sign by the path.

"They're called irises," Evelyn explained. "They're rather unassuming plants. The flowers are kind of small. But they're nice to look at and relatively easy to care for."

Evelyn glanced at the writing on the sign. Each sign had the name of the plant, some information about its history, how to care for them, blooming or fruiting seasons, and what amounts of sun it preferred. For the flowers in particular, there was always an extra section on the meaning of each flower when gifted to another. For the iris, it represented royalty, respect, and wisdom. Evelyn didn't really care about what it represented, but she appreciated that other dragons would.

"They're quite pretty," Alita said, looking over the flowers. "Some of them look a bit like Luana's cloak in colour."

Evelyn looked at the flowers again and suppressed a sigh. Of course Alita was thinking about Luana still.

"I suppose they do," Evelyn said. "Let's keep going. There's a lot more to look at before the day is done."

"Alright," Alita said as Evelyn continued down the path.

Evelyn didn't want to admit that the mention of Luana was the reason she was so quick to move on. How could Alita be so enthralled with Luana that even a simple flower could evoke memories of her? Evelyn wondered for a moment if she would be able to change Alita's mind on that matter. But she swiftly pushed that thought from her mind. She would have to if she wanted to follow through with her plan.

Chapter 45

Evelyn and Alita continued through the gardens, stopping every now and then to admire particular plants. Evelyn found herself enjoying the day more and more as time went on. She explained how the fly traps worked when they passed the greenhouse full of insects. She laughed when Alita tried smelling the citronella, only to cough at its musky scent. They even got to run through a field of sweet smelling moss roses, though the flowers stuck to their legs and they had to wash them off afterwards.

By midday, Evelyn was eager for a break from walking and chose a shady spot under a maple tree to sit down. It wasn't as delightfully romantic as the cherry blossom tree in the Noble Districts, but it was more than enough for a rest and some food. Alita lay down on the grass next to her and sighed deeply.

"Those flowers smelled really sweet," she said. "What did you call them again?"

"Moss roses," Evelyn said. "They do have a bit of scent to them. At least they smell nice."

"Can flowers smell any other way?" Alita asked.

"Some can," Evelyn said. "There aren't many on the island since they're more tropical, but the corpse flower smells rancid!"

"Corpse flower?" Alita wrinkled her nose. "That sounds horrible."

"It's best to visit it in the morning or early afternoon," Evelyn explained. "Its smell is most potent in the evening and at night."

"Is there one here?" Alita asked.

Evelyn nodded. "There's one in the tropical greenhouse near the gazebo."

"Perhaps we can look in from the window," Alita suggested.

"Maybe." Evelyn couldn't help but smile. "It really doesn't smell too bad during the day. We can head over there after some lunch."

"Lunch sounds great. What is there to eat?" Alita asked.

Evelyn nodded her head to a cart down the path. "They sell bread rolls with meat and orange or lemon around the gardens. There'll be water too."

"Meat and citrus together in the same piece of bread?" Alita tilted her head and made a face. "It doesn't sound very appetising."

"It's better than it sounds," Evelyn said, standing back up. "Besides, it's all part of a healthy diet."

Alita heaved herself up and started following Evelyn to the cart. "Is that a big deal here? We didn't worry about that much in the Tribe."

"Well, in the Tribe there wasn't a concern over the food in our diets," Evelyn explained. "But the Calndom has all sorts of foods that the Tribe doesn't have. Some dragons here have started studying the food we eat to see what's good and what's not."

"That's... new," Alita muttered.

"Perhaps I can find you one of the books they've been releasing," Evelyn suggested.

When they reached the cart, Evelyn paid for two rolls of bread and passed one to Alita. The meat in the rolls were cooked today and smelled like musky poultry. The tart smell of the orange slices helped make it more appealing. Evelyn had never been a big fan of cooked meat, but it was commonplace in the Calndom, especially when prepared by Fire Dragons.

Alita took a bite of the roll and her eyes widened. Evelyn smiled as she chewed on her own roll. She was glad Alita's sense of taste was still predictable. Evelyn could taste a hint of salt on the poultry and knew Alita would love it. Something about growing up by the ocean made salt a very homey flavour.

"This is pretty good," Alita mumbled through a mouthful of food.

"I told you." Evelyn grinned. "There's more to meals than just fish and rabbits."

"I thought fish was your favourite," Alita said.

"It is. But there's so many other flavours you can try as well," Evelyn said. "In the Calndom, dragons try all sorts of combinations in the hopes of getting a better flavour profile."

"Where does all the food come from anyway?" Alita asked. "It's not like dragons are hunting all day here."

"No need to hunt. The edges of the Calndom are reserved for farmland," Evelyn explained. "There's deer, sheep, dwarf buffalo... and ticking fowl."

"Ticking fowl?" Alita raised an eyebrow.

"Yup. Crazy birds. Not easy to farm unless you know what you're doing," Evelyn explained.

"I know what ticking fowl are, Evelyn. I just can't believe dragons managed to tame and farm those things," Alita said. "I tried to hunt one once and it nearly pecked my eyes out."

"Well now you know what they taste like without having to hunt for one," Evelyn said, nodding to Alita's roll as she popped the last bit in her mouth.

Alita hummed as she chewed. "Farming is good."

Evelyn smiled. "There's other great things about the Calndom too. Every district is unique in some way. Their markets are on different days. Shops and elemental demographics vary. I've even heard that the Northern Districts have festivals throughout the year."

"That's pretty cool. But we live in the castle," Alita pointed out. "We're never going to see any of that."

"We can see some of it," Evelyn said, "At least there's more variation here than the Tribe."

196

"Do you miss the Tribe?" Alita asked.

Evelyn blinked a few times. She hadn't been expecting that question.

"Sometimes. I don't miss it every day. Some of the laws there were annoying or pointless. But there's some of that here too," Evelyn explained. "To be honest the only thing I truly miss from the Tribe isn't there anymore."

"What's that?" Alita asked.

Evelyn shook her head. She wasn't ready to admit it yet. "Don't worry about it. If you're done eating, we can go down to the greenhouse to see the corpse flower."

"Alright. Let's go," Alita said with a nod. "But we'll stay outside. I don't think I want to smell it right after eating."

Chapter 46

After some rest, Evelyn led the way down the path to the tropical greenhouse. Thankfully, it wasn't too far to walk and they were standing outside it within a few minutes. The greenhouse was a little taller than the previous ones they'd seen and a lot longer and wider. The glass was clear and clean but it was hard to see past all the leaves that brushed the inside edges of the greenhouse.

"There's a lot of plants in there," Alita commented, peering through the windows.

"It's the only greenhouse in the gardens that houses tropical plants," Evelyn explained. "A lot of work goes into making sure there's a good range of plants and that all of them are healthy."

"Are we going to be able to see the corpse flower from here?" Alita asked. She ducked her head from one spot to the next, trying to see everything inside the greenhouse despite the foliage blocking the way.

Evelyn looked at the half blocked windows. "Perhaps not. The corpse flower is in the centre of the greenhouse. I've never tried to view it from outside before."

"Hey, what are these?" Alita's ears perked up as she peered through a larger gap in the leaves.

Evelyn leaned close to her to get a look. There was a bench on the opposite side of the glass with several flower pots lined up on it. The leaves of the plants were thick and nearly circular in shape. Their flowers had five petals of varying colours. Some were pink, others purple, and a few even had frilly white edges encapsulating the bright colours.

"They look like tropical violets," Evelyn said, pulling her head away from the glass. "There'll be an information board by the gazebo about them."

"Why by the gazebo and not here?" Alita asked, turning to look at her.

"There's a board inside the greenhouse for them but there's also common violets growing by the gazebo. The two kinds are mixed up by dragons who don't know any different, so both the boards have information about both violets and how they differ," Evelyn explained.

"Sounds interesting. Can we go have a look?" Alita asked.

Evelyn smiled. "Of course. The gazebo's this way."

She took Alita a little further down the path to the gazebo. It was on the opposite side of the path from the greenhouse, allowing space for both to expand if there was ever a need. Various flowers grew around the base of the gazebo, including Evelyn's personal favourite.

"So these are the common violets," Alita muttered as she scanned the board next to a patch of small purple flowers. "They look a lot more delicate than the tropical violets."

"They might look fragile but they're actually quite hardy," Evelyn said. "I think I read once that the tropical violet is harder to care for than the common violet when you don't know what you're doing."

"Amazing," Alita breathed. Her eyes were wide as she read the information about the violets.

Evelyn glanced over the board. The symbolism of the violets stuck out to her. It represented watchfulness, faithfulness, and modesty. Did Alita know she embodied the same characteristics? Evelyn wondered if the flowers even meant anything to her.

As she pondered, Evelyn's eyes slid over to a patch of different flowers. She smiled as she recognised her favourites, the bleeding heart flowers. They flowered differently from most flowers. Instead of upward facing blooms, the plant sent out tendrils, each of which would grow several hanging flowers. The petals formed the shape of a heart with a droplet underneath it in vibrant pink and stark white colours. It was almost as if each flower on the plant were bleeding, mourning their inevitable deaths as the seasons changed.

"Oh, darn it."

Evelyn pulled herself out of her thoughts at the frustrated tone of the caretaker in the gazebo. It seemed that Alita had heard her too, as she wasted no time in approaching the dragon.

"Are you alright?" Alita asked.

The caretaker sighed. "As alright as I can be. I've been trying to nurse this plant for months but it just won't respond to anything."

Evelyn joined Alita at the edge of the gazebo and looked down at the wilting plant. She recognised the long points and deep green of the leaves in an instant.

"That's a Winter Star," she said before she could stop herself.

The caretaker nodded. "Laird Markos was kind enough to give me a cutting from his personal plant when I expressed interest in having one in the gardens. But no matter what I try, it just doesn't seem to want to grow. I don't understand what I'm doing wrong, I know the one at Everhart Manor is thriving and I'm following Laird Markos's instructions to the letter."

Alita crouched down next to the plant to inspect it. "That is peculiar. Markos showed us his Winter Star the other day and mentioned the strong connection he has with the plant.

Evelyn remembered the conversation in the Manor gardens and shuddered at the memory. If Gerold's plant died the same day as he had, and now no one but Markos could get one of these to thrive, surely there was more to the Winter Star than met the eye.

"I don't think we can help you, I'm afraid," Evelyn said, backing out of the gazebo.

Alita turned to follow her out with questioning eyes. "Are you alright? You look a little pale."

Evelyn forced a smile. "Yeah, I'm fine. That flower just freaks me out a little. Too many coincidences with it. How about we keep going?"

"Alright. Maybe we can find some plants that don't make you uncomfortable," Alita suggested.

Chapter 47

Luana sat quietly, frowning at nothing. Her ears twitched with each distant noise. She and Markos had been waiting outside Everhart Manor for Evelyn's visit for hours and she still hadn't arrived.

"I don't think she's coming today," Luana muttered.

"I think you might be right," Markos said. He had been oddly quiet the whole morning. Luana got the sense that he was a little on edge, though she couldn't figure out why.

"Do you think Modesty did something to Evelyn?" Luana asked, taking a guess at what was bothering him so much.

"No, we'd have heard something by now," Markos said.

Luana sighed and pushed herself to her feet. "Come on. If Evelyn isn't coming, I want to visit our friends."

Luana began walking through the streets with Markos close behind her. She appreciated that he didn't try to lead her anywhere, though she could still tell he was worried about something. She pushed the thought aside and focused on locating Victoria and Zina. She'd heard Zina's laugh coming from the streets and guessed that they were hanging out together.

It didn't take long for Zina's voice to become clear. Victoria was naturally quieter than Zina, but Luana could hear her nonetheless. She was definitely going the right way.

Luana turned a corner and their voices picked up significantly. They were just down the street; Markos could probably see them by now.

"Zina! Victoria!" Luana called, raising a wing in greeting to them.

"Luana!" Zina cheered, pouncing over to her.

"What are you doing here?" Victoria asked. "We thought you were with Prinze Evelyn today."

"She never showed up," Luana said. "I can only wait so long before I do something else."

"That's odd. I wonder where she is," Victoria muttered.

"Don't worry about that. She doesn't matter," Zina said.

"Zina, that is your Prinze and future High Caln." August's voice came from between Zina and Victoria. Luana hadn't realised she was there too. Perhaps she could help bring Markos out of his thoughts.

"Hey August," Luana greeted her.

"Good to see you, Luana," August said. "And Markos too."

"Hey," Markos said, though he sounded distant.

"What have you guys been up to today?" Luana asked.

"Well, Zina's been teasing me for my crush on Adair again," Victoria said.

"Those were only suggestions," Zina said. "I wasn't making fun of you."

"I know, Zina," Victoria said. Luana could hear the hint of a smile in her voice. Zina loved to tease but she usually meant well. Especially when it had to do with her closest friends. It was something Luana and Victoria were used to at this point.

"I think you and Adair would be cute together," Luana said to Victoria. Adair was one of the three sons of the Peacock family. Each one was slightly different in personality and drastically different in appearance. Adair was a gentle soul. Luana knew he and Victoria would get along well.

"Thanks Luana," Victoria said, an appreciative smile clear in her voice.

"Yeah, but he's so tall and you're so short," Zina said.

"Taller than you," Victoria shot back.

Zina stuttered. Luana couldn't help but laugh. Victoria wasn't always witty, but this time she'd managed to catch Zina out. Zina didn't really like being reminded of her height, but she knew by now that Victoria could give as good as she got.

"I hate to ruin this delightful little conversation, but I think I know where Evelyn might be," August said.

"You do?" Zina asked. "How do you know where she is?"

"I don't know for sure, but I saw her and Alita leaving the noble districts this morning," August explained. "I think I heard her mention the Calndom Gardens."

"The Calndom Gardens?" Luana echoed. "What would she need to do there?"

She recognised a rustle as August shrugged her wings. "I'm not sure. But I got the feeling it was more about who she was with than where she was going."

Zina hummed loudly. "You don't suppose she's got a special interest in her bodyguard, do you?"

"It would make sense," Victoria said. "Why else would she go all the way to Tribe-Ali to choose a bodyguard? She chose an old friend right? What if she feels more than just friendship there?"

That did make sense, given the timing. Luana and Evelyn's betrothal had come just a few weeks before Evelyn chose a bodyguard. If she was trying to get out of marrying Luana, it would make sense that Evelyn would choose a dragon she actually liked to be close to her every day. But what would happen if Evelyn told Alita how she felt? Luana doubted that Alita was already aware. Would she reciprocate if Evelyn confessed? Luana suddenly feared losing her first and only love to the dragon that brought them together in the first place.

Interlude VIII

Modesty sat in the sunroom, staring out the window. The late afternoon sun was warm. Disgustingly warm. It was quiet, though, and she could see any dragons that approached or left the castle.

The rest of the castle was in chaos. Adelaide reported that Evelyn never came to see Luana. Ever since that report came through, all the guards were searching the castle grounds and scanning the Noble Districts for any sign of Evelyn.

But she wasn't anywhere to be found. Modesty already knew that Evelyn had left the castle with her bodyguard that morning. She'd been in the sunroom then, too, when she watched them leave and turn away from Everhart Manor.

The door opened and Clement poked his head in. Modesty barely glanced at him as he entered.

"There you are. Mother and I have been looking all over for you," he said.

"I'm not hiding," Modesty said. "I haven't done anything."

"So you don't know where Prinze Evelyn is?" Clement asked. His tone was guarded. Modesty sneered at what he might be suggesting.

"All I know is that she never intended on going to Everhart Manor," Modesty said. "When she left this morning, I saw her turn towards the next gate out of the Noble Districts. Though, I suppose it's possible that she was running away with that bodyguard of hers."

"Why would she do that?" Clement asked.

Modesty shrugged her wings innocently. "How would I know? I don't spend every second of the day trying to track and understand her."

Clement frowned. "I know that's not true, Modesty."

"Whether you believe me or not, that's the only answer you're going to get," Modesty said. "Can I have some peace and quiet now?"

Clement sighed. "I'll tell Mother where you are. Don't be surprised if she comes to check on you."

Modesty didn't say anything in response. Clement quietly left the room, letting the door close behind him. Modesty returned her focus to the window. Something deep in her gut told her there would be a moment to enact her plan soon. Perhaps not tonight, but soon.

Chapter 48

Alita sat on a hill facing the western horizon. The sun had just set and the stars were starting to make their appearances in the sky. It was a clear night, so the stars and moon shone brightly down on them. Evelyn was curled up beside Alita, resting her head on Alita's shoulder. Alita figured she was tired from a full day of exploring the Calndom Gardens. Alita was worn out too. But she was still technically working until Evelyn went back to her room for the night.

"This has been an amazing day," Evelyn sighed blissfully.

"It has been pretty fun," Alita said. "And I learnt a lot of new things."

Evelyn hummed quietly, a small smile on her face. Her eyes were closed and her whole body was relaxed. Alita didn't think she'd seen Evelyn this at ease since they'd been fledglings. As much as she wanted to get back to the castle and sleep, she figured staying out here a little longer would be better if it meant Evelyn had more time to feel relaxed.

The peaceful silence only lasted a few more minutes before Evelyn sat up.

"Alita, there's something I have to tell you," she said quietly. Her voice had turned solemn and her expression anxious.

"Is something wrong?" Alita asked.

"No, nothing is wrong. But I can't keep this to myself any longer." Evelyn paused and stared at the ground for a long moment. Then she took a deep breath and looked up at Alita again. "Alita, I like you. I really, really do. More than just a friend. It's why I hired you as my bodyguard. I wanted to have you back in my life, close to me, constantly by my side. I wanted you to see the life I've been living the past seven years. But more than that, I wanted you to be part of it. I never wanted to marry Luana. But I figured if I could find you and bring you here, I might be able to marry you instead. Since you've been here, I've been happier than I have in the past seven years. I... I really want to be with you."

Evelyn touched Alita's shoulder with her wing. Alita stared at her, then blinked a few times, and looked down at Evelyn's wing. She never realised that Evelyn wanted to be more than friends. She'd never even considered Evelyn in a romantic way before. But as she tried to comprehend what she was hearing, Alita realised there had been signs. Hints that this would happen. Even back when they were young, Evelyn had always stuck to Alita more than anyone else. She always suggested things that would have the two of them together alone. Perhaps she should have seen this coming. And maybe if she had she could have spared her friend's feelings.

Alita looked back up at Evelyn. She was still waiting for Alita's response. Alita took a moment to consider a life where she married Evelyn. She really tried to imagine what it might be like. But the longer she thought about it, the tighter her chest felt. Thoughts of Luana flooded her mind. She couldn't possibly turn her back on a love like that, even if they had only known each other a short time. No matter how hard she tried, Alita knew she would never have those feelings for Evelyn.

"Evelyn... I'm really sorry, but... I don't feel that way about you," Alita said slowly.

Evelyn pulled her wing back to her side and lowered her gaze to the grass.

"You're my best friend," Alita said. "But I've never felt more than that. I'm sorry."

Evelyn closed her eyes and shook her head. "I didn't think you would. I just had to know for sure."

Silence stretched between them for several agonising seconds. Then Evelyn sighed and turned back towards the pathways.

"Come on. It's probably time we returned to the castle," she said quietly.

Chapter 49

It was dark when Alita and Evelyn returned to the castle. The stars and moon were the only source of light. Evelyn was silent the whole way back. Alita's mind was swirling with thoughts as they walked. She knew she'd never have romantic feelings for Evelyn, but she couldn't stop thinking about it. If Evelyn liked her, what did that mean for their friendship? Alita still believed Evelyn was her best friend. That wouldn't change. But how could it not now that she knew how Evelyn felt?

Alita's pondering stopped as she followed Evelyn into the castle and the sound of dragons rushing over echoed through the room. Griffin, Misti, and Heather were hurrying over to them.

"Thank goodness you're okay!" Misti said.

"Where have you been all day?" Griffin asked. His voice was tighter than Misti's. There was less relief and more anger.

"I went to the Calndom Gardens," Evelyn said flatly.

"What were you doing out there?" Griffin asked, his voice lowering further. "You were supposed to spend the day with Laird Luana, *inside* the Noble Districts."

"What does it matter where I went or who I was with?" Evelyn snapped.

"Don't start with me, Prinze Evelyn," Griffin growled. "You'd better not run off like that again, or I will be forced to change your bodyguard to someone who will ensure your safety."

"Don't worry. It won't happen again," Evelyn muttered. "I'm going to bed."

Evelyn marched for the stairs with Griffin and Misti close behind. Alita went to follow them but Heather stuck out a wing.

"Alita, what exactly were you and the Prinze doin' outside the Noble Districts all day?" Heather asked.

"We went to the Calndom Gardens and looked at the plants there," Alita explained.

"Did it not occur to you that the Prinze should stay within the Noble Districts?" Heather asked.

"My job is to protect her from danger, not stop her from doing what she wants," Alita said. "I'm pretty sure royalty has more power than I do about where we go."

"When it comes to keepin' Prinze Evelyn safe and on track, you should be reinforcin' her schedule and responsibilities," Heather said.

"I don't even know what she's going to do from one day to the next. I only ever know when I ask her," Alita explained. "I don't exactly have an itinerary of all of Evelyn's duties to follow. Nor would I even force her to follow it. She was my friend before she was Prinze and I'm not about to get in the way of her freedom."

Heather narrowed her eyes at Alita. "Perhaps there's more goin' on here than meets the eye."

"What makes you say that?" Alita asked.

"This mornin' I went to Prinze Evelyn regardin' your recent behaviour. The way you sneak out at night and how you spent your day off with Laird Luana," Heather said. "Now, we find out that you and the Prinze have spent the whole day out together, avoidin' responsibilities. Since you arrived, Prinze Evelyn has been spendin' less time with Laird Luana and causin' more and more trouble. Either you have somethin' to do with that, or she is actin' out all on her own, perhaps in reaction to your interest in her future wife."

"So what if she is?" Alita asked. "I certainly didn't ask for any of this. I happen to like Luana, and Evelyn is my best friend. I'm not about to change any of that."

"Then I'll change it for you," Heather said. "From now on, you are not allowed to leave the castle without my permission. Unless it is as part of your duties as Prinze Evelyn's bodyguard, you are to stay within the castle at all times. I will inform the gate guards of my decision."

"Fine," Alita said, barely holding back a growl. "I'm going to bed."

Chapter 50

Evelyn was slow to wake the next morning. Her wings felt heavy and she didn't want to lift her head. The only thing she could think about was how Alita had rejected her last night. They'd had such a good day, yet it was all for nothing. Alita didn't feel the same way. They would only ever be friends.

Worst of all, it was the last day of Alita's trial. She would be assessed for her work the very next day. Alita had proven her worth as a bodyguard, but Evelyn couldn't decide if she wanted her to stay or leave.

Evelyn forced herself out of bed before realising she'd woken alone. Lily hadn't come to prepare her for the day yet. Perhaps she'd be there soon, though. Evelyn decided to put on her cloak and crown herself. It was the least she could do while waiting.

Voices from outside the door drifted in. Evelyn recognised Crystal and Lucas talking to Alita about the castle.

"Where does that door go?" Alita asked.

"That leads to the viewing room, also called the sunroom," Crystal explained.

"And the Gallery, which can only be accessed through that room or the throne room," Lucas added.

"What's in there?" Alita asked.

"The sunroom is just a room for enjoying the sunlight and watching dragons come and go through the gate," Lucas explained. "There's not much in there aside from a massive window and some cushions."

"The Gallery is far more interesting," Crystal said. "But only certain dragons are allowed to go in there."

"Seriously?" Alita asked.

"The Gallery has paintings of past High Calns and their families," Lucas explained. "Most of them are old. The more recent ones tend to be hung around the castle."

"Seems like a ridiculous idea to hide a room full of paintings away from dragons," Alita said.

Evelyn decided to stop listening and join the conversation. Perhaps she could show Alita the Gallery. She pushed open the door and exited her room.

"Prinze Evelyn! You're not meant to be up yet," Crystal exclaimed. "Lily hasn't come to wake you."

"I don't need to be woken with you three chattering like birds," Evelyn said. She looked at Alita. "Would you like to see the Gallery?"

"I- uh... sure," Alita replied, tripping over her own words. "We didn't mean to wake you."

"Don't worry. It happens sometimes," Evelyn said, walking over to the door of the sunroom.

Evelyn pushed her way into the sunroom. It was warm from the morning sun. Almost warm enough to make her forget the way her heart had twisted upon seeing Alita. Wordlessly, Evelyn led the way into the Gallery past the sunroom.

The gallery was impressively big. It wasn't as brightly lit as the sunroom, but light still filtered in and illuminated it with a soft glow. Most of the paintings were covered with sheets, protecting them from light and dust. A few frames hung on the walls, displaying their paintings to the world. Evelyn looked around the room while Alita marvelled at the sight. There were several shades of blue in a lot of them. Many of the paintings were from Griffin and his family throughout their lives. Evelyn was only in two paintings. One where she sat next to Griffin, looking regally bored, and another where she was pictured in a field of snow. Evelyn regarded the second painting.

"You look so young in these," Alita said.

"They were painted five or six years ago," Evelyn explained. "All the High Calns have a painting done with their chosen Prinze. The snowfield one was submitted by an artist who wanted to sell his works in the mid-week market. Griffin decided to keep it, though I have no clue why."

"Did the artist get into the market?" Alita asked.

"He didn't at first. But I told Griffin that his skill would be appreciated by the nobles," Evelyn explained. "You see, this picture never happened. The artist saw the debut painting of me and Griffin and chose to imagine a scene that matched my colours from the painting. You can tell it's made up because I don't have my crown or cloak, two things that I would have to wear in every painting. To be honest, it's my favourite."

"Wow," Alita breathed.

Evelyn smiled slightly for a moment before it fell away. How she wished she could go back to a time when she didn't have to wear a cloak or crown at all. They were so heavy on her head and shoulders, especially today.

Alita's gaze continued to a pair of paintings near the corner. One painting was of Griffin with an orange Fire Dragon. They were similar in age and both wore crowns embedded with jewels. The Fire Dragon was wearing a translucent cloak with the Everhart crest etched on the button. The second painting had the same Fire Dragon, but much younger, next to a colourful dragon with a long, thin body and intricate wing patterns.

"Who are these two?" Alita asked.

"That's Rana and Gerold," Evelyn explained. "Rana Peacock was High Caln before Gerold. She chose him as her heir through a competition, I think. Gerold was best friends with Griffin when they were young, so he made Griffin his heir when he became High Caln."

"So that's... Luana's father?" Alita asked. "She looks quite a bit like him."

Evelyn regarded the painting for a moment. "Yes, I suppose she does."

Gerold's eyes were green, just like Luana's, but they were brighter, instead of the pale green of Luana's eyes. He had a short, curly mane that bordered on unruly, much like Markos, but the colours were shades of orange and red-orange like Luana. The resemblance brought back the pain in Evelyn's heart. She couldn't bear to look at the painting any longer.

"We should go," she said. "Griffin will be mad if I'm late to breakfast."

Chapter 51

"No, that won't do. It needs to be extravagant for the ball." Adelaide said as a servant held a cloak against Luana's side.

Luana rolled her eyes as the servant pulled the cloak away. She had no idea what colours her mother was picking out, but she was certain that she hated all of them. Markos, Jakob, and Hamlet were by her side, trying on their own cloaks for the event.

Luana didn't even know why there had to be a ball. It wasn't to celebrate a holiday. The most she could conclude was that the ball was to celebrate her betrothal to Evelyn. The reminder made the fire in her chest flare.

"Mum, this one is too big," Hamlet complained. "I keep standing on the edges."

"Oh, that won't do," Adelaide said. "We can't have you tripping over yourself all night at your first ball."

"I want to dance with Evelyn again," Hamlet said. "Like I did at the market."

"Prinze Evelyn will be too busy tonight, dear," Adelaide said. "She has responsibilities during the ball. Besides, she will be dancing with your sister."

Luana frowned. The thought of having to dance with Evelyn made her want to rip off her cloak.

"Don't make that face, Luana," Adelaide said.

Luana felt a wing press against hers as Markos said, "Don't worry,

Luana. Alita will be there too."

Luana smiled at Markos. "Thanks. I just hope I can spend some time with her."

"Why on Laili would you want to spend time with the bodyguard?" Adelaide asked. Then she gasped. "You're not trying to court her are you? You're betrothed to Prinze Evelyn!"

Luana rolled her eyes again. "I don't care about Evelyn. Alita's nice and she actually likes me."

"I should have known there was something going on. I heard Markos mention how you snuck off with the bodyguard during your trip to the Northern Districts," Adelaide said. "You'd better not do anything like that tonight, Luana. I'll be watching you."

"Oh, please. It's not like you can stare at me all night," Luana said. "You'll get caught up in conversation with Griffin and the other nobles like you always do."

"I don't appreciate that tone, Luana," Adelaide warned. "If you're not careful, I'll have to give you a bodyguard as well."

Luana shivered at the thought of having someone following her and correcting her behaviour every day. That was the last thing she wanted.

"Don't worry, Sis," Markos said. "I'm sure tonight will be everything you need and more."

Chapter 52

The day went uneventfully for Evelyn. Her mind was focused on the evening. She hadn't told Alita yet, but there was going to be a ball. Dragons from every noble family would be there. Everyone would be dressed up for the event. Alita would need to look nice too.

Late in the afternoon, Evelyn went up to her room, with Alita diligently following her. There were no guards posted, but they weren't needed during the day. Evelyn pushed the door open and looked back at Alita.

"Come in," she said.

"Uh... I thought no one was allowed in your room except for Lily," Alita said.

Evelyn nearly rolled her eyes but forced a smile instead. "I can give dragons permission to enter my room when I want. Such as right now. Come with me."

Alita nodded hesitantly and followed Evelyn into the bedroom. She stopped just inside the room and looked around with wide eyes. Evelyn guessed she was surprised at the size and extravagance of the room. While Alita was looking around, Evelyn unclipped her cloak and let it fall to the floor.

"Wh-what are you doing?" Alita asked.

"There's a ball on tonight," Evelyn explained as she slid her tail out from under the cloak. "I'm getting ready for it. Lily will be here in a moment with something for me to wear."

"You're not going to wear the same cloak?" Alita asked. "What is the ball for?"

Evelyn shrugged. "They happen sometimes. There's not really much reason for them, though I suspect this one is meant to celebrate my betrothal to Luana."

Evelyn scowled as she said the words. It left a sour taste in her mouth. She wanted to be dancing with anyone but Luana.

There was a knock before the door opened and Lily came in. She was dragging a rack of cloaks behind her. Evelyn saw cloaks in various shades of blue and purple with lots of sparkle. She wasn't a big fan, but it was required to look formal for the ball. Besides, she needed to have dressed Alita in something nice too.

"Prinze Evelyn, sorry I'm late," Lily apologised. "I was trying to pick out the best cloaks for you to choose from."

"Thank you, Lily, I appreciate it," Evelyn said.

She went through the cloaks on the rack, making sure to look at each one. She finally picked out a sparkling indigo cloak made of translucent silk.

"This one will do," she said.

"Excellent choice, Prinze Evelyn," Lily said. She took the cloak and wrapped it around Evelyn's back and shoulders. She straightened it out carefully before doing up the golden button.

"Why doesn't the button have your crest on it?" Alita asked.

"Because these are temporary. They are only intended to be worn at big events," Evelyn explained. "We're all expected to know each other anyway. The crest is more for everyday life, not these big parties."

Lily went back to the rack and picked out a pair of silvery earrings and showed them to Evelyn.

"I thought you might like these," she explained. "They're made of glass from the sands of Tribe-Ali. I know your home means a lot to you."

Evelyn stared at the earrings, wide eyed. Her chest tightened. She wasn't sure what to say.

"You got earrings made from the same sand I used to walk on?" she asked quietly. "That's amazing."

Lily smiled and offered the earrings to Evelyn. She happily took them and put them on. She rarely wore earrings, though she'd had her ears pierced soon after becoming Prinze for situations such as this. The need to wear earrings somehow happened just often enough that Evelyn didn't need to re-pierce her ears every time.

"How do I look?" Evelyn asked, turning to Alita.

"Very sparkly," Alita said. "The earrings are a nice touch."

Evelyn smiled. "Thanks. Now it's your turn."

"Wh-what?" Alita stammered before Evelyn pulled a cloak from the rack and placed it on her back.

"You'll need to look nice too," Evelyn said. "You're going to be following me around all night after all."

Evelyn paused to inspect the colour clash of Alita's brown skin and the translucent blue cloak she'd just picked. It wasn't quite right. Evelyn put the cloak back on the rack and picked out another one. It was more purple and looked a little better, but the cooler colours really didn't mesh well with Alita's warm shades of brown.

"Are you sure?" Alita asked. "It wouldn't be weird or inappropriate?"

Evelyn shook her head and turned back to the rack. "I think it would be weird if you *didn't* dress up a little."

"What about this?" Lily whispered, offering Evelyn a purple-red translucent cloak.

Evelyn took the cloak and held it up to Alita's skin. It meshed very well. Evelyn smiled and draped the cloak over Alita's back and wings. She pulled the front of the cloak around Alita's neck and carefully did up the button. She tried not to think about how she was close enough to feel Alita's warm breath on her head.

"There we go," she said, stepping back. "You'll be the prettiest dragon there."

Alita ducked her head. "I-I really doubt that. There'll be so many dragons who live and breathe this sort of life."

"Never doubt your beauty, Alita," Evelyn said. She tried not to look at the jadeite earrings. The green of the earrings and the purple-ish tone of the cloak reminded Evelyn too much of Luana. Evelyn suddenly wished she didn't have to go to the ball at all.

Chapter 53

"Alright, we're ready to go," Adelaide said. "Where has Markos gone?"

"He's in the garden. I'll go get him," Luana said quickly. She slipped out the side door of the Manor before her mother could stop her.

As soon as she had stepped outside, Luana sighed. She was well and truly over her mother's fussing. Adelaide had dressed Luana in a sparkly, scratchy sheer cloak. It was thinner and lighter than her usual cloaks, which meant her wings caught on it more often. She wasn't used to how the cloak moved against her body.

Luana pushed aside her thoughts about her cloak and focused her hearing on locating Markos. She detected his quiet breathing and subtle movements across the gardens, near the tree where he grew the Winter Star. Luana crossed the gardens in a few paces and stopped behind him.

"Markos, it's time to go," she said.

"I'll join you soon," Markos said, his voice hollow.

"Don't be too long," Luana told him, too absorbed in her own thoughts to dwell on the shift in her brother.

She hesitated. This was a good opportunity to ask Markos for some advice. Perhaps he could see a way she could get out of marrying Evelyn.

"I don't suppose you might have thought of a way I could get out of the betrothal with Evelyn? Perhaps even tonight?" Luana asked.

"The violet and the iris bring more joy than the lamprocapnos," Markos said. His voice was flat and distant. The tone alone sent a chill down Luana's spine.

"Okay. I don't really know what that means," Luana said, turning back for the Manor. Markos's words had confused her more than if she hadn't asked for his advice in the first place.

"Did you find him?" Jakob asked as Luana rejoined her family.

"Yeah, he'll be in soon I think. Hey, Jakob, do you know anything about plants?" Luana asked.

"Not really. Why?" Jakob looked as confused as Luana felt.

"I asked Markos for some advice and he said something strange. Do you have any idea what a lamprocapnos is?" Luana asked.

"Sorry, Luana, I wouldn't have a clue," Jakob replied. "And before you ask, looking it up would take too much time away from my work translating the old language. You already got me looking at law books to help you."

"That's too bad," Luana sighed. Perhaps she could ask Markos what he meant later.

Chapter 54

Alita followed Evelyn and Lily out of Evelyn's room after some more adjustments. She felt unnecessarily fancy with the glittering cloak on. But Evelyn had insisted on it, and she didn't want to argue.

When they reached the main room of the ground floor, Alita was surprised to see how different it looked. There were flames of different colours scattered around the room and over a hundred dragons in sparkling and glittering cloaks. Many wore necklaces, earrings, bracelets, and golden lines of thin chains. Suddenly, she felt underdressed.

"Lily, you are excused to help with the party," Evelyn said. "Alita, your job tonight is the same as always. Follow me and keep an eye out for danger."

"Are there any real threats here tonight?" Alita asked, scanning the many, many unfamiliar faces.

"Just the same ones as always," Evelyn said. "But I doubt the Duchies will do much of anything tonight. They'll be too busy keeping up appearances."

Evelyn nodded to a small group of dragons across the room. Alita recognised Modesty and Clement talking to Zina and Victoria. Modesty looked like she wanted to be anywhere but there, though Clement's face was tinted as he smiled at Zina. All four dragons were dressed in shiny cloaks and various jewellery.

"Prinze Evelyn, there you are," Griffin said, approaching them.

"Laird Luana will be staying by your side tonight."

Luana was standing beside Griffin and nodded slightly. She was wearing a shiny cloak of lilac and had her jadeite necklace around her neck. It was a simple outfit, but Alita found herself mesmerised.

"Very well, Griffin," Evelyn said. She turned to Luana and said, "I suppose we should start with our required dance."

"That would probably be best," Luana agreed.

Evelyn glanced back at Alita and said, "Alita, you stay here while Luana and I dance. We'll only be a few minutes."

Alita nodded, barely taking her eyes off Luana.

Evelyn stretched out her wing to Luana. Luana stretched hers out to meet Evelyn's halfway and they walked into the crowd of dragons. Alita stayed where she was and watched as the crowd moved to create a clearing. The quiet music that had been playing in the background suddenly grew louder as Luana and Evelyn began to dance. It was a reserved dance. They didn't look at each other. Evelyn's eyes were trained on the ground while Luana kept hers closed for most of the song.

But as Alita watched, she noticed Luana open her eyes. They locked onto Alita so intently she almost believed Luana could see. There was something in her gaze. Luana smiled slightly and Alita felt her heart flutter. She was so beautiful.

When Alita glanced at Evelyn, she realised Evelyn was watching her too. But Evelyn's expression was near unreadable. It seemed solemn, almost sad. Remembering the evening before, Alita could only bear to hold Evelyn's gaze for a moment before looking at Luana again. Alita's heart felt tight with emotion. She wanted to be out there, dancing with Luana, like they had at the market. There was something that felt so right about dancing with her.

When the song ended, Luana and Evelyn exited the dancefloor with refined elegance. They returned to where Alita was standing and the act dropped immediately.

"It's over. Can we do something more pleasant now?" Luana asked.

"We have to go around the ball and talk to everyone," Evelyn told her.

"I said 'pleasant,'" Luana muttered. A small wisp of smoke started rising from her nostrils. "That somehow sounds even worse than dancing with you."

"Ouch," Evelyn said flatly. "Let's get it over with then, and try to be pleasant. You're representing our future tonight."

Luana frowned but followed Evelyn as they re-entered the crowd. This time, Alita followed them. She wondered how much longer it would be before one of them broke down and started yelling at the other.

Chapter 55

Evelyn led the way as she and Luana navigated the maze-like crowd of dragons. She wasn't thrilled about having to spend her time with Luana during the ball, but it was required. They had to portray the image of a happy couple. After all, nobles weren't the only dragons attending the ball. Journalists for the newspapers were attending as well.

Evelyn and Luana stopped to talk to several dragons as they went around the room. Alita trailed after them. Evelyn would glance back at her every now and then to make sure she was still there. Alita looked beautiful with the cloak over her vest, though she still scanned the room with observant eyes and twitching ears. Evelyn could tell she was trying to do her job despite all the noise.

"Prinze Evelyn! Laird Luana! How wonderful to see you again!" Carmina's shrill voice made Evelyn cringe.

Carmina was the daughter of High Caln Rana, though her brilliantly red and pink skin was quite different from the greens and blues of Rana in paintings. Evelyn had learned to be extra nice to Carmina. She could be quite sensitive when she wanted to be.

"How is the happy couple?" Carmina asked.

"What happy couple?" Luana grumbled quietly.

"Shh!" Evelyn nudged Luana with her wing, forcing a smile to Carmina. "We're good. Please forgive Luana's attitude. She's just overwhelmed by all the noise."

"Of course, dear," Carmina said. "It must be so hard to get around in your state."

Evelyn simply smiled and nodded. She hoped Carmina couldn't hear the small growl coming from Luana.

"Such a shame you didn't choose one of my sons as your betrothed," Carmina continued. "But love is love. My mother knew that better than anyone."

I would never have chosen one of you sons, Evelyn thought bitterly, still forcing a smile.

"Perhaps I could convince Duchy Modesty to court one of them," Carmina said. "She's such a lonely hen."

"I don't think that's a good idea," Evelyn said. "Modesty isn't exactly easy going."

"Oh, I'm sure I can convince her," Carmina said. "I must go find her. I'll see you both later."

"Goodbye," Evelyn called as Carmina disappeared into the crowd.

"She's going to get stabbed," Luana muttered.

"Luana, stop being such a downer," Evelyn said. "If you weren't such a puddle of ice melt, this ball could actually be enjoyable."

Luana shot a glare at her. A fresh wave of smoke rose from her nostrils. Evelyn frowned and nudged her towards the wall with her wing. Luana followed obediently, though she still frowned.

"Don't do that here," Evelyn said quietly once they were in a secluded corner of the room.

"Do what? Be honest?" Luana questioned.

"No, the smoke. You have no control over your element," Evelyn said. "If you keep fuming like that, dragons are going to notice. I can't lie to cover your bad behaviour forever."

"I don't want you to cover for me," Luana growled. "I don't want to be here at all. If you let one more dragon believe that I'm overwhelmed because I'm blind, I will personally burn your tail off."

Evelyn hissed, fighting to keep her voice low. "If you do that, I will gladly throw you in the dungeon."

"So I can never see the light of day again? Great joke, Evelyn," Luana muttered. "I'm going outside. Don't follow me."

Evelyn watched Luana pace away. Ice had formed over her feet and she had to consciously melt it. She couldn't stand Luana's attitude. They were both equally annoyed to be betrothed. Why couldn't Luana just try to be pleasant?

Evelyn took a breath to calm down and turned to Alita. She was standing a few metres away. Evelyn couldn't help but smile when she saw Alita in her sparkling purple-red cloak. She managed to push aside the twist she felt in her heart.

"Sorry for that, Alita," Evelyn said, walking over to her.

"Is Luana alright?" Alita asked.

"She just needs to calm down. Leave her be," Evelyn said. "Would you like to dance with me?"

"Uh..." Alita's eyes darted around the room. No doubt she was looking at all the other dragons present. "I don't think it would be a good idea... f-for dragons to see you dancing with someone other than Luana. Especially me."

Evelyn struggled not to show her disappointment. But deep down, she knew Alita was right. She also knew that wasn't the only reason Alita had declined. She would have been thinking about Evelyn's confession the previous night.

"Sorry. You're right. Forget I asked," Evelyn muttered.

She looked around the room, at all the faces present. She recognised most of them. The few she didn't know were the journalists. They were talking to the nobles or keenly observing the room. There were so many watchful eyes and far too many of them wouldn't hesitate to talk and speculate and spread rumours. Suddenly, Evelyn didn't feel like staying at the ball any longer.

"I think I'll go to bed," she said.

Evelyn started for the grand staircase, but stopped when she realised Alita was following her. Suddenly she wished Alita didn't have to follow her around all the time. She looked around and spotted Lucas standing nearby.

"It's okay, Alita," Evelyn said. "I'll take Lucas with me. He'll need to go up there eventually anyway. You're relieved for the day."

Interlude IX

Modesty suppressed a groan as she weaved through the crowd. Her cloak for the night was extra heavy and made from a rough, scratchy material. Her mother had insisted on sparkly earrings and silver bangles for her legs. Modesty hated the way the bangles clattered together and pinched her fur.

But that was the least of her trouble for the moment. She had been strategically moving around the room, away from Carmina. Her shrill voice somehow still filled Modesty's ears as if she were standing right beside her. Modesty just knew that Carmina would try to marry her off to one of her three sons.

"Modesty, why do you keep moving?" Clement asked. He'd been staying by her side all night.

"I'm avoiding the precious mother of the colourful family," Modesty muttered.

Clement blinked at her, frowning slightly. "You mean Carmina? She's not doing anything wrong."

"If she talks to me, I can't promise not to stab her," Modesty growled. She idly picked up a lemon slice from the buffet table beside her and popped it in her mouth. It was sour and made her jaw clench.

"You know, Modesty, it *is* possible to talk to others without wanting to kill them," Clement said. "You could try being polite, listening to what they have to say, and gently declining any offer you don't like."

"Oh, please. I'm not going to listen to anyone's mindless prattling,"

Modesty sneered. "That includes you, too. Just leave me alone."

Clement sighed. "Very well."

Modesty watched Clement turn and cross the room from the corner of her eye. As he joined Griffin and Misti on the far side of the room, Modesty spotted a blue figure climbing the stairs. She quickly realised it was Evelyn, followed by the Water Dragon guard that sat outside Modesty's room every night.

Modesty frowned and quickly scanned the room for Evelyn's bodyguard. She spotted Alita standing in a corner by herself, looking a bit lost. If Evelyn was going to bed early, and without her Rock Dragon bodyguard, or any half useful dragon for that matter, Modesty could have a chance to take her out. The Water Dragon would be less than useless against her in combat.

But as Modesty's gaze slid back over to Griffin, she realised her plan would have to wait. Griffin was surrounded by nobles and journalists, along with having Misti and Clement on either side. He was too well protected. Doing anything now would ruin her chances at getting the crown.

Chapter 56

Alita watched Evelyn go in silence. She suddenly felt very small and very lost amongst all the chatter and music. She stayed near the edge of the room, simply watching the dragons move around her.

Many were dancing in pairs in the centre of the room. The band was situated near the front door. They were playing a lively song while the pairs of dragons danced in time with the beat. Other dragons stood in clusters around the room. Alita spotted Griffin talking to a dragon with a notepad. Next to him, Clement was still talking to Zina and Victoria, his face a reddish purple.

Alita could also see Markos. He was dancing with August, a big grin on his face. Another pair of dancing dragons, Alita noticed with surprise, were Heather and Henry. What had happened to keeping their relationship secret?

Alita wasn't sure how long she'd been standing there, but she suddenly felt a nudge and turned to see Luana standing next to her.

"Hey," Luana said.

"Hey. Are you alright?" Alita asked.

"I'm fine now," Luana said. "I don't like Carmina very much and Evelyn let her believe I was in a bad mood because I was blind. It's insulting."

"I'm sorry you had to deal with that," Alita said.

"It's okay. You couldn't have changed anything about it," Luana said. "Do you want to go outside?"

"That sounds nice," Alita said.

Luana smiled and turned for the door that led to the gardens. As soon as they were outside, a sense of peace washed over Alita. It was so much quieter. The chill of the night air was a relief compared to the stuffy heat of the castle.

"I haven't been out here since Dad died," Luana said. She took a deep breath and let it out slowly. "I forgot how peaceful it is."

"How did he die?" Alita asked.

"The doctor said it was cancer," Luana explained. "It was a lump growing from his leg. We had no idea how to stop it. He got so sick in his last months of life."

Luana lowered her head and her wings drooped a little. Alita put a wing around her. The cloak made it tricky, but she managed.

"It's hard to imagine how he saw it coming," Luana continued. "But he knew. He knew for a while how he was going to die. The only ones he ever told were me and Markos. He didn't tell Jakob, or even our mother."

"He must have loved you a lot," Alita said.

Luana smiled. "He did. He loved all of us. Even Hamlet, though he never got to meet him."

Luana leaned on Alita with a sigh. Alita held her close with her wing. Luana soon stepped back and raised one of her wings.

"Would you like to dance?" She asked.

Alita smiled. "How can I say no?"

She raised her wing to mimic Luana's movement. Their wings brushed gently. Alita didn't know how to dance. She knew that for certain. But much like when she had danced with Luana in the market the other day, the steps suddenly came to her. On instinct, she knew when and where to move her feet and how fast or slow to move. She knew when to turn, when to spin, and when to stop. The rest of the world disappeared and it was just her and Luana.

When their dance ended, Alita found herself much closer to Luana than when they had started. Their noses were almost touching. She wasn't sure if she felt excited or nervous by the closeness.

"There's a dance performed at weddings that's meant to display the closeness of the pair," Luana said quietly. "It's not really performed much anymore, but weddings among nobles and royalty require it. It's usually staged rather than the true instinctual dance that's supposed to be done."

"I've heard of that," Alita said. "It's called a courtship dance, right?"

Luana nodded. "Yes. I think we just did it."

"I would do it again in a heartbeat," Alita said softly.

Luana smiled. Her cheeks tinged slightly redder and a small wisp of smoke rose from her nostrils.

"I'm glad you feel that way, Alita," she said. "I feel the same."

Luana stepped closer and ruffled her wings. Then she hissed and stepped back.

"This stupid cloak," Luana growled. "I can't use my wings properly with it on."

"Isn't it meant to gather on your back for flying?" Alita asked.

"Yes, but it only works if you unfold your wings the right way," Luana explained, tugging at the button, "It doesn't work if you only want to move your wings a little bit."

Luana fiddled with the button of her cloak a little more before hissing in annoyance. Smoke started to rise from her nose as she tried to rip the cloak off. Suddenly, the cloak burst into flames and fell off her back. Luana sighed and waved her wing over the fire. The flames dulled to embers but the cloak was already destroyed.

"Not the first time I've burnt one of those," Luana muttered. "Sorry."

"Don't be," Alita said. "I'm surprised the necklace is still intact though."

Luana touched the jadeite necklace around her neck and smiled. "Gold is much harder to destroy with heat. The cloak was only a thin sheet of cotton. It burns easily on Fire Dragons."

"You're kidding," Alita said.

"Not at all. My mother takes pride in wearing cotton cloaks because she never burns them," Luana explained. "It's a bit like a statement of emotional and elemental control, to wear something that doesn't work with your element."

"Is that why High Caln Griffin wears thick fleece?" Alita asked.

"Yup. The idea that he can wear something so warm and not constantly feel the need to cool his own body is a power statement," Luana explained.

The cloak had stopped burning now. All that remained were the charred remains of the wooden button. Alita decided to remove the silk cloak she'd been wearing all night. It was getting in the way a little anyway.

Chapter 57

Alita left her cloak by the discarded remains of Luana's and they continued walking through the gardens. Luana walked so close to Alita's side that their wings brushed. Alita wrapped a wing around her and Luana was sure her heart would melt. She snuggled up to Alita and flared the heat in her chest until her skin was warm to the touch.

"This is perfect," Alita said after a while.

"It is," Luana agreed. "Just you and me in the night air. There's nothing better."

Alita stopped to rest her head on top of Luana's. Luana couldn't help but smile as a purr rumbled in her throat. It was a sound of pure, uninhibited bliss. She couldn't recall ever feeling so content that she had purred, but doing it here, now, felt right. Especially once she heard the same low rumble coming from Alita.

After several minutes, Luana felt Alita's head dip down. Her nose brushed Luana's face and she felt her heart speed up. Wordlessly, Luana tilted her head so that her nose met Alita's. Alita hummed quietly and leaned into it until their foreheads touched as well.

Luana didn't want the moment to end, but they couldn't just stand there all night. She pulled back and picked a soft spot on the grass to lie down.

"Come sit with me," she said to Alita.

Alita obeyed wordlessly, sitting so close that their sides pressed together. Luana leaned against her happily.

"Did you figure out how to get out of the betrothal?" Alita asked.

"No. But I asked Markos for ideas," Luana replied. "He said, and I quote, 'the violet and the iris bring more joy than the lamprocapnos.'"

"The lamprocapnos?" Alita repeated. "That sounds familiar. I think I read about that at the Calndom Gardens yesterday."

"Is that where you and Evelyn went all day?" Luana asked. She immediately shrugged off any need for an answer. "I know it's a flower, but I'm not sure which one."

Alita hummed quietly. "I think I saw it near the gazebo. It was pink... but the other name for it has slipped my mind."

"I'm sure it's not that important," Luana said. "He did seem distracted when I asked him."

"Distracted?" Alita asked. "How so?"

"It's hard to explain," Luana said. "He was tending to his Winter Star in the garden and barely seemed to notice me. His voice was kind of flat, like he wasn't really there."

"That's... concerning," Alita said.

"He gets like that sometimes," Luana said. "I trust him though. If only I could understand what he meant."

"Perhaps Jakob would know," Alita suggested. "He might be able to find something about flowers in the library."

Luana shook her head. "He's too focused on translating old texts at the moment. I tried asking him for help in researching the flowers Markos mentioned but he said he didn't have time."

"Well... what if I helped you?" Alita suggested. "Heather doesn't want me leaving the castle anymore but I could go through the castle library in my free time. Perhaps I'll be able to remember what I read in the Calndom Gardens too."

Luana smiled and rested her head on Alita's neck. "I appreciate that, Alita. I'm sorry I can't help you when it comes to written word."

"That's not your fault." Alita wrapped a wing around her. "Besides,

239

you're great in so many ways; I'm glad I can help you in this one."

Luana hummed and closed her eyes. She let herself fully relax in Alita's embrace. She was ready to just fall asleep.

Interlude X

"Oh, Modesty, you would *love* Brighton," Carmina said. "He has such a strong spirit. I think he'd really help you... uh... relax."

Modesty's eye twitched. She was barely holding back a snarl. "No, Carmina, I'm *not* interested."

Of course it had only been a matter of time before Carmina cornered her and started going on about her 'amazing' sons. Modesty hadn't been able to weasel out of the conversation yet.

"Well, how about Adair?" Carmina suggested. "He's a sweetheart, really caring. With your blues and his reds, any offspring you had would have such interesting colours."

Modesty cringed at the thought of having eggs with anyone, let alone Carmina's son.

"As I said before, Carmina, I'm not interested. Perhaps you should keep your nose out of other dragons' business before someone scratches it," Modesty warned before pushing past Carmina, just about knocking her to the ground.

To her relief, Carmina didn't call after her or try to chase her down. Modesty could barely keep the ice off her claws as it was. If Carmina had tried calling after her, Modesty might have just ripped her throat out then and there.

Modesty glanced around the room, she spotted Griffin and Clement heading up the stairs to the second floor landing. She watched as they walked to the spiral staircase in the corner and disappeared into it.

Where could they be going? She knew Griffin would never turn in from a party before its conclusion. Perhaps he'd noticed Evelyn's absence and was going to get her.

Which meant this was the perfect opportunity for her to strike.

Modesty pushed her way through the crowd and ducked around the dancing dragons as she headed for the stairs. She would only have a few minutes to execute her plan before they came back. She had to make the most of it.

Modesty stalked up the main stairs, allowing her feet to coat themselves in a smooth layer of ice. Her claws sharpened into thin icicles and the frozen points scratched the floor. Just as she was nearing the spiral staircase, Griffin and Clement emerged again, this time with Evelyn and the Water Dragon guard.

"You must stay at the ball until it has ended, Evelyn," Griffin was saying. "It would be inappropriate for you to hide away in your room all night."

Evelyn simply nodded. Her eyes were red with dark bags underneath them. It seemed like she'd been crying. Modesty didn't care enough to wonder why. She hadn't expected them to come back down so quickly. But she didn't want to let the moment go. Carmina's shrill laugh echoed across the room, giving Modesty a fresh burst of anger. She was done waiting.

"Father. Evelyn," Modesty said when she reached them. Her voice was thick with contempt. She couldn't hide it any longer.

"Modesty, daughter." Griffin blinked warily at her. "What is it?"

"I need something from you," Modesty said.

"What would that be?" Griffin asked.

Modesty cracked a grin. "You're crown."

In one smooth motion, Modesty plunged her frozen forefoot into Griffin's chest and wrapped her claws around his heart. Griffin gasped and jerked but couldn't move away. Modesty's grin stretched further as she yanked his now frozen heart out and smashed it on the floor. Griffin stumbled, then collapsed to the floor.

The whole room went quiet. Everyone on the ground floor could see what had just happened. Modesty didn't care though. It felt too good to see her father's corpse crumble as his eyes faded into death.

"M-Modesty," Clement gasped. "What have you done?"

"I got rid of a problem," Modesty said. "Would you like to help, dear brother? I could give you the simple task of taking out that Water Dragon."

Clement's face was pale and he visibly swallowed. He looked at Lucas, then back at Modesty. She knew his answer before he'd even said it.

"I-I can't do that. I-I-I won't," Clement said.

"Then don't get in my way," Modesty said, lowering her tone.

"I-I can't let you get away with this," Clement said shakily. He took a trembling step forward.

Modesty could almost laugh. "Then you'll be next."

She lunged at Clement and tackled him to the ground before he could move. Clement struggled against her but his movements were too shaky. Modesty swiftly slashed his throat and plunged her icy claws into his chest. She willed the ice to swallow him, only leaving his slit throat unfrozen. He would bleed out as his body melted. If the freezing didn't kill him, the blood loss would.

Modesty stepped back from Clement and was caught in the side. She fell with a snarl and bunched her legs together beneath her attacker. She kicked with all her force and sent Lucas flying into the railing. The wood cracked loudly at the force. Lucas groaned and forced himself back up. Modesty growled and got up to lunge at him again.

Lucas met her attack with claws slashing and teeth bared. Modesty ducked underneath him and slashed at his foreleg as hard as she could. Lucas cried out and fell to the ground. His leg gave out beneath him and he collapsed on top of it with a sickening crack.

Modesty grinned, breathing heavy, but feeling alive. More alive than she'd ever felt. She turned to look for Evelyn and spotted her running down the stairs. She was going to try and disappear into the panic below. Modesty couldn't let that happen. If she got away, the Calndom would still have a ruler. Modesty needed to be the only one left to take the crown.

Modesty charged after Evelyn, leaping the railing in a single bound and aiming her glide to land her on top of her. Evelyn tripped on her cloak and collapsed on the floor. Modesty grinned and tucked in her wings to dive. The crown would be hers.

Chapter 58

Alita gave Luana a gentle shake. "Luana, it's getting late. I think the party is finishing."

Luana sighed. "I guess we should go then."

Alita withdrew her wing and stood up. She immediately missed Luana's warmth. But she knew it was time to go. Luana was slower to get up. Once she was on her feet, they started walking back to the castle together.

"This was nice," Alita said.

"It was," Luana agreed. "There's one more thing I want to do."

"Yes?" Alita turned to face her.

Luana stretched her head up and gently touched noses with her. Alita leaned into it with a happy little sigh. Luana held the touch for a long moment before pulling away slowly.

"I think you did that already," Alita said quietly.

"I know," Luana said. "I wanted to do it again."

"I wanted to do it again too," Alita admitted.

Luana smiled. Then her ear twitched and she frowned.

"What's wrong?" Alita asked.

"The ball isn't ending. Something's happening," Luana said. She stepped back, tilting her ears towards the castle. "I can hear screaming."

"Screaming?" Alita's eyes widened and panic filled her chest. "We need to go!"

Luana nodded and they both ran for the castle. Alita was the first to burst through the doors. The room was a mess. Dragons were scrambling around, some fleeing out the main doors, others cowering in corners. Alita immediately spotted Evelyn collapsed in the middle of the room. Modesty was in the air above her, tucking in her wings and extending ice over her claws.

Alita reacted instantly, leaping to catch Modesty mid-air. She hit Modesty's side and they went tumbling to the ground. Modesty snarled. It was a nasty, sickening sound that no dragon would normally make. Alita growled in response and grappled at her. Modesty struggled against her, tucking in her legs. Alita felt that she was about to be thrown off and dug her claws into Modesty's shoulders.

When Modesty kicked, the force was stronger than Alita had anticipated. She was thrown over Modesty's head and hit the marble floor. Alita raised her head, dazed from the collision, but Modesty was already on her feet. Bright red streaks of blood lined her shoulders. At least Alita had left some marks when she'd been tossed.

"I've had enough of you being in the way," Modesty snarled. She stalked towards Alita menacingly. "I'm not holding back anymore. I'll kill you, and anyone else who tries to stop me."

Alita forced herself up. Pain shot through her wing where she'd landed on it.

"My job is to protect Evelyn." Alita said through gritted teeth.

Modesty smiled menacingly. "You won't stop me now. No one will."

Modesty leapt at Alita, ice turning her claws and teeth into sharp frozen points. Alita had just enough time to catch Modesty before being forced back to the floor. Alita scrabbled at Modesty's chest and neck, trying to keep her teeth and claws from scratching her.

But as Alita struggled, she felt small, chilly scratches appearing on her skin. Modesty had an advantage on Alita now. No matter how much she struggled, Alita could tell she was fighting a losing battle. If Modesty killed her, she would go after Evelyn and Luana next. The thought struck her with more fear than Alita thought possible. She had to make sure they were safe.

"Luana! Run!" Alita called out. "Take Evelyn and get out of here!"

Chapter 59

Luana heard Alita's cries. She'd been listening to the entire fight. Alita was losing. Modesty had her pinned. Luana couldn't just run and hide or stand around while Alita was killed.

Luana crouched down, gathering all her strength to her legs, then leapt at Modesty. She let a growl escape her as she crashed onto Modesty's back. Modesty gasped and snarled. Her attention turned away from Alita as she bucked and kicked and wriggled around, trying to throw Luana off.

Luana dug her claws in as deep as they would go and let her fury fuel the fire in her chest. Her body began to heat up. Modesty growled in anger and pain and reared up.

Luana slid off Modesty's back, still heating her body. Fire emerged from her mane, brushing her skin. The warmth fuelled her. She'd never done this before, but she knew she could. She heated herself a little more and her body burst into flames.

The fire on her skin didn't burn her. It barely even felt hot. It was more like a warm embrace. The flames hugged her skin and tickled her mouth. Any breath she exhaled would only be fire.

"That's how you want to do this? Fine," Modesty growled.

Through the crackles of her fire, Luana heard the sharp crack of ice. Modesty was covering her entire body with ice to combat Luana's fire.

Luana crouched, readying herself. Her ears twitched alertly for any sound of movement. She heard a scrape and tinkling as Modesty lunged at her. Luana reared up to meet Modesty's attack. Modesty slammed into her and dug her icy claws into Luana's skin. Luana snarled and pushed back, summoning more heat to her skin.

After a moment of wrestling, Modesty cried out and pulled back. Luana didn't wait to breathe out a burst of flames. Modesty shrieked. Luana soon felt a chill passing over her and knew that Modesty was throwing her own ice breath back at her. Luana channelled the flames from her breath into her skin, allowing her body to heat even more. Her flame breath stopped but her body was starting to burn from the extensive fire use. It was time to end this.

Luana ran at Modesty and slammed into her. Modesty screamed in pain. Her ice was little use against Luana's white hot fire. Smoke filled Luana's nose, bringing with it the sickening smell of burning dragon. She swallowed and wrapped her wings around Modesty's body. Modesty's scream increased in pitch, becoming an outright wail. Luana winced at the sound.

"This is the end, Modesty," she said quietly, though she wasn't sure Modesty could even hear her. "Perhaps in another life, you might learn to let go. Goodbye."

Luana stepped back from Modesty, allowing the fire on her body to flicker out. Modesty's cries died out as the burning smell strengthened. Luana could hear the crackling fire that covered Modesty's body. She sighed, her ears drooping. Her energy had been completely sapped. Her legs gave out and she collapsed to the ground.

"Luana!"

Alita was at her side in an instant. Luana forced her head up. Alita touched her nose, then jumped back. Luana smiled weakly.

"I just lit myself on fire, Alita," she said hoarsely. "I need time to cool down. And a lot of water. I'll be fine."

"We'll get you some water," Misti said. "We also need medics to check everyone here."

Misti's voice was hollow, yet somehow she was still able to coordinate the different rescue and medic dragons that had swarmed the room. As dragons brushed past her, Luana knew Misti was only holding herself together out of necessity. She had just lost her entire family after all.

"I'm so glad you're alright," Alita muttered.

"Are *you* alright?" Luana asked.

"I think so. My wing hurts though," Alita said.

"You've dislocated the wing from its socket," a gentle voice came from beside them. Luana guessed it was one of the castle's medics. "You've also bruised the outer edge. I can put the wing back in place but it will still hurt for a few days. You won't be able to fly while it's healing."

"Okay. Thank you," Alita said.

A voice came from the second floor, echoing around the room, "Caln Misti! Lucas is still alive!"

"How bad are his injuries?" Misti asked.

"His leg is bleeding badly and the bone is broken," the medic said. "We'll have to amputate it, but he'll survive if we act quickly."

"Make it so," Misti said. "And while I'm thinking about it, we will need a new leader now that my husband is dead."

Misti's voice thickened with grief and she paused. Luana managed to prop herself up a little. Misti was about to announce Evelyn as the new High Caln. The least she could do was be slightly upright for the moment.

"Prinze Evelyn," Misti began.

"Actually, Misti," Evelyn interrupted her softly, "I can't."

Chapter 60

Evelyn forced herself to her feet despite the aches forming in her legs and the pit in her stomach.

"What do you mean 'you can't?'" Misti asked.

"I can't be High Caln," Evelyn said. She took a breath to steady herself and continued, "I never wanted to be High Caln. I never even wanted to be Prinze. I... I formally renounce my title as Prinze."

Evelyn took the crown off her and tossed it across the room. It clattered against the marble floor. When it stopped moving, there was a new dent in the soft gold.

"That... is very unfortunate," Misti said. "Without a Prinze or any Duchies to become High Caln, a decision will have to be made."

"Who becomes High Caln when no Prinze or Duchy is present?" someone asked. Evelyn couldn't see who it was, but their voice was young and shaky. Had that been Hamlet? She had forgotten that he'd even be there that night.

"In ancient times, rulers were found in distant blood relatives," Jakob said. "But in those societies, the crown was passed through the family and relatives were kept in the loop on how to rule."

Misti hummed with thought. "Perhaps it should be someone from the Everhart family."

"Y-you want one of my sons to be High Caln?" Adelaide asked shakily.

"Well, it would have to be someone we trust to run the Calndom,"

Misti said. "They should be an adult, which would rule out your younger two, and the dragon we choose should be ready to step up to the challenge."

"And whoever it is will need to choose a Caln to marry before their official coronation," Adelaide added. She turned around abruptly. "Markos, how is your relationship with August Waltz going?"

Markos blinked, looking blindsided. "With all due respect, Mother, I don't want to be High Caln. I wouldn't be a good choice."

Evelyn was surprised that he would turn down the offer. He had grown up in the castle when Gerold had been alive. Markos was the oldest of Gerold's offspring. Surely he would know better than anyone how to be High Caln.

"That leaves Luana," Misti said, turning to Luana and Alita, who were still crouched on the floor. "Luana, would you accept this responsibility?"

Luana was quiet for a moment. At first, Evelyn expected her to say no as well. But then Luana heaved herself to her feet and faced Misti directly. Alita stood up beside her.

Luana nodded, resolve clear on her face. "I will, and I choose Alita to be my Caln."

"M-me?" Alita stuttered, eyes wide.

Luana smiled softly at her. "I wouldn't want anyone else by my side. I love you."

Alita's face flushed, but her expression softened into a dopey smile. "I love you too."

"Then it's settled," Misti said. "Luana will be the new High Caln. Perhaps we can rework the original wedding plans to include a coronation so that we don't have to delay the event. Given the circumstances, Alita's work trial is now void. I will personally teach you the responsibilities of being Caln instead."

"Luana, are you sure you can do this?" Adelaide asked.

Luana nodded. "Yes. I can do anything as long as I have Alita with me."

Evelyn knew Luana would be a good High Caln. She was kind and smart. They may not have gotten along while betrothed, but Evelyn didn't doubt that Luana would be perfect for the role. Her gaze settled on Alita, who was still smiling at Luana. Alita would never love anyone else again. Evelyn could see that clearly. Perhaps it was time for her to leave.

She left wordlessly through the main doors. The night air was cool and calm. There were no dragons around, not even the gate guards. Dragons had either fled from the castle entirely or rushed in to see the commotion when Modesty attacked.

The sky was clear above her. The moon shone down, washing everything in a silvery light. A gentle breeze brushed at Evelyn's wings, practically willing her into the sky. She undid the button on her cloak and allowed it to fall off her.

"Evelyn?"

Evelyn turned to see Alita a few metres behind her. Her wing sat awkwardly at her side and her cloak and vest were completely missing. Small streaks of blood through her fur highlighted her battle with Modesty. Despite all that, the jadeite earrings still clung to Alita's ears.

Evelyn hadn't realised Alita had seen her leave. Surely, she should be inside with Luana. Evelyn turned her gaze back to the sky.

"I've been Prinze for so long," she said. "And now, it's over."

"What are you going to do?" Alita asked.

"I'll go home. Back to Tribe-Ali. I'm not needed here anymore," Evelyn said.

"Don't say that," Alita said. "I'm sure you'd still be welcome."

Evelyn turned her head slightly to glance at Alita. "Do you really think I should stay? After everything that's happened?"

Alita lowered her gaze to the ground. She knew the answer just as well as Evelyn did.

"You don't have to go back to the Tribe if you don't want to," Alita said, looking up at her again. "You could live somewhere else in the Calndom."

"Alita, you don't understand. Tribe-Ali is my home. It always has been." Evelyn looked back up at the sky. "I want to feel the sand under my feet and smell the ocean on the breeze. I've missed it so much."

Alita sighed. "Alright. I won't try to stop you."

"Thank you, Alita," Evelyn said quietly.

She stretched her wings and took to the sky. With no gate guards around to stop her, she could fly over the gates freely and head for home. Her eyes burned as tears began to form. She would miss Alita. They had been friends their whole lives. But it was for the best that Evelyn didn't stay. She couldn't watch Alita marry someone else. At least Alita would be happy with Luana. That was the only thought that would keep her heart from breaking completely.

Chapter 61

Alita pushed her way into the guardroom and quickly located Lucas lying on the floor, surrounded by blankets and pillows. It had been three days since Modesty was defeated. Lucas was recovering well. His leg stump was bandaged, with a few extra lengths wrapped around his chest and shoulders. He smiled as she sat next to him.

"Hey, how are you doing?" he asked.

"I'm good," Alita said. "The real question is how are you doing?"

"I'm not going to lie, I'm still a little gutted about losing my leg," Lucas admitted. "It's a bit itchy but the doctor says it's healing well."

"Will you be able to walk again?" Alita asked.

"Yeah. I'll probably use my wing to support myself," Lucas said. "How's Luana?"

"She's doing much better. She was so dehydrated. I was getting worried. But she's keeping up with the fluid intake," Alita explained.

"That's good," Lucas then asked. "What about Evelyn?"

Alita sighed. "She's gone back to the Tribe."

"That's too bad. Will she come back for the wedding?" Lucas asked.

"I don't think so," Alita admitted. "I think seeing Luana and I get married on her intended wedding day would just be too much after everything that happened... between all of us."

"She's still got three weeks to change her mind," Lucas pointed out.

Alita shook her head. "It'll be better for her. Probably better for me and Luana too."

"Are you talking about me?"

Alita looked up to see Luana standing in the doorway. She couldn't help but smile.

"Just about the wedding," she said.

Luana smiled and walked over to them. She touched her nose to the side of Alita's face as she sat down.

"I'm glad you guys got your happy ending." Lucas smiled.

"I'd call it more bittersweet," Luana said.

"I agree." Alita nodded. "But you can have a happy ending too. There's plenty of dragons you could pursue instead of Priscila."

Lucas ducked his head. "Crystal has been bringing me extra food every day. We never talked much during our night watches but in the past few days we've... kind of clicked."

"There you go." Alita smiled. "Sounds like you two will be happy together. And I promise, no more night watches for either of you."

"I've already started going through the guards' and servants' routines to improve it all," Luana said. "With Misti's help of course. Until I'm actually crowned, I don't get the final say."

"I appreciate the effort," Lucas smiled.

Epilogue

The wedding and coronation happened on the same day, three weeks later. It was a pain to replan everything in such a short time, but it was easier than moving the date, and with no High Caln, the Calndom was at risk of uprisings. As Markos watched his sister dance with her new wife, he reflected on everything that had led to this moment.

He saw a lot of possibilities in his dreams. He knew Luana would be the best fit for High Caln out of all the options, including himself. He wasn't built for the role. He'd end up like his father, so stressed about giving everyone else a perfect future, that he couldn't predict his own death until it was too late to change it. He didn't want that for himself. Using his powers just to bring about this moment had been exhausting enough. He was pretty sure Alita thought there was something wrong with him.

But now he could relax and use his foresight casually again. He could take solace in the knowledge that his sister would be the best High Caln that Hiza Calndom had ever seen and her reign would bring about many changes and improvements for Laili Island as a whole. He certainly didn't have to worry about that metal structure floating in the sea that kept popping up in his dreams, or the visions of Evelyn's future. Nope. Not at all.

As more dragons joined the dancefloor, Markos started to weave through the crowd. He spotted Victoria dancing with Adair from the

Peacock family. He was much taller than her, which made for an interesting dynamic, but somehow they made it work. Meanwhile, Zina was sneaking extra food and chatting with her mothers. He felt a premonition in the back of his mind. She would have a good life.

Markos kept working his way through the crowd until he spotted the dragon he was looking for. Her sandy yellow skin was well complemented by her pink sheer cloak. Her tail twitched as she watched the dancefloor hungrily.

"Hello August," Markos greeted her with a nod.

"Laird Markos," August said. "Or is it Duchy again?"

Markos laughed. "No. Just because Luana's High Caln now doesn't mean I have any different title. I'm still the same old Markos."

"You seem a lot more relaxed today," August said. "I haven't seen you this laid back in months."

Markos shrugged his wings under his cloak. "I'm enjoying the celebration. Would you care to join me for a dance?"

"Don't mind if I do," August said with a smile.

Markos smiled back. He knew they'd have a good life together if they wanted to. But he didn't let that sway him. Too often, his visions led to knowing more than he should. He wanted to get to know August and experience what their life could be if they just let it be. Markos extended a wing to August. She extended her own in response so it brushed his, and they walked out onto the dancefloor.

Samantha Edwhan is a budding new author from New Zealand. Her lifelong interest in creating and sharing stories, coupled with her special interest in dragons, led to her first book, Intertwined. When she isn't planning or writing stories, Samantha is revising, editing, or over-researching her ideas.

Did you enjoy Intertwined?

Leave a review with your thoughts on Amazon!

What to read more of Samantha Edwhan's work?

Check out her website for FREE reading material!

www.edwhanbooks.com

End of the
Winter Star

Griffin's Choice